Praise for Bianca D'Arc's *Jaci's Experiment*

Joyfully Recommended "...other worldly and hot, hot, hot...a story about growth with lots of love and laughter, as well as an action-packed story that made me want only good things for Jaci, Mike..."

~ *Jambrea, Joyfully Reviewed*

Rating: 5 Bookmarks "I am absolutely wild for these stories and cannot wait for the next one!"

~ *Jennifer, Wild On Books*

Rating: 5 Red Tattoos "An emotional thrill ride... Jaci's Experiment is not a book you'd want to start late at night as it is absolutely impossible to put down."

~ *Megan, Erotic Escapades*

Blue Ribbon Rating: 4.5 "...a testimony to [D'Arc's] ability to formulate, plot, and invariably write some of the most risqué but sweetest ménages I have ever read... I couldn't put JACI'S EXPERIEMENT down."

~ *Natasha Smith, Romance Junkies*

Look for these titles by *Bianca D'Arc*

Now Available:

Wings of Change
Forever Valentine
Sweeter than Wine

Dragon Knights series
Maiden Flight (Book 1)
Border Lair (Book 2)
Ladies of the Lair—Dragon Knights 1 & 2 (print)
The Ice Dragon (Book 3)
Prince of Spies (Book 4)
FireDrake (Book 5)

Tales of Were series
Lords of the Were (Book 1)

Resonance Mates series
Hara's Legacy (Book 1)
Davin's Quest (Book 2)
Jaci's Experiment (Book 3)

Brotherhood of Blood
One and Only (Book 1)
Rare Vintage (Book 2)
Phantom Desires (Book 3)

Print Anthologies
I Dream of Dragons Vol 1
Caught By Cupid

Jaci's Experiment

Bianca D'Arc

A Samhain Publishing, Ltd. publication.

Samhain Publishing, Ltd.
577 Mulberry Street, Suite 1520
Macon, GA 31201
www.samhainpublishing.com

Jaci's Experiment

Print ISBN: 978-1-60504-304-3
Digital ISBN: 1-60504-127-0

Editing by Angela James
Cover by Anne Cain

First Samhain Publishing, Ltd. electronic publication: August 2008
First Samhain Publishing, Ltd. print publication: June 2009

Dedication

To those who boldly go where none have gone before and to those who support them. My hat's off to the explorers, the dreamers, and those who make the future possible.

That includes, most importantly, my Dad, the man who gave me my love of science—both fiction and fact.

Chapter One

Lita 498 was in medical, seeking treatment for a broken leg. She'd fallen that morning and as a result, Jaci 192 had to take up the slack and try to do both Lita's job and her own. She didn't mind too much, except that Lita was a lower level tech and part of her day was devoted to collecting samples from the elite.

Jaci hadn't done sample collection since her promotion, but she didn't mind filling in under the circumstances. She knew if the roles had been reversed, the agreeable Lita would be more than willing to help her out.

So Jaci went to the sample collection unit to find Lita's single appointment for the day already waiting. The first thing she noticed was his size. He was huge. Obviously a warrior, and not just any warrior, but one of the best of the best. She'd seen him from afar many times and people did talk—especially about the elites. This was Grady Prime, top of the Grady line on-planet, and perhaps in the known universe. The ultimate soldier, the consummate warrior, with skills unmatched among the warrior class. And an extremely handsome male, to boot.

Jaci hadn't realized that Lita serviced Grady Prime and for a moment she felt the tiniest flicker of envy for the younger girl and her biweekly appointments with such a man. Jaci had never been near enough to see the incredible blue of his eyes before, but as he looked down at her from his much superior height, she found herself noting the azure effect with a new awareness.

"Where's the other girl?" Nothing in his voice indicated anything other than a mild sort of interest.

Jaci smiled professionally as she closed the door to the room behind her.

"Lita 498 fell this morning and broke her leg. She's probably still in medical. I am filling in for her today. I am Jaci 192." She offered the traditional respectful bow of her head after the introduction and he replied in kind, impressing her with his manners. For a warrior, he at least knew how to act in polite company.

"Grady Prime." She liked the fact that he bothered to confirm his identity to an underling when almost everyone on-planet had to know exactly who he was.

Jaci strode to the examination table and he followed, unbuckling his pants as he went.

"Would you prefer manual, oral or vaginal stimulation?"

"I'm in the mood for pussy." The growl in his deep voice did something to her insides she'd never encountered before. He helped her to jump up the short distance to sit on the table facing him as she removed the lower part of her uniform and spread her legs.

She'd done this many times before, but something felt different this time. Something almost wistful entered her thoughts, surprising her. Could the odd, emotional thought have anything to do with her accident? She put the thoughts aside and made herself focus on the task ahead. She had a job to do and she would worry over the accidental exposure she'd suffered later.

Grady Prime's cock was as handsome and huge as the rest

of him and she admired it as she prepared to sheathe him in the ultra-thin collection sack that would capture and preserve his seed. She stroked him to hardness with expert hands, then followed his lead as he pushed her head down to take him in her mouth. Apparently he wanted both kinds of stimulation and it was her job to make certain he was satisfied. For not only did he outrank her, he was also much more important to the breeding program than she would ever be. He was one of the elite. One from whom future generations would be created. Only a few in every line were chosen for such an honor at any one time, and only the best and brightest were ever considered.

She sucked him deep, following the pressure of his hands as he moved her head on his enormous shaft. She was enjoying his dominance in a way she'd never before experienced. Sure, she'd never been with a soldier of his caliber before, but many Alvian males exhibited the physically dominant tendencies of their ancestors when in coitus.

The difference here was her response. She discovered she felt some kind of emotional response to his dominance, which was unnerving in the extreme. She watched her reactions as if from a distance, needing to observe what had changed in her previously unemotional makeup to evaluate how badly the accidental exposure had affected her.

But Grady Prime was making it difficult. She couldn't concentrate when he hoisted her closer on the table. One of his large hands reached for the lubricant kept nearby, but hesitated at the last moment as his gaze focused on the pouting lips of her pussy. She knew she was wet already and didn't want to wait, but also knew her role. She had to be submissive to the Prime's desires in all things, despite the fact she wanted to force him onto the table so she could climb on that hard cock and have her way with it.

Instead she waited as he slid two large fingers into her

channel while his hot palm covered her pussy. It felt delicious. He smiled when he discovered her wetness, sliding his fingers around a few times before withdrawing. She almost whimpered when he left her, but held back by the sheerest thread. It only took a moment for him to move into position, then slide into her pussy with one hard, ecstatic shove. She wanted it hard and that's exactly what he gave her. Grady began pummeling her, his huge arms trapping her on the table while his cock shuttled in and out of her body. She squirmed with nearly uncontrollable desire.

She'd never felt anything like it. She'd always enjoyed a moderate amount of pleasure from vaginal stimulation, but nothing like this. She pulled at his arms, urging him to move faster, though she couldn't speak a word. Her breath came in fast panting gasps, her eyes closed in shuddering bliss as she hurtled into the most intense orgasm she'd ever had.

Her inner muscles clamped down around him and a moment later, she felt the spasms of his cock that told her he was coming too. He strained against her, setting off yet further explosions in her body as he came long and hard, his own breathing rough above her.

After long, satisfying moments, he disengaged and moved back, those deep blue eyes watching her with interest. She tried to get a grip on the unfamiliar emotions flooding her, but it was difficult. Still, this man was a danger to her. He would undoubtedly report any truly odd behavior on her part, so she had to tread lightly.

She put her head down and saw to the final stages of sample collection, unsheathing him, depositing the receptacle in a special sample pouch lying next to her on the table. She couldn't meet his eyes but felt the weight of his gaze as he followed her every movement.

While she'd finished her task, he dressed and straightened his clothing, and she held tightly to her sigh of relief as he walked toward the door. She needed time to examine her responses and decide her next course of action.

But he turned back to her just before he reached the doorway to the small examination room. She wasn't in the clear yet, she reminded herself sternly as she fought to meet his cool expression with unemotional eyes.

"Will you be here next time?" His question surprised her.

"Probably not. Lita 498 should be healed sufficiently in a day or two, at which time she will resume her duties."

"Pity." He tilted his head. "I very much enjoyed our time together today, Jaci 192. Thank you." His voice was unemotional, but warm and rumbly in that supremely masculine way, and she was oddly touched that she'd somehow pleased him. He was, after all, one of the elite, and the way he was looking at her made her almost wish she would be able to repeat their encounter. "Maybe it's because I'm of soldier stock, but I truly like the sensation of a woman's sheath contracting around me. It heightens my pleasure considerably and you have a very tight channel to begin with."

She didn't quite know how to respond to that, so she just nodded.

"I mean no insult, but if you were ever inclined to seek sexual pleasure, I hope you would consider me as a potential partner."

She was flabbergasted by his offer. He was a Prime, after all. He could have his pick of females from any line, even if he was a soldier.

"I am flattered, Grady Prime, and I will remember your words. Thank you."

He smiled softly at her before leaving the room and she

collapsed with a sigh, knowing she'd just had a rather narrow escape.

§

Above all, she couldn't let on that she'd been accidentally exposed to the experimental therapy. She was only 192nd in the Jaci line on this world, which meant if her superiors found out she'd botched up this badly, she would either be summarily put down or imprisoned. For certain, she'd be demoted. Possibly booted out of the science sector completely.

She wasn't, and would never have been, among the select group chosen from volunteers for this all-important experiment. She'd only been meant to prepare the skin patches of the new therapy, not take the dose herself. But sloppy handling and fatigue from overwork had caused one of the patches she'd been making to adhere to the bottom of her forearm and she hadn't noticed until the next day when she'd bathed.

At first she noted the skin patch with her usual detached observation, realizing the patch had turned color from green to blue, indicating the entire dose had been successfully delivered. She remembered thinking through her options clinically, deciding on her best course of action.

The panic didn't hit until a few days later. Subtle at first, she began to *feel* things—emotional responses she'd never experienced before in her life. She realized then that her genetics were being manipulated on a molecular level. She was becoming more like her Alvian ancestors, and her new emotions were beginning to display themselves when she least expected it.

She buried herself in her work for the next few days. They

were gearing up for the grand experiment and final decisions were being made as to who would receive the therapy and who would monitor. They moved slowly, being as certain and deliberate as they could because this was a very big step for the Alvian race as a whole.

Jaci knew Mara 12 had done a prior, top secret experiment using an old soldier Prime as test subject, but he'd mysteriously disappeared before any data could be collected. Rumor had it—among Mara 12's personal staff, of which Jaci was a part—that he was dead. That didn't bode well for the next group of test subjects, or Jaci herself, but hopefully Mara 12 had refined the DNA cocktail a bit since that first, unsuccessful trial.

That the Alvian High Council was even considering reversing ten generations worth of genetic manipulation and public policy was an enormous undertaking. But their interactions with the native inhabitants of their new planet made the radical step seem increasingly necessary. The native inhabitants—those left alive after the cataclysm the Alvians had wrought—were called Breeds, a native word adopted as a proper noun that had no real explanation in the Alvian lexicon. Only a few in the scientific community knew they were the improbable descendants of the very first Alvian explorers and native humans of Earth.

The Breeds were very emotional, while Alvians had deliberately bred aggression and emotion out of their people. It was hard for Alvians to understand Breeds, but steps had been taken of late to do more. This test was a further step to see if Breed genetics could help the Alvian race improve itself yet again.

Only the geneticists and the High Council knew the experimental treatment was designed to introduce a bit of human DNA into the pure Alvian genome of the test subjects.

Already, Jaci was feeling the effects. She was so much more emotional than she had ever been on so many levels and she feared—actually *feared* for the first time in her life—the changes weren't over yet.

The idea for this experiment actually started more than a decade ago, when a top Mara scientist came back to the city after an information gathering mission to announce to her staff that there was Hara DNA on Earth. She'd found three brothers, all named O'Hara, who carried Alvian DNA of one of the greatest heroes of the Alvian race.

Hara was a legend. He'd been a soldier, explorer, scientist and savior of their very race. It was his party of explorers that had sent back the means by which they could save their people from extinction as their own sun went supernova. He'd sent word of this planet and a few others to which the Alvians had dispatched worldships. They'd taken those planets and changed them to suit the very specific Alvian resonance needs, settling them as colonies from which to restore and continue the Alvian culture and race.

The planets were chosen for their rare crystal deposits. Work had been done before the worldship arrived to begin the tuning of the Earth's crystals, but much destruction and damage had been done to the existing society. In her people's defense, they hadn't known the humans had progressed so far in their evolution from the time thousands of years before, when Hara had sent his instructions.

It took time for information to flow between such distant worlds and then the time to construct the satellite platforms and ships. They divided the population into several different ships bound for distant worlds and began the long journey. Hundreds of years passed on the little blue rock called Earth before the Alvian worldship appeared in their solar system. The automated crystal seeding platform had already begun the bombardment from space that would begin changing the raw quartz deposits of the planet to something the Alvians could use to survive even before the worldship began deceleration. A year after the seeding, the worldship began to deploy all over the globe, breaking apart into its various sections to set down the kernels of cities, engineering facilities, military garrisons, scientific institutions and other necessary structures from which the Alvians would begin to rebuild their civilization.

The Alvian crystal seeding of the Earth killed many millions of natives. Scientists theorized that the new resonances of the planet allowed only those humans with traces of Alvian DNA to survive comfortably. Most Breeds fled to the wastelands of the planet before the tsunamis and earthquakes that had helped reshape the world for Alvian colonization, but many died along with their human brethren in the large cities and population centers all over the globe.

Of the Breed survivors, there were few women. The three O'Hara brothers had protected the wife of the eldest, but when it became apparent the other two would never find mates among their own kind, they decided to share her. The apparent success of that arrangement was something Jaci didn't understand. She had witnessed the barbarity of rough Breed men as they fell upon females put in their pens for experimental purposes. The Alvians had captured a great number of Breeds for study and kept them confined below the cities. Part of Jaci's duties each day was to observe them. From those observations, she didn't see how the women survived.

Alvian scientists tried to study Breed emotion—even if they didn't understand it. The Breeds didn't seem as aggressive as their Alvian ancestors had been, but there were some very aggressive traits in human DNA that made it a risky venture to mix it with pure Alvian. Which was why the upcoming clinical trial was so controlled and so important.

Well, it *had* been controlled, until Jaci had blundered by accidentally introducing the test agent into her own body. Of all the stupid moves she'd ever made in her life, that had to have been the stupidest.

Now she was changing on a genetic level and she couldn't tell anyone about it for fear they would either pen her up or kill her outright.

She went back to her tasks, trying desperately to hide the changes in her responses. She strove for outward calm and that same, emotionless, blank look of moderate inquiry on the faces of all Alvians. It was hard, especially when her work brought her into the Breed pens.

She'd come to know many of the Breeds kept in the underground pens and now that she was changing, she felt more kinship with some of them than ever.

There were two men she wished she could speak to most of all. They were different from the other men kept in nearby pens. These two special men had been educated before the cataclysm. They'd been businessmen with their own company, they'd told her, though she didn't quite understand how the commerce system in what they called the "old world" had worked.

She'd talked with them far more rationally than she'd ever spoken with any other Breed males while she did her rounds in the pens each day. She considered them friends of a sort, as she did some of the Breed females she also cared for. They made her saddest now, of course, thinking what these poor women had been put through at the hands of her Alvian brethren, all in the name of experimentation.

These poor women hadn't deserved the emotional pain they'd been subjected to by beings who could neither understand it nor appreciate it. Most of the women wore defeated, dead looks on their faces, but there was one who had been friendly toward Jaci even before she'd accidentally injected herself and begun to notice.

Ruth had been pregnant when Jaci had first been assigned to her care. Ruth had been despondent until Jaci was instructed to deliver a note to the Breed woman from Caleb O'Hara, one of the three Breed brothers with Hara DNA. It was believed that Caleb O'Hara had the ability to see events in the future. The Breeds called him a precog, and Jaci had been interested in the idea that such psychic abilities could truly exist.

She'd seen a change in Ruth after the woman read Caleb O'Hara's note. For one thing, she smiled more and started to take an active interest in her pregnancy. Jaci had read the contents of the note, but at the time she hadn't understood what the words meant on an emotional level. Ruth had been subjected to "testing" by her captors, sent into a cell with four Breed males where she was raped repeatedly.

One of the males tried to protect her and was beaten by the others for his trouble. As a further part of the experiment, she and her injured protector were put in a cell by themselves where she tried to heal him with what little equipment they had in the cell. She washed him with water from the sink and used the bandages and rudimentary medicines they'd supplied. Over time, she bonded with Sam. Ruth even claimed to have fallen in love with him, though Jaci had no real understanding of what love was, except as a textbook definition of something she would never be able to feel.

She thought she understood Ruth a little better now. Jaci could easily see the love Ruth had for her baby. It was on her face every time she looked at Samantha. Caleb O'Hara's note had helped Ruth find love for the life inside her, for Caleb O'Hara had foreseen the baby was Sam's and not the result of rape. Once Ruth believed that, she became interested in her pregnancy and in the child she bore nine months later.

"Something's different about you, Jaci, but I can't figure out what it is." It was Ruth who first noticed the changes in Jaci as she moved about the small cell doing routine health checks on both mother and child.

Jaci's breath caught. She knew the pens were monitored closely, but she also held the control to the monitors, since system maintenance was one of her assigned tasks. Jaci made no comment to Ruth until her work brought her to the monitor. She surreptitiously shut it down for the moment it would take to talk to Ruth. She was taking a chance, but she needed to talk to someone who might understand and Ruth was as close as she could come to a friend among the Breeds. She believed in her newly awakened heart that Ruth would not betray her.

"You're right, Ruth, and I'm scared to death."

The real agony that must have shown on her face clearly shocked the other woman.

"What's going on, Jaci? I thought your kind didn't have emotions. How can you feel fear?" Ruth was clearly perplexed, but willing to listen. Jaci nearly broke down in tears.

"There's a big experiment going on. You're not supposed to know about it, but I've got to talk to someone!" She hugged herself tightly around the middle, in agony as everything she'd been feeling welled up inside her. "I was assigned to prepare the doses and accidentally dosed myself with the agent. I didn't mean to do it, and now I don't know how to deal with these...*feelings*!"

Ruth stepped closer. "What was this agent supposed to do, and why can't you tell your bosses? Wouldn't they help you?"

Jaci shook her head vigorously. "They'll kill me. Or lock me up. I wasn't supposed to be involved. I'm not worthy of this honor. The subjects have been carefully chosen and most are among the elite of our society. They'd never have let me take part in the experiment." She fought down her hysteria. "It's a genetic manipulation agent. It's reformulating my DNA and reigniting the sequences that theoretically might allow us to feel again, and it's definitely working. I'm feeling all kinds of emotions I've never experienced before and I'm not prepared to deal with it. It's ripping me apart."

Ruth came over and put her arm around Jaci's shoulder, hugging her close. It felt so good to have even this small comfort from another being.

"I think you're just overwhelmed. It happens to most human youngsters during puberty. All these hormones release suddenly in their young bodies and their emotions go a little crazy until they get used to it."

Jaci looked up at her hopefully. "How long does it usually last?"

"A few years."

"Years! I can't wait that long!"

Ruth chuckled and squeezed her shoulder before letting go.

"You need to tell David about this."

"David?" Jaci was startled by Ruth's suddenly businesslike tone. She knew who the other woman was talking about. David was one of the pair of cousins she liked best of the male Breeds.

In fact, the room that housed the two cousins was right next to Ruth's and was Jaci's next stop on her rounds in the semi-private section of the pen complex. The test subjects housed here were granted more freedom than the others, earned by good behavior or other special circumstances. Each cell had solid, opaque walls for improved privacy, but the entrance was an energized archway that was open to the hall. The temptation to talk to the man next door was enormous, but she didn't know what good David could do for her.

"Yes, David. And Michael too. But David especially might be of some use to you."

"Why?"

"In the old world, David was a psychiatrist. We talk sometimes, late at night when I can't sleep, through the wall. He's helped me a lot, and I know he likes you. Both of them do."

"What is a psychiatrist? What does that mean?" Jaci was confused and suddenly feeling a bit jealous of the other woman's late night conversations with the man she admired. It was unsettling to say the least.

"It means that he had to go through a lot of schooling, first to attain his medical degree, then his specialty in psychiatry. He's a very smart man and I like to think he's a good friend."

"He's a doctor?" Why did she suddenly feel sad that he'd never told her about his past?

Ruth nodded, compassion clear her eyes. "Go talk to him," she urged. "I know you've done something to the cameras in here. Do the same in their cell and talk it out. They can help you and they will. They like you, Jaci. They wouldn't give the time of day to most of your kind, but you've been kind when you could, even though you didn't understand our emotions. Now I think, they'll have pity on you and help you through your rough patch. Trust them, and know that I won't tell a soul what you've told me. I don't want you hurt. I like you and consider you a friend."

Tears traced down Jaci's face, much to her astonishment, and she wiped them away, looking at her wet hand with confusion. She didn't know how to describe all the different things she was feeling. Ruth was so good, such a kind person, and so forgiving of her earlier unfeeling treatment. Jaci didn't feel worthy of being called friend by this noble woman and it touched her deeply. She bowed her head.

"I am honored by your friendship, Ruth, and I thank you. I'll try to do as you suggest, but I don't know if I'm brave enough."

But Ruth just smiled. "I think you'll find that you're brave enough for just about anything, Jaci. All you have to do is try."

Jaci restored the monitors and moved on to the cell next door in her normal rounds. She was eager now to try as Ruth suggested, but fearful as well. What if the men she'd come to think of so fondly rejected her. It would crush her.

Having emotions was a tough thing to deal with. Suddenly she had new respect for these Breeds and the upheaval her kind had put them through. Most of them were truly remarkable, and now she understood a little better the ones who had been driven insane or close to it by her people.

She couldn't wait to talk to David and Michael. She moved straight to the monitor when she entered the room. Normally she would mask her maintenance of it with her other tasks so the subjects would have no idea there was any sort of equipment in the room at all. This time, she didn't care about protocol. She needed to talk to these men without the monitors and she would do so now, before she lost her nerve.

She disabled the system and turned to face them with her hands behind her back and her breath caught in rather desperate apprehension. Both of them were watching her carefully, inquisitive looks on their handsome faces. The moment of truth had indeed arrived.

"What's wrong?"

David's concern brought another of those amazing tears to her eyes. She wiped it away, noting their stunned expressions and sank onto the edge of the table behind her, resting wearily against it as she explained her tale of woe.

She told them all about how she'd exposed herself to the agent and it was tall, muscular Michael who came over to gather her into his strong arms, not David as she would have expected. David, instead, watched her in a way that was unnerving. He watched her as if she was some kind of experiment, and she suddenly understood how and why these Breeds resented their captivity and the constant monitoring.

"I'm so sorry." She sobbed, turning her head into Michael's strong chest.

"For what, Jaci? You've never done anything to harm either of us. You've been as close to a friend as one of your kind could be given your lack of emotion. We liked you regardless."

She cried a bit more, waves of emotion hitting her that she didn't know how to deal with. Michael seemed content to let her ride the storm out in his arms and she didn't want to move. He felt so good. So powerful and protective. She wanted to stay in his embrace, safe, for as long as she could.

Of the two, Michael was the larger and physically stronger. David was more cerebral and handsome in a way that made her stomach clench. He had a cunning smile that hinted at deviltry and close-cropped hair that she'd wanted to touch for a long time, just to see if it was as soft and fuzzy as it looked. His sharp features and intelligent, dark blue eyes were aphrodisiacs of a sort different from that of his more muscular cousin.

Because of his almost frighteningly strong masculine form, Jaci would have thought Michael would be less likely to offer her comfort. He had a rough demeanor and more athletically defined physique. He spent a lot of his spare time doing push-ups and other kinds of physical exercise that kept his body at a peak of conditioning unmatched by any of her other charges. She'd been surprised when he'd been the one to gather her close to all that amazingly warm muscle and brawn, but she loved the feel of him against her. With such a man holding her, Jaci felt like nothing could ever harm her.

Mike looked from the sobbing woman in his arms to his watching cousin. Dave was taking it all in, but he hadn't yet made a move to help the confused young woman, and Mike was surprised. He knew Dave liked the look of Jaci. They'd had enough conversations about her since she'd become their jailer to know that for a fact. She was easy on the eyes and had a graceful manner, plus she never used her position of power to intentionally harm any of her charges. She was thoughtful and kind—or as kind as a person without any understanding of emotion could hope to be.

"Why won't you help her?" Both men were reasonably strong telepaths and had other gifts as well.

"She needs to cry," Dave said firmly in his cousin's mind. *"When she's got this out of her system, we can begin to work on integrating the emotions."*

"This could be the break we've been looking for." Mike was excited by the possibilities. *"If the aliens are experimenting with reintroducing emotions into their people, it could help us all. I bet the O'Haras had something to do with this development."*

The rumor mill among the Breeds was fast and furious. With so many telepaths among their number, even the separation into cells couldn't keep many of them from communicating with each other. Word had spread quickly about the O'Hara brothers when an old O'Mara woman and her husband and daughter had been captured. She'd stood right up to the aliens and told them what the eldest O'Hara had told her to say and surprisingly, it had worked. She'd mentioned her maiden name and suddenly the family had been whisked out of the general population. They had friends down in the pens and they'd kept up the communication, telling them what had occurred.

Mike knew there were free humans working to better conditions for them all and the O'Haras were at the forefront of the fight. He'd even heard tell of the half-alien boy one of the brothers had fathered and his work to help his human kin. Harry, they called him, but the aliens called him Hara in almost reverent tones. Mike had watched and listened carefully, compiling information and looking for his own way out of the cells.

Whether that meant a breakout or cutting some kind of deal, he'd had enough of captivity. It was slowly driving him mad. Only his cousin's calming influence had helped him through the worst of it. Of the two, Dave was the thinker and Mike was the doer. It had been that way since they'd been kids. They'd worked together to build their business. Dave had written the books and Mike had marketed them. Together they'd made millions, but it was all gone now, and Dave was putting his education and talents to use, simply helping those few people he came into contact with stay sane—or as sane as they could given the circumstances.

"From what we've heard, the O'Haras have influenced the aliens more than anyone could have guessed. Maybe you're right," Dave mused silently to his cousin as he moved nearer the sobbing girl. *"Maybe after studying humans for more than a decade, the aliens are finally coming to realize their own lack of emotion and what it's cost their people as a whole. We've heard the rumors about the throwback crystallographer, right? He's teaching humans now, so maybe they've found some link between emotion and their prized crystal gift."*

"We've speculated about that before, Dave. We have no evidence to support that theory, but now that we know they're

experimenting on themselves to this radical an extent, it makes sense to think something's spurring them on."

Mike stroked her hair as his mind raced. Dave drew nearer and reached out his hand. Mike knew his cousin had a healing touch and he could feel Jaci's tears winding down.

"Give her to me."

Mike relinquished her without a word, knowing Dave would work his magic on her. He was glad of his cousin's gift. He liked Jaci and didn't like to see her suffer, even if she was an alien. After this he figured, if she survived her unintentional experimentation, she'd be less like the aliens and more like them. Maybe they could truly be friends now. Or more.

After all, she was a beautiful woman. Tall, lithe and pale, she was prettier than most human women he'd been with, and he'd been with a lot of human women before the cataclysm. Opportunities were rarer now that most human women were gone, but since their capture two years before, the aliens had given him and Dave chances to fuck other captives, which they only did if the woman they were thrown in with wanted it. Of course, with Dave's extraordinary ability to heal the mind as well as the body, most women wanted to fuck them in thanks after he'd laid his healing hands on them.

But Mike didn't love any of those women. Hell, he barely even knew them. He'd always needed at least to be friends with the woman beneath him in bed. He believed it made the sex better, and he knew Dave needed emotional attachment as well, due to his rather unique gifts. It had been hard for the cousins and though they'd never even considered enjoying a ménage before the cataclysm, the rarity of women had brought them to realize they enjoyed sharing the few women they'd found who wanted the pleasure they could bring.

Mike watched Jaci shift into Dave's arms with speculation.

They'd never fucked an alien woman but they'd heard about it from another captive who'd been asked to do it. Their body temperature was hotter and their pussies tight, or so the man had claimed. Mike licked his lips, thinking he'd really like to find out the truth of it for himself, and he knew just the woman he'd like to discover it with.

Chapter Two

Dave took her into his arms. She didn't weigh much for such a tall woman. He was more than a few inches over six feet and she only came up to his chin. He was amazed by the turn of events that brought her into his arms in need of his healing touch, but he'd learned that things generally happened for a reason. As his cousin had said, this could be a chance for them to regain their freedom. He didn't quite know how yet, but such an odd occurrence had to be significant in some way.

"David," she sobbed, her tears starting to ease as he stroked her hair.

"I'm here, Jaci. Just relax. Listen to my voice and relax, okay? I'll try to help you."

"How?" She hiccupped and he had to smile. She was cute when she was upset.

"I'm a healer." He'd never admitted his real talent to any of his captors before, preferring to let them think he was just a mild telepath. He didn't want to cooperate with them any further than he had to.

"Ruth told me you were a doctor before."

So she'd been talking to Ruth. He took in the information, realizing he should not have been too surprised. Ruth often spoke to the cousins about the things Jaci had told her about the outside each day. Little things, like whether it was raining or sunny, what the temperature was doing or what small furry creature she'd just discovered in the park area the aliens had set aside for walking. Jaci had tried to be kind in her way, and had succeeded even before her emotions had been released. He thought that was significant.

"I was a medical doctor and a psychiatrist, but what I really meant is that I can heal with my touch." He let a small pulse of his energy tingle along her skin and she jumped, making him smile.

"But I am not physically injured." Her voice was muffled against his chest and he found he liked the feel of her slight weight resting against him. He stooped his head to speak into her ear, his breath teasing her sensitive skin, raising goose bumps, he was pleased to note.

"I can heal physical injuries, it's true, but I also have a special gift, Jaci. I can heal the mind."

She drew back from him, wonder in her wide eyes.

"Truly?"

He nodded slowly, holding her gaze.

"But you never told Mara—"

"I'm a prisoner here against my will. I have no desire to cooperate with Mara or any of your people. I told them only what I wanted them to know."

She thought hard for a moment, he could tell, then her eyes brightened. A few new tears leaked out.

"That's how you've been helping Ruth and the others. I thought I noticed some of them were better after talking to you, but I never put it in the logs. I wasn't sure enough to record the observation. I'm not a real scientist after all, just a tech. Jacis practically never rise higher than tech level."

"You don't give yourself enough credit. There are countless

tales in human history about people overcoming humble beginnings to become great leaders and innovators. You're more than your genetic code, contrary to your people's beliefs. We all have greatness within us. We need only tap into it."

She tilted her head, considering his words. "I'm feeling something odd. I've never felt it before, but it feels light and bubbly and...yearning. I think it's hope." Her eyes dilated with pleasure as he watched.

"You're on the road, Jaci. Mike and I can help you, but you need to walk part of the way to meet us. Do you think you're up to it?"

She didn't understand what he meant, but she felt this...hope...bubble and swell within her. She felt like these men cared for her—even if they had no real reason to—and that they would help her.

"Did you heal me just now?" She couldn't be quite sure.

He shook his head. "I'll touch you, if you consent, but from what you said, your emotions seem to be manifesting gradually. You're going to have to deal with them as they come to you. Since it's a natural process there's not much I can do except ease your confusion. You have to integrate the emotions into your being, but I have no doubt you can. Just come to me if you start to feel overwhelmed, okay, Jaci? I'll do what I can to help you."

She nodded, moving back from him as he positioned his hands on either side of her face. He held her gaze as he let his gift delve deep, stroking and easing her suffering as best he could. Really, it was mostly reassurance he sent her that made her feel better. She was feeling overwhelmed and panicky, but he realized his and his cousin's presence and understanding helped calm her.

Maybe she would be theirs after all. God knows he'd

fantasized about her often enough, jerking off at night when the pressure got too great. He leaned forward, unable to stop himself from depositing a soft kiss on her warm lips.

She gasped and pulled back.

"Feel better, sweetheart?" He knew she was calmer after receiving his healing energy, but he wanted her to acknowledge it.

She smiled faintly and his hands fell back to his sides.

"Why did you kiss me?"

He shrugged, a roguish smile on his lips. "I couldn't help myself. I've dreamed about you, you know."

"Don't rush her, idiot!" Mike's scowling voice sounded through his brain. *"We can't afford to scare her off."*

"I know what I'm doing."

She tilted her head and smiled up at him, slightly embarrassed at his admission.

"I'm glad, though I don't deserve your attention. I've been so callous to you both. I don't understand how you can be so kind to me now."

"Join in anytime here, Mike. She needs to see us as a pair. If we're going to get her help getting out of here, she has to realize from the start that we travel as a set."

Mike came over to stand beside his cousin, facing her.

"You were always as fair with us as you could be given your lack of understanding of our emotions. We like you, Jaci." Mike dared to stroke her cheek and move in closer.

"Kiss her, Mike."

Mike needed no further urging from his manipulative cousin. He pulled her into his arms and bent slightly to take her lips more fully than Dave had, sending his tongue to stroke her hot lips and slide intimately within. She squirmed closer, her temperature rising appreciably as he delved deep into her mouth.

"That's enough. We don't want to scare her off, I believe you just said?" Dave's voice was disapproving as he watched them with narrowed eyes. Mike winked at him over her shoulder as he lifted away from her all too tempting lips.

"You kiss like a dream, Jaci." He liked the look of her flushed face, the sparkle in her eyes. "I'll dream of you tonight." He kissed her eyes, eliciting a soft moan from deep in her throat.

Dave came up behind her, sandwiching her warm body between the two cousins, surrounding her in their heat. They both could feel her increased heart rate as Dave leaned in to nip at the tender skin where her shoulder met her neck.

"My people don't dream much, but since the accident, I've been waking in the night with strange images in my head."

"Did your ancestors dream before they started tinkering with your genetic code?" Dave kept his tone gentle.

She nodded, leaning back against him. "There are stories of dreams so violent that warriors would wake with their weapons in their hands and kill the first person they saw. My ancestors were even more violent than your human predecessors."

"Well, I want you to dream only of us, Jaci. Happy dreams. Dreams of pleasure and understanding." Mike breathed in her ear as Dave laid his healing hands on her once more, reinforcing the thought.

"Dream of us tonight, sweetheart, and know that you are not alone." Dave whispered into her other ear as his energy zinged through her once more, calming and reassuring.

"Someone's coming to check on Jaci."

The message came unbidden into their minds, a forceful

voice neither of them had heard before. They drew away from her with a final caress and pushed her toward the monitor in the corner.

"Someone's coming. Can you say there was trouble with the equipment?" Mike walked with her to the place where he knew the monitor resided then moved past her to sit nonchalantly on the cot against the far wall.

She shook herself as if to gather her cool. "Telepathy, right? That's how you know someone's coming."

"I always knew you were smart." Mike smiled at her.

She grinned back at him, her smile full of pleasure. He felt as if he'd just praised his puppy and received a full-body tail wag in reward. She was just that cute and so freshly innocent on her journey of emotional discovery.

"Get to work, sweetheart," Dave reminded her in a low voice from the other side of the room, "and wipe that killer smile off your face. It's most un-Alvian looking."

His conspiratorial wink softened the chastising words as he pretended interest in the viewer the cousins had earned for good behavior. They were slowly learning the Alvian language and were permitted to read certain histories and other entertainment texts to keep their minds occupied. That had been a new development instituted by the Maras. Apparently they'd learned from their studies that captive Breeds fared better when there was sufficient activity for their rather advanced brains.

Jaci schooled her thoughts and her expression in preparation for the arrival of one of her people. She realized in that moment, she truly did feel better. Ruth had been right. David and Michael both had helped her acclimate some of the overwhelming emotion into her being. She felt better than she had since the accident and she knew she would come back to this cell to be with these men as often as she could in the coming days. She needed them if she was to survive this transformation and more than that, she liked them and wanted to get to know them on a more personal level than just as jailor and inmate.

"Jaci 192, is everything all right? I was sent to check on your progress."

Jaci sighed with relief as she recognized the new voice at the energized arch that was the only opening into the cell. She turned to her subordinate with a calm expression on her face.

"I am well, Lita 498. I am also pleased to see that your injury is healed. How does it feel?" She made small talk as she moved toward the arch, indicating with a small nod they would discuss the matter of the monitor outside the range of the Breeds, as was only prudent.

She left the monitors off as she lowered the energy field and left the room with the other girl. She reenergized the arch, but had left the monitors off inside the cell. To switch them on so quickly after Lita's arrival would only raise suspicion. She turned to Lita 498, explaining the supposed monitor malfunction to the other woman. The lower-graded tech took Jaci's explanation at face value. After all, the monitors were not entirely infallible and failures were more common than the Maras wanted to admit. Lita left to report back to their superiors and Jaci calculated in her mind a reasonable time for fixing the malfunction she'd claimed.

It gave her just a few minutes with the cousins to explain before she'd have to turn the monitor back on. It would have to be enough. She reentered the room calmly, then broke into a grin as she reenergized the arch behind her.

"I only have a few minutes." She moved to the area by the

monitor so she'd be ready when the time came to turn it back on. "I turn this off every day when I come in for routine maintenance. Once each week, I also run a self-diagnostic program that takes approximately ten minutes. It is offline during the diagnostic, so we can talk freely. Every once in a while, perhaps once a month or sometimes twice, the device will jam. That's what I told them happened today. Such problems can be cleared up usually in about twenty minutes." Her orderly mind wanted to give them all the facts.

"So you're saying you won't be able to spend this much time with us very often." Mike nodded. "We'll work with that, now that we know what to expect."

She sighed with relief. "Thank you." Her eyes sought each of them. "Thank you both. I honestly don't think I could face this without your support. I was so frightened."

Dave moved forward and hugged her close, bending to place a fierce kiss on her lips. He was making up for the kiss Mike had given her, wanting his share and cementing his claim. The message was clear. The cousins wanted her. Both of them. Equally.

"Dream of us."

He sent one last tingling jolt of his healing power through her in reassurance, then drew back. She knew the time had come to switch on the monitor and go back to her emotionless existence. Emotionless on the outside at least. Inside she was dealing with amazing changes she was only just beginning to understand.

Jaci slept well for the first time since accidentally exposing herself, and dreamed of four strong arms holding her close within a tight circle of security. She dreamed of the kisses she'd shared with the two cousins and more that she could only imagine.

She'd had sex with several different partners as part of her duties, but she'd never made love. That last encounter with Grady Prime was perhaps as close as she'd ever come. In the rare free moments since her exposure, she'd begun to review the databases of human writings and even some from her culture's long-distant past. She knew intellectually there was supposed to be a difference between having sex and making love, but she'd never experienced it. Maybe with the cousins, she could find the exchange of emotion that would elevate the sexual act to that sublime level of which the poets in both their cultures wrote.

In her dream, Michael and David were in her room with her. They were in her bed and all three of them were naked. While Michael was the brawnier of the two, her desire flared at seeing that David was just as fit and had the same wide, strong shoulders. His deep blue eyes glittered down at her as his cousin's warm brown gaze flowed over her body like a caress. She was in the middle of the suddenly expanded bed with Michael leaning on his elbow on one side and David on the other. Both cousins were about the same height but Michael's bulk always made him seem somehow bigger, but not now. Now, with their clothes off, both men were equally devastating, equally masculine, and equally desirable. Jaci felt her temperature spike with the undeniable heat of passion.

"Well, is it like you expected?" Mike wanted to know.

"Is what like I expected?"

"Having us both in bed with you." David's voice was accompanied by a sweep of his big hand down her arm. She was under a thin sheet but both of them were gloriously nude above it where she could look her fill.

"I hadn't given it much thought until just recently."

"We have." Michael reached over and kissed her sweetly, one hand cupping her cheek. "Almost from the first moment we saw you, we dreamed of you in our arms, and in our beds. We've wanted to be with you for a very long time, Jaci."

"Really?"

David captured her attention by pulling the sheet down and placing his warm palm over one of her breasts, cupping her and toying with the hardening peak. She hadn't known her sensitive skin could enjoy such stimulation, but then she was learning a lot from these two men that she'd never even contemplated before.

"Really," David said, just before his lips latched onto her breast, sucking with gentle but exciting pressure. Michael moved down and swirled his tongue around her other nipple before sucking it into his mouth, tugging with the same rhythm as his cousin.

She noted the expressions on their handsome faces, so tender they nearly stole her breath. She held them to her with trembling hands, sinking her fingers deep into their hair—Michael's short and fuzzy, tickling her palm and David's longer waves that teased her senses with luxurious silkiness. She'd never known such pleasure just from having a man—no, make that two men—lick her skin.

Michael ripped the sheet away from her body, his fingers roaming downward to the juncture of her thighs. David pulled at her leg, urging her to make room for their hands as both men laved at her sensitive breasts. She spread her legs and they moaned in near unison as they zeroed in on her most sensitive areas.

David lifted her leg over his hip, attacking from underneath, using his long fingers to push deep into her channel, taking the wetness gathering there and moving it down just a bit to the pucker of her ass. Michael's skilled fingers played along her folds while his other hand shaped her breast, kneading as he began to nip at the peak in a way that excited her beyond all reason.

"Do you like that?" David raised his head to watch her reaction. "Do you like him biting you, nipping at your tasty skin?" Mutely she nodded, unable to speak beyond her incredible excitement. "Good." His murmur of approval was followed by a satisfied smile as he moved down her body, lifting her leg over his shoulder as he left her field of vision. She didn't know what to expect but when his wet tongue dove into her channel, she nearly screamed.

Michael lifted his head and looked down her long body to where his cousin was feasting on her, a smile of envy and mischievous delight on his beloved face. He rose up and kissed her hard and deep, both hands shaping her breasts as David paid homage to her lower regions.

"Dave eats pussy really well." Michael let her up for a breath of air between kisses. "Don't you think?" He tugged hard on her nipple when she didn't respond. "Don't you?"

Jaci clutched his broad shoulders as David nipped her clit, bringing her closer and closer to a perilous edge. "He's a master."

Michael laughed and looked down her long body at his cousin. "You hear that, Dave? She called you Master."

"About time." David's words rumbled against her excited skin as he growled in male satisfaction.

"I'll tell you a secret." Michael leaned down to blanket her upper body with his. "David likes eating pussy almost as much as he likes a woman's ass. Do you think you can handle that? Do you think you can handle both of us inside you at the same time? Because that's what's coming."

She gasped as David moved his talented tongue down to circle her anus. "I've never done that before."

David growled, driving her higher. "I think he likes that." Michael chuckled. "Come to think of it, I like the idea too. I like that we'll be the first men to have your ass and your pussy at the same time. The only men. After us, you'll never have another."

His arms grew tight around her as David redoubled his efforts. She was so close!

"I don't want other men. Only you. You and David!" She practically screamed then as she came. The cousins held her, never letting up as she spasmed in their strong arms. They held her tight as she came down from the highest precipice she'd ever climbed. She remembered their soft kisses on her body as she fell into a deep sleep and didn't dream again until morning.

§

Jaci hurried through her morning duties and made her way to the cells, intent on completing the list of tasks that would bring her to the cousins' cell once more. Ruth, too, was someone she wanted to speak with.

Before long, she was facing the other woman in her cell, having just shut down the monitor.

"You were right and I want to thank you for helping me yesterday. I had a long talk with David and Michael and they were wonderful to me. Thank you, Ruth."

Ruth moved forward, cradling her baby in her arms as she smiled softly. "I'm glad." She nodded with her chin toward the monitor. "I hope you don't mind, but they told me about the monitor last night."

"You're telepathic too, aren't you?" It was something the woman had never admitted to, but Jaci suspected it strongly now that she was getting to know and understand these people better.

Ruth blushed and dropped her eyes. "A little. I need to be in close proximity for it to work. A few yards are about my limit, but I can communicate with a few people in the cells around me who also have the gift."

"Amazing," Jaci shook her head, experiencing true wonder at the Breeds' abilities. "I'm glad you've been able to talk to someone besides your baby. I never liked the idea of these cells, but the Maras are in charge and they designed this place."

Ruth reached out to touch her arm gently. "I never blamed you for this prison. Don't fret. I know you don't have much power among your people."

"I'm a Jaci and only ranked 192nd. You're right. I have no real power. My purpose until now has been to serve. Jacis are bred to work in the labs. We have orderly, scientific minds, but we rarely rise to the level of skill and innovation necessary to be top scientists. We are mostly lab techs, though a few of my relations have the crystal gift."

"What's that?"

"Each child is tested at age thirteen for the crystal gift. If they prove any level of the skill they are moved into the engineering program. As you may have realized, our technology is all based on crystals, but it's the power of the crystallographer's mind that tunes the crystal and allows us to harness its energy." She went about her tasks in the cell so she'd be ready to move on when she switched the monitor back on. "The Maras would not want you to know, but the crystal gift is leaving our people. Each generation breeds fewer and fewer crystallographers. Our greatest at present is a throwback and under normal circumstances, he would not be permitted to breed, but he's found a mate. It was a huge scandal, but he claimed a resonance mate from among your people. She has proven to have an amazing level of crystal skill herself. Together, they are unstoppable, and I personally think their success is what has made the High Council consent to this experiment to bring back some of my people's emotion."

"Without the crystal gift, you can't power your cities." Ruth caught on quickly.

"And without emotion, the crystal gift is leaving our people."

Ruth shook her head in wonder. "I would never have thought of that, but we've all been speculating."

Jaci had to grin. "I guess the telepathic grapevine is quite active down here."

"You can say that again." Ruth laughed outright. "We don't have much else to occupy us down here, except Dave and Mike make an effort to find entertaining and educational things on their viewer and share them as often as they can with the rest of us who can hear. We've been learning a lot about your people since you installed it in their cell."

"And speculating a great deal, I imagine." Jaci found herself astounded by their ingenuity. "I'd be willing to help you decipher anything that might be confusing. Just ask."

Ruth's smile lit her whole face. "That's great! Thanks."

She found herself in the cousins' cell shortly thereafter, a smile full of apprehension on her face as she faced them.

"It's off," she said as calmly as she could.

She didn't want to appear weak, but she really needed a hug. The emotions were flooding her again and each cell she visited made her want to break down and cry. But she had to be strong. She couldn't show the changes that were happening to her.

"Come here, sweetheart." Michael's tone was gentle as he tugged her into his arms.

She felt at peace for the first time since leaving her dreams of these two men. She snuggled into Michael's embrace, unsurprised when David moved up behind them, placing his soothing hands on her head and neck, massaging away her tension with his magic touch.

"How's that? Better?" David asked at her ear, making her shiver.

She heard a sound come from her throat that she'd never made before. It was a hum of pleasure and it alerted her to another sound, a low pulsing hum that had started sometime after Michael had opened his generous arms to her.

She stood back from them with wide eyes, breaking contact and the hum stopped.

Could it be?

"Blood of the Founders!" Her whispered exclamation caught their attention.

"What's wrong?" David's voice was a little sharper as she looked at him.

"I don't know. Maybe nothing, but..." She moved forward, her hand outstretched to touch his cheek, gently, with great uncertainty.

And there was the Hum. She knew what it was now, with dreadful certainty. Her heart was both elated and troubled.

She let him go and turned to Michael, repeating her action. As she touched him, the Hum returned. But how could this be? Her thoughts whirled. They only had about five minutes left for her to tell them what she suspected, but it was much too complicated.

She firmed her shoulders and turned to face them both, touched by the concern on their faces. She'd just have to do the best she could.

"I don't understand this, but have you ever heard the term 'resonance mate'? It is part of my culture's distant past. There might be something in the ancient texts they've given you access to that could help you learn more, because there's no way I can tell you much in the time we have remaining before I have to turn the monitor back on."

Her eyes grew wild and the men moved closer, seeking to calm her. They touched her, David first, taking her into his arms, then Michael surrounding her from behind and the Hum returned, pulsing through her entire being, making her feel warm and comforted in a way she had never before experienced.

"Take it easy, sweetheart. Whatever has you troubled, you can tell us in your own good time." David was so kind, his words gentle as he kissed her cheeks and eyes with a softness that nearly broke her heart.

"You can't hear it, can you?"

"Hear what?" Michael asked from behind, stroking her waist and hips with his hands as his mouth burrowed under the hair at her nape, placing soft kisses on her heated skin.

"The Hum. When I touch you—both of you—we Hum. It's the first of the tests for resonance mates. There's supposed to be only one perfect match for each person, but I Hum with both of you. I never noticed it before."

David pulled back to look down at her. "This sounds serious."

"It is."

She gasped as he leaned in and kissed her once, very thoroughly before releasing her. She was spun around and Michael took an equally devastating kiss from her lips before she could form a coherent thought. He released her abruptly and set her away from them.

"God, but I've been dreaming of that all day. But we're running out of time."

She was glad someone was keeping their wits about them. She moved back toward the monitor.

"Look it up on the viewer if you can. There's too much for me to explain now, but please, I hope you don't mind. I never expected that I would ever Hum with anyone. It's not something that happens to my people anymore."

"Not since they bred emotion out of them, right?" David's voice was knowing.

She was amazed. "You're right! And now that I'm changing, this has changed too. Amazing." She shook her head in wonder. "I'll have to test this further."

Michael drew her attention back to him by taking her around the waist and dropping a small kiss on her brow. She'd never felt so cherished.

"Just don't go around kissing all the boys. I think Dave and I would have something to say about that."

He smiled and she laughed, but it made her warm to think that these two handsome men would care what she did and with whom. But then, she'd been their only link to the outside world for months now. Perhaps they cared for her in some odd fashion. She'd heard that prisoners sometimes fell in love with their jailors.

Her face fell at the thought as she left Michael's embrace. She wasn't very good at hiding her emotions in front of these men. They knew her too well.

"What you're saying doesn't make sense. I know I'm the only woman from the outside that you have contact with. I can't trust that if things were different you would still feel the same."

"Stockholm Syndrome, you mean?" David asked, coming forward, looking intrigued. "I'm aware of the implications in our situation but I don't think either Mike or I would fall victim to such feelings. I know for a fact we both want to rip the legs off the bastard who hunted us down and captured us like dogs." His expression turned violent. "I heard his men calling him Prime. A prime asshole, I figure."

She realized suddenly that these men hadn't gone quietly into imprisonment if they'd sent their best troops after them.

"Grady Prime," she said softly, nodding to herself.

"Yeah, that was the bastard's name. Grady," Michael growled, his eyes going cold with hatred. "You know him?"

She felt uncomfortable. She could hardly tell these two that she'd serviced him just days before. She somehow understood just the idea of it would make these men violent. But she couldn't lie either. They would know. They could read her too easily, with their lifetimes of experience with the emotions she was only just starting to feel.

"I know him, thought we do not interact often. He's an elite, a Prime. He outranks me to a very considerable degree, even if he is of soldier stock. In the normal course of things, a Jaci would rank slightly higher than any soldier, but not a Prime, and especially not Grady Prime. He is the best of the best."

Michael snorted. "Well, at least there's that. It took their best man to take us down. We'd been on the move for years, but this Grady bastard had us on the *run*. Until he came along, the patrols were easy to outmaneuver, but this guy was downright spooky. He always seemed one step ahead of us."

"That's because I was."

The cold male voice sounded from the archway, startling all three of them. And there he was. Grady Prime, in the flesh.

"Holy shit," Michael cursed softly, moving in front of Jaci as if to protect her from the soldier.

Dave was more direct as he faced the other man. "You have some nerve showing your face here, scumsucker."

Grady just watched them with mild curiosity. "I've come for the girl."

David stepped in front of Grady, blocking his path across the room to her.

"You'll have to go through us to get her and I see you've left your goon squad at home this time. I've been waiting two years to get a piece of you, so just try to take her. Make my day."

She'd never heard David sound more lethal and the look in his eyes truly scared her. There was only one way out of this situation. She had to bluff them all, but she didn't know if she had it in her. Still, she had to try. She didn't want any of them getting hurt over her.

She took a deep breath, schooled her features and stepped out from behind Michael. He tried to grasp her arm, but she evaded him.

"What do you require, Grady Prime?"

"Mara 12 has ordered that you accompany my team on a short mission. There is some technical data that must be gathered and you were chosen to do it."

She carefully hid her relief. "I am almost finished with the maintenance of this cell and can be with you momentarily." Without waiting for acknowledgment, she turned back to Michael, gave him a look that begged him to stand down and moved to switch on the monitor.

She tried her best not to look at either of the cousins as she finished her duties and walked straight to Grady Prime. The soldier had not eased his vigilance with the two Breeds, but stood ready should they offer him trouble. She had to respect all three men for standing their ground, but not giving in to their baser emotions.

She'd almost gained the door when David shot out his hand, catching her arm in a light grip. He held her by the wrist, his skin against hers and the air filled with the low, throbbing Hum she'd only just recognized.

"Will you be all right with him?" His concerned expression demanded an answer.

She nodded, trying to convey all that she was feeling without giving herself away to the soldier who watched with great interest. "Grady Prime is our greatest warrior. There is no shame in having been captured by him."

"I didn't mean—"

"What is that noise?" Grady was looking at them strangely, thankfully distracted by the noise that only he and Jaci could hear with their more sensitive Alvian ears.

She tried to look innocent while tugging her wrist free of David's light hold. The Hum stopped and Grady eyed them suspiciously.

"I don't hear anything." Michael stepped up to face the soldier, belligerence in every line of his hard muscled body.

"You wouldn't," Grady said quietly, his voice calm and not at all mocking. "I doubt human ears would pick up something this low frequency." He shook his head. "But it's gone now. Must have been some equipment somewhere that's just switched off."

Jaci tried not to show her relief, nodding calmly. "Must have been." She stepped forward to stand next to Grady. Ever the soldier, he hadn't let down his guard for a moment with the men in the room. "I am ready to depart with you, Prime. Will the journey be long?"

"We should be back by nightfall."

She turned to the cousins. "Then I will see you tomorrow, gentlemen, unless I am reassigned. Have a nice day."

It was her standard parting from all her charges and had been for years so there was no way it would raise any alarms with those who watched over the monitors. Still, she wished she could say something more private to the two men who had become so important to her. Any other time, she would have jumped at the chance to be assigned to Grady Prime even temporarily. It was a sign the Maras were pleased with her work and it could mean advancement was not far off for her, but just now, with so much happening to her inner being, any further change was unwelcome.

She couldn't let it show, of course. She couldn't let anything show.

She went as calmly as she could out the cell door with Grady Prime to face whatever the future held in store for her.

Chapter Three

Their destination was the Southern Engineering Facility. Jaci had never been there before, and she found it quite an amazing sight. The facility was built in dense green jungle that sparkled and sang with natural crystal deposits. She felt an energy in the air that she'd never felt before and she realized what it was almost as soon as she saw the small woman bounding toward the shuttle.

She was a Breed! Roaming free about the facility and even carrying advanced crystals on her person, she greeted Grady Prime by name, even daring to reach up and place a kiss on his cheek. Jaci had never seen the like.

The woman's broad smile turned to her and suddenly a puzzled frown replaced her open expression. Jaci immediately felt fear. This woman could see right through her, she realized, and it could spell disaster.

The woman stepped forward, offering her hand. Jaci had no polite choice but to accept the human gesture of greeting.

"I'm Callie. You must be the lab tech Mara was sending along to take samples."

Jaci pulled back from the disturbing contact with the woman's cool skin.

"I am Jaci 192 and you are correct. Mara 12 sent instructions on my duties here, which I studied on the trip. I am ready to collect the samples once I am directed toward the patient."

Callie chuckled. "That would be me."

"You're pregnant then?"

Jaci found it hard to believe. This small woman seemed too delicate to be carrying a baby. According to Mara's notes, Callie was supposed to be just entering her second trimester and Jaci couldn't see much of a bulge around her middle.

Callie nodded with a broad smile that Jaci found infectious.

"Yes. I'm having a girl and she's quite active already."

"Congratulations," Jaci said with some confusion as the bubbly woman escorted her into the facility. The soldiers were doing various tasks around them, loading and unloading crates of supplies and equipment which had been their primary task on this trip. "But how do you know it's a girl? Mara seemed to indicate that you have not yet had medical testing."

"I don't need medical testing to know. This child is telepathic, as am I. She's talking to me already. Well, not *talking*, but sending me images at least." Callie opened a door to the landing control room and breezed through, sweeping Jaci along a series of corridors that she hardly noted.

"Amazing." Jaci's mind was moving quickly. "I'd heard of these abilities, of course, and encountered them among my charges from time to time, but I had no idea a child in the womb could communicate with its mother."

"And its father, even if he's not telepathic at all." A deep voice sounded from the back of the large workroom they'd just entered and a tall, fair, Alvian man stepped forward to wrap his arms around the Breed woman.

"I am Jaci 192."

She had to remember her manners though she was secretly

astounded by the obvious relationship between these two people. The man especially surprised her. There was emotion in his eyes and joy on his face as he hugged the small woman. She'd never seen an Alvian face so animated before.

The man nodded at her respectfully but did not loose the woman. "I am Davin."

Suddenly it all made sense.

"Chief Engineer." She tried desperately to keep her voice even, but she knew she failed when the woman's eyes flashed up to hers. "I am honored to be of service."

The man seemed to look her over more thoroughly then, placing a kiss on the crown of Callie's head before releasing her. He faced Jaci with narrowed eyes.

"It is to my mate that you will be of service. I expect you to show her the same courtesy you would show me. Is that clear?"

"Perfectly, Chief Engineer. Again, I am honored."

She could feel the caution emanating from him. She knew he was a throwback. Everyone knew it. Unlike the vast majority of Alvians, Davin's genetics were very much like that of their ancestors, an aberration that happened every once in a while even in the best of laboratory conditions. He had emotions and had dealt with them all his life. Stories abounded about his finding of a resonance mate among the Breed women.

The High Council hadn't liked it at first. Under normal circumstances, a throwback would never be allowed to procreate, but Davin was unique. He was the most gifted crystallographer in generations and his skills could not be lost to the madness that would claim him had he not found his mate. Neither could the High Council afford to alienate him. If he wanted to have a child with his Breed mate, then there wasn't much they could do to prevent it.

Which brought her back to why she'd been selected to come

here. They weren't happy about it, but the High Council wanted to monitor the child's development. Not only was Davin the greatest crystallographer in many generations, but his mate was also highly skilled with the crystal gift. Rumor had it that their abilities had expanded when they came together, to the point where the High Council could not do without either of them.

That explained why this Breed female was given extraordinary freedom in this secure facility. Without her and her mate, it would cease to operate and all the Council's technology would eventually falter and die without the crystals these two were tuning for their use.

Davin appeared highly protective of his mate. Undoubtedly he'd had a hard life among the Alvians before he'd found her. Jaci felt sympathy welling up inside her no matter how hard she fought against it. She wanted to put this man's mind at ease. Jaci would never do anything to insult or hurt his mate and she sought for some way to express that without blowing her own secret.

"I have heard rumors about your mating, Chief Engineer. I enjoy reading our people's histories and I'm gladdened by the idea that you have found your resonance mate. Such things should not have been lost to our people, though I believe that is the case."

Davin looked at her sharply, but seemed to relax as his mate put her hand on his arm. Jaci became aware of the Hum between them and smiled. That sound was fast becoming familiar to her and she welcomed the evidence that what she'd heard when she'd touched the cousins had been the genuine article.

"You are an odd creature, Jaci 192. I am glad Mara sent you. Perhaps in this instance, she knew what she was doing."

Davin retreated, stepping aside so the women could make their way to a small door set in the rear of the room.

Jaci followed meekly behind Callie, realizing the woman was taking her to their private quarters. Suddenly she was alone with the Breed woman.

Callie shut the door and turned on her, hands on her hips.

"There are no monitors of any kind here. We may speak freely."

Jaci swallowed hard. This woman's look was too knowing and she feared what she might say. Jaci turned to her small medical kit to busy herself.

"Shall we begin the sample collection? I will need a blood sample."

When no answer was forthcoming, Jaci had to raise her eyes. The woman hadn't been fooled at all.

"I'm an empath, Jaci. I feel your fear and your turmoil."

"Shit."

Callie laughed as she moved to the couch and sat down. "Now that's a very human expression. I wonder where you picked it up?"

"I maintain some of the cells where the Maras keep their Breed subjects."

"Prisoners, you mean?" Callie's voice had turned cold and Jaci felt uncomfortable in the extreme. "So you're a jailer? Funny for a jailer to feel the level of guilt you just put out."

"I don't like that they're prisoners. But honestly, it never bothered me before."

"Before what?"

"Before I could feel." Jaci's voice was very soft, almost a whisper as emotion threatened to overwhelm her.

Callie just watched her with non-judgmental eyes. "So what happened? Why can you suddenly feel emotion when every other Alvian but Davin, can't?"

Jaci knew then she was done for. She pitched herself into a chair and told this strange woman the whole sordid story. She didn't care anymore. The burden was too great.

"Just do me one favor," Jaci asked tearfully, her emotions flooding her in a way she just couldn't handle. "Get word to Michael and David—and Ruth too. Tell them I never meant to hurt them. I considered them friends and their friendship meant a lot to me. Please, just tell them that."

Callie put a hand over Jaci's, bridging the distance between their two chairs and suddenly Jaci started to feel better. It wasn't the same kind of healing touch David had, but it was soothing and definitely had the flavor of this woman's psychic abilities. She was calming her, soothing her distraught emotions.

"Come now," Callie said, compassion in her eyes. "You sound as if you'll never see them again."

"I probably won't. When the Maras find out what's happened, they'll put me down or imprison me. I wasn't worthy of testing the agent. What's one more Jaci?"

"I don't know, but I think *this* Jaci is very important." Callie's smile calmed her senses and stopped her tears. "And Mara 12 won't hear about this from me, or from either of my mates."

Jaci was stunned for a moment by her use of the plural. "You have more than one? Is that possible?" She hadn't dared hope.

Callie smiled softly. "I can guess what you've heard on the rumor mill. Davin is my true resonance mate, and I love him dearly, but so is Rick. We all found that out in a rather upsetting way when Rick had to save my life. They didn't get along too well at first, but we've all come to accept the arrangement now. After all, I keep telling them, my own mother has three mates, so they should count themselves lucky." Callie chuckled, but Jaci was astounded by her words.

"But the ancient texts say there is only one resonance mate for each person."

"Been studying up on the topic, have you?" Callie gave her a knowing smile.

Jaci blushed. "There are two men...I Hum with them and I was wondering if maybe..."

Callie jumped up and went to the cabinet on the far side of the room. She opened a few drawers until she found what she was looking for, then came back to stand before Jaci, holding out her hand. Jaci reacted to the motion by raising her palm and a pure, clear crystal dropped into it.

"Kiss them both. Use this. See what happens."

"I couldn't." Jaci immediately recognized the worth of the small, absolutely perfect crystal Callie had given her.

Callie closed Jaci's fingers over the warm stone. "You can and you will. It's quite possible they are both your resonance mates. My mother has three true mates. I have two. Only testing will reveal the truth for you."

"But there's only supposed to be one."

Callie sank back on to the sofa behind her. "We have a theory about that, but it's a little farfetched. I think it has to do with the shortage of women on Earth. There's no way there's one female for every male, even counting your people, so nature, or God, or whatever higher power you believe in, has decided we have to share."

Jaci paused to consider her words. "I suppose it could be

possible." But she wasn't convinced.

"Or maybe just one of the men you Hum with will turn out to be your true mate. Or worst case, neither will. Just because you Hum doesn't mean you are mates." Callie paused. "Test them. See what happens. And I promise to keep your secret. I agree you probably should keep this hidden as long as you can. Things are changing for my people, slowly but surely. If you can hold out a bit longer, you might find it all works out for you and your potential mates. Have faith."

They talked a bit more and Jaci took the samples Mara had requested. She tried not to jump when a Breed man came into the room and pulled Callie into his kiss, but she did check the crystal glowing in her hand.

"This is Rick," Callie introduced him with a smile. "Rick, meet Jaci."

"Jaci 192," she clarified, reaching out to accept the other man's handshake as was customary between Breeds.

"I don't hold with numbering people, so I'll just call you Jaci, okay?" Rick seemed somewhat unfriendly at first, but when Jaci smiled at him, he eased up a bit, confusion on his face as he truly looked at her for the first time. "Have you had contact with a human healer recently?"

Jaci was astounded and not a little afraid. "How can you tell?"

Rick looked at her closely, putting Callie back on the couch. "That sort of energy is rare and it leaves traces another healer can sometimes sense. Your healer is strong. Very strong. What happened that he had to expend so much energy on you?"

Jaci was afraid, but Callie came to her rescue. "I'll fill you in on all the details later, but suffice to say, poor Jaci has been through a huge upheaval lately. Is the healer one of the men you mentioned?"

Mutely, she nodded.

"Then he expended a lot of his energy on you. How is he doing?"

Jaci's eyes widened in shock. "It could hurt him? Healing me can harm him? Why didn't he say something?"

Rick tilted his head, watching her most un-Alvian responses. "It would weaken him. All healing does. Some kinds of healing gifts work differently, but the few healers I've known have all experienced power drain of one sort or another. We give it to the people we heal, you see."

"Oh, no." Jaci collapsed into her seat. "He touched me earlier today, but he did it yesterday too. Several times. It felt so good. He calmed my turmoil. But I don't want to hurt him in order to make myself feel better."

"He's a mind healer?" Now it was Rick who sounded shocked.

Jaci nodded. "He said he can do both. He can heal physical injuries, but also problems of the mind."

"Wow." Rick sat on the couch next to Callie, putting his arm around her shoulders, playing absently with the ends of her hair. "He must be something. I've heard rumors of mind healers, but they're few and far between. The power needed is enormous, and the drain of that kind of work is serious."

Jaci shot to her feet. "I've got to get back! I've got to check on him!"

Callie could feel the Alvian woman's panic and she knew it would do her no good.

"Wait, Jaci. Think. You can't show them your fear and I might just have a way to check on your man without your people knowing. Will you let me try?"

Jaci sank back down still agitated, but willing to listen. "How?"

"My brother is a strong telepath. You probably have heard of him. The Alvians call him Hara."

"Hara is your brother? Holy shit!"

"She's definitely been hanging around with humans," Rick observed with a chuckle at the earthy expression coming out of this very proper Alvian woman.

Callie smiled. "Are any of your Breed friends telepathic at all?"

"David is. And so is Michael. Ruth too, but she has to be close to someone to hear them, she said."

"All right," Callie said, leaning forward, "here's what we're going to do."

After a bit of planning, Callie contacted her brother using a secure crystal. Jaci was warmed by the obvious love in his voice as he talked with his sister and she filled him in on Jaci's situation. She was growing uncomfortable with how many people were learning her secret, but she realized quickly that she needed them. She needed a support system of some kind if she were to survive, changed as she was.

Hara was in the northern city and took only a moment to seek out David's mind in the pens beneath. He reported back that David was tired, but otherwise all right. David himself had said he was fine, but Hara could see deeper. He could use his extraordinary gifts to feel the energy levels of the mind he contacted, and he reported the truth back to his sister.

"Dave wants to know how Jaci's doing. Actually, both he and Mike are a bit irate. They're worried about her going off with someone they're calling 'that scumbag Grady'. Do you think they mean our old pal Grady Prime?" Callie chuckled at her brother's humor but Jaci was too on edge.

"Tell them I'm fine. Grady Prime would never harm me."

Apparently he heard that through the communication crystal because he answered her directly. "I think they're more worried that he's going to put the move on you. They sound very possessive. Why's that?"

She didn't understand all of his words, but the tone was clear. "I don't want him."

Callie caught her attention. "You and I both know with a man that highly ranked in your society, it's not a matter of what you want."

Jaci shrugged uncomfortably. "Yes, he has asked me to consider having sex with him again, but I don't think he would force the issue. He seems to think that even with his rank, because he's a soldier, he'd be insulting me."

"Again?" It was Rick who caught her guilty flush. "You've had sex with him before?"

"Only once," she admitted uncomfortably, "and only because it was my duty. He's an elite. I was filling in for the girl who usually services him for sample collection. It was last week, just after the test agent started to change me and he seemed to notice how much I...uh...well...how much I enjoyed having sex with him. He told me he liked it and wanted to do it again, but he gave me the choice to seek him out. I haven't and I won't. I don't want him."

Two pairs of Breed eyes watched her in shocked silence. It was Hara who came to her rescue, his voice sounding through the room over the communication crystal.

"I can't tell them that."

"No!" she shouted in alarm. "You can't!"

"I just said that, didn't I?" He seemed to chuckle a bit at her vehemence. "I'll tell them not to worry. I've known Grady Prime all my life and I know he wouldn't force himself on any woman. That's a truth they can find some comfort in, but if I were you, I'd straighten out this thing with them when you get back. They are jealous men and they really seem to hate Grady for some reason."

"He's the one who finally captured them," she told him despondently. She wasn't looking forward to facing her men—her friends, she corrected herself—with the news.

She heard Hara sigh on the other side of the connection. "That explains it then. I'm impressed it took Grady to get them. They only send him out for the hard cases." He paused just a moment. "Look, Jaci, when you get back I'm going to track you down. Mara 12 won't suspect anything if I make friends with you now that you've met my sister. I'll find you to thank you for treating her so well. Praising you can only help your career, right?"

"I don't give a shit about my career."

Rick chuckled at her use of the human expletive that seemed to have become her favorite.

"I can understand that, given what's been happening to you, but you can't let my mother and her pals know that."

Suddenly she remembered just who she was talking to. Hara was the son of Mara 12 and a Breed male with Hara DNA. Jaci knew because she was a member of Mara 12's staff, though Hara's origins weren't a matter of public knowledge. He was half-Alvian and related to one of the most important scientists in the city. Undoubtedly he was watched closely, but he also deserved great respect, just by virtue of his DNA—Mara and Hara together was a formidable mix.

"So, I'm going to find you when you get back, to thank you for being nice to my sister and you're going to become my friend. My mother knows how close I am to Callie."

"Why would you want to be my friend?" She was dumbfounded by the generosity of these people she'd only just met.

Hara chuckled and it warmed her. "I think you need all the friends you can get right now, Jaci. There are precious few of us with entry to the Alvian culture who can understand and experience emotion. I'm hoping in the long-term we can help our human friends and family by influencing Alvian society for positive change and understanding."

"I'd be happy if they'd just leave me alone," Jaci grumbled.

"I understand your feelings, but what about your friends? What about Mike, Dave and Ruth and her baby? Don't you want them to have a better life too?"

"I do," she said softly, "but what can I do to help that? I'm only a Jaci and not of high rank."

"Let me worry about that, sweetheart." Hara's voice was calming and soothed her distraught senses, even over the crystal. Only one other man had ever called her by that human endearment and she desperately wanted to feel his arms around her again.

"Tell David I miss him," she said softly, "and that I won't let him touch me again unless he promises not to drain himself."

There was a short silence while she imagined Hara passing on the message telepathically.

"He says you can try to keep him away, but you won't succeed." He chuckled. "And Mike's jealous as hell."

Her heart lifted for the first time. "Tell Michael not to worry. I miss him too. Just as much."

"Just so you get the full picture, she Hums with both of them." Callie chimed in, sharing Jaci's secret with her brother.

"Really?" Hara sounded interested and a bit amused. "Well, that's a nice development. Shall I explain to them what it could mean?"

Jaci's heart started pounding. "I tried, but there was no time. We only have about ten minutes each day. This is all still so new."

"Well, I have all night to talk with them now that we've established contact. I can tell them about the tests if you like, and my own observations of my father's mating with Mama Jane, as well as my sister's experience. It might help. Resonance mates are a wholly Alvian concept and not something they would have experienced in the old world."

"I think that's a good idea, Harry," Callie told her brother. "I've given her a small crystal she can use to do the tests. If they are mates..." She let the sentence drift off.

"If either or both of those men find that Jaci is their true mate, I'll do all in my power to see they can be together. It's the least the Alvians owe humanity for taking and changing their world. But we have to take this one step at a time, and I'm going to talk to Papa Caleb too. Maybe he's seen something."

"Thank you, Hara. I fully realize that you don't have to do any of this for me and I can only surmise you are a wise and kind person. You have my gratitude." Jaci's formal words rang clear through the room and her heart was a bit lighter. Somehow that feeling of hope was bubbling up to the surface again, even if she had no real reason to think the future would be any better than the present.

"I think we're going to be good friends, Jaci. I'll look for you in a day or two. Until then, take care."

Jaci took his words to heart. She would have to be extra

careful not to show her expanding emotions. They were getting stronger all the time now and each new revelation stunned her with its intensity.

"I love you, Harry." Callie said to her brother, signing off with clear affection for her sibling, so far away.

They ended the communication and Jaci just sat there in shock for a moment. So much had happened in such a short time.

"I don't know what to say."

Callie laughed, putting her small hand over Jaci's and passing some of that amazing empathic warmth to her, making her feel slightly better. Jaci marveled at the small Breed woman's intense power.

"Say you won't mind when I request Mara sends you from now on to check my baby's progress. I like you, Jaci, and I want to help you."

Jaci felt a tear slip from her eye. This woman had a huge heart and Jaci could learn a thing or two from her. Silently, she nodded, unable to speak lest her emotions get the best of her. It was a terrifying feeling, but it was also sublime in its way.

Chapter Four

"You're the one who warned us when that other tech was coming," Mike accused the new voice in his mind telepathically. They'd been talking back and forth for a good half hour or more now since Harry had sought them out.

"Guilty as charged. I monitor the pens from time to time to see how they're treating everyone, but my mother doesn't know it. She'd be pissed if she found out, so keep it quiet, okay?"

"Why? Who's your mother?" Dave's tone was suspicious. They really didn't know who this guy was except that he was an incredibly strong telepath and undoubtedly human. Or was he?

They could actually feel his sigh in their minds. *"I'm half-Alvian. My mother is the lead scientist in this city, Mara 12. My father is human. His name is Justin O'Hara. The Alvians call me Hara, but I prefer Harry."*

"We've heard rumors about you, kid. Son of a bitch. They actually did it. They bred with a human just to see how the baby would turn out." Mike was clearly disgusted by the idea.

But Dave was more understanding. *"You've probably had it pretty rough, Harry. Thanks for leveling with us. And thanks for the warning the other day. You saved Jaci a lot of trouble."*

"My sister filled me in on what happened to her. Tough break. But my Uncle Caleb says it's one more link in the chain that will save humanity. He's a strong precog and he hasn't been

wrong yet."

"You think what happened to Jaci is a good thing?" Dave's question was cautious.

"More importantly, does your precognitive uncle believe it?" Mike was more practical, as usual.

"Let's put it this way," Harry said seriously, *"if she turns out to be compatible with one or both of you, you'll celebrate the day she got sloppy in the lab. Having a true mate is a blessing, especially now that human women are so scarce. I know, I've seen the relationship my father has with my step-mother and the one my sister has with her mates. They're lucky people and if either of you are so lucky as to have already found your mate, you'll have my eternal envy."*

"So how do we know if she's this—what did you call it—resonance mate? She told us about the humming phenomenon, but she didn't have time to tell us the rest and we weren't able to find much on the viewer." David's question was clinical, but excited nonetheless.

"My sister gave her a crystal. The next time you've got her to yourselves, put the crystal nearby, then take her in your arms."

"I think I like the sound of these tests," Mike murmured with a touch of humor that all three men enjoyed.

"The first test is the Hum. She said you both Hum with her. That's good. One down, two to go. The second test is the Kiss. With the crystal nearby, kiss her and the crystal should glow reddish-orange. The Hum will increase too, but I guess you won't be able to hear it since you're human."

"What's the third test? Is there a third?" Mike wanted to know.

"The third test is the Embrace. Touch her skin on skin and deepen the kiss, fitting your body to hers intimately. The crystal

will shine yellow like the sun and the Hum will increase as well. After that, there's only the Joining and from what I've heard, when you join with your true resonance mate, the crystal will shine with the light of a thousand stars. I've never experienced it myself, but to give you some idea, my sister and her mate caused such an energy rush during their first joining, half the crystals in this city glowed and she was over three thousand miles away."

"No shit?" Dave used his favorite expletive though there was a bit of awe in each of the three men's joined minds.

"One or both of you could be her mate, so you might have to get used to the idea of sharing," Harry warned.

"I think we can handle that. We're not proud of it, but since the cataclysm, we've shared women." Again it was Dave who was so forthcoming with details Mike would rather have kept to himself.

"Are you brothers? I only ask because my step-mom is mate to all three O'Hara brothers. I was working on that theory until my sister found her mates who are completely different species." They could hear the dismay in his voice even telepathically.

"We're cousins. We had a business together before the cataclysm and we've always been close. Being gifted in the old world, you know, it made us stick together."

"Yeah, back then we had to hide our psychic abilities, now it's the thing that saved us." David's tone was dry.

"You're both telepathic, but I sense more. Dave, you're a healer, right? That's what had Jaci so up in arms that they called me. But what about you, Mike?"

"I've got a tiny bit of empathy and sometimes I can mind read, but my biggest skill is that I'm a dreamwalker." Mike used the slang term for telepaths who had the ability to insert themselves into other people's dreams. It was a rare as well as a somewhat tricky gift, just like mindreading, which was another

slang word for high-level telepaths who could pick up on the thoughts of other people even when they were not being directed to them.

"Made me a bit of a shark in business," Mike continued, *"but I tried never to abuse the information I learned from my rivals too much. It's hard to believe that was over twenty years ago now. I'm getting to be an old man. What day is it, kid? Do you know?"*

"September twenty-second. Why?"

"Damn, my forty-sixth birthday just passed. Jaci's too young for me."

"Well, actually, Alvians don't age like you did. She's probably about the same age as you chronologically, but you'll have to ask her to know for sure. Their lifespan is about five or six hundred years, as is yours now."

"What?" David was clearly shocked.

"Oh, I guess you didn't realize. When Mara first took my Uncle Caleb from the family for study, I brokered a deal with her. By then she realized the humans left on Earth after the cataclysm most likely carried at least some Alvian DNA. Hara was one of their famous explorers and he was lost to them. He probably stayed here on Earth and was one of my distant ancestors. You two probably also have Alvian ancestors back in your family's far past. Anyway, you have the gene that would make you age like an Alvian, but it was turned off by your human side. I asked her to turn it back on so my father, uncles, step-mother and siblings could live longer, but I recently found out Mara's been doing it to all the human prisoners so she can study them longer. She doesn't want to take the risk that she might lose the traces of Alvian DNA you all carry by taking too long to discover its uses."

"Holy shit." Dave was as eloquent as ever. *"So you mean*

that she turned off our aging gene two years ago when we were caught?"

"Probably, but I can try to check your records to be absolutely sure."

"Do that, would you, kid? This is big news and a little hard to take in." Mike picked up the slack for his shocked cousin.

"Hang on a second, I'll be back shortly."

And with that, Harry was gone from their minds.

The two cousins stared at each other.

"We're going to live five hundred years?"

"Or maybe six." Mike added helpfully, equally stunned as his cousin.

"Holy shit."

Far above the pens in the city, Harry was hacking into his mother's computer system. He chastised himself for not looking for this information before, but he was glad he'd checked now. Mara had apparently decided, with the High Council's approval, not to take any chances on losing more of their ancestors' DNA. She'd blanketed the remote areas of the Earth with an airborne agent that would infect every human who breathed it, altering their DNA so they ceased to age as a normal human.

That meant his new friend Mike wasn't actually forty-six, but more like thirty-six or even younger, depending on when he'd been exposed to the agent. She'd started distributing it almost fifteen years ago. This news was too big to keep to himself. He had to tell his family, but first, he had to tell Mike. He owed the man that much for giving him a reason to check.

He reached out gently with his mind, finding the man easily now that he knew the path.

"Hey, Mike, I have good news, I think. They didn't

administer the agent when they caught you. I just discovered my mother's team started blanketing the Earth with a gene-altering agent about fifteen years ago. You were probably exposed back then because they tested you when you were caught and your Alvian aging gene had definitely already been activated. Dave's too."

"So what you're saying is I've got basically forty-six years worth of living in a thirty-one year old body? And I'll age about one year physically for every fifty years of actual time?"

"That's about the size of it."

"Holy shit."

§

Grady Prime was the perfect gentleman on the trip home, but he did look at her oddly a few times. He'd had to come get her in the Chief Engineer's quarters when they were ready to go and he'd almost caught her in an emotional display. But Davin had chimed, giving them a bit of warning before the other man knocked on the door and she'd had a precious few moments to school her features.

She couldn't believe what she'd seen in the engineering facility. Not only was Callie a Breed, but she was a truly gifted crystallographer who had found not just one, but two resonance mates. She was also one of the nicest people Jaci had ever met. As was her brother, Hara, whom she had yet to meet in person, but if what he'd said was true, he would seek her out soon.

It felt good to know there were other people who knew about her problem and who thought they could at least try to help her. They would help her friends too, if they could. Suddenly she was aware of an underground movement to make life better for the native inhabitants of this world and just as suddenly, she found herself hoping they would succeed.

Anyone with feelings could see what her people had done to these earthlings was wrong. Destroying their way of life, changing their very planet was a grievous sin, only compounded by what they'd done since. Capturing the survivors, separating families, forcing them into experiments without regard for their emotions was unforgivable in her newly awakened mind. She vowed silently to put all her energies towards helping them achieve some bit of freedom.

But first she had to deal with the looks Grady Prime kept shooting her. She had to tell him that there was no chance of a repeat between them, but she had to do it in such a way as to not insult him. He was still, after all, a powerful Prime, one of the elite.

So just after they landed back in the northern city, she sought a private word with him as they walked from the shuttle port to the main part of the city.

"Grady Prime, I have something to say that I think you will not like, but I must say it to clear the air between us."

"Say what you wish, Jaci 192. I'm not an unreasonable man even if I am a soldier."

She smiled softly, trying not to show too much emotion.

"I have no disgust of soldiers, Grady Prime. I'm only a Jaci, after all."

"Even a Jaci holds higher station than a soldier."

She was surprised by the bitterness in his voice. While she'd always been taught that soldier strains had more aggression left than any other, she'd never realized they could experience other kinds of emotion too. Suddenly she felt sorry for him.

"I've always thought such rankings were stupid, really. I admire your achievements, Grady Prime, and under other circumstances, I would welcome the opportunity to be your bed partner. In fact, I'm flattered that you asked in the first place."

"Yet I sense you're about to turn me down." He was taking it well, all things considered.

She smiled to soften the blow.

"As I said, I would welcome your invitation under other circumstances, but I have a prior commitment that is incompatible with starting a relationship with you."

"There's someone else?"

"I'm sorry, Grady Prime. I truly enjoyed our time together, even if it was duty."

"I know. I could tell." His smile was devilish and made her shiver in memory of that great orgasm he'd given her.

"You're gifted at giving a woman pleasure. You surely don't lack for women eager to bed you."

Grady looked wistful. "I enjoy my share of female companionship, but I do like you, Jaci 192. I like the look of you and the feel of you. I'm sorry we can't share more outside of duty, but perhaps it is for the best. I've volunteered for a medical test that I have been warned may change me for all time."

She caught her breath. "You're going to be part of Mara 12's new experiment, aren't you?"

He looked at her sharply. "How do you know about it?"

"I prepared the dosages last week. I'm one of the higher ranking lab techs on Mara 12's personal staff."

She thought he looked mildly relieved. "Then you know what it could do to me?"

By the First Shard, did she know! But she couldn't tell him

what she'd learned firsthand about the agent they would administer to him.

"I have some idea, yes. You're taking a great chance, Grady Prime, but for what it's worth, I think what you're doing is a noble thing. I'm only a tech, but even I can see that our people are stagnating the way we are. These humans..." Her voice trailed off as she thought about the people she'd met over the past week and the amazing things she'd learned. "These humans are much more than most of our kind gives them credit for."

Grady watched her with interested eyes. Perhaps she didn't realize she'd called the Breeds by the term they used for themselves, but it hadn't slipped past him. He was trained to be observant after all. This lab tech was more than she seemed but he would reserve judgment until he had more evidence. Still, he would watch her. Carefully.

"I agree that the Chief Engineer's living situation was surprising to me when I first learned of it, but then, he is a throwback, so he's bound to be eccentric. You spent time with his mate, didn't you?"

She nodded. "Yes, Callie is a fascinating woman."

"I've known her and her family for years now. She was a precocious child and has grown into a lovely woman. Her family reports that she's happy with her mating and she looks well."

"But you barely spoke to her while we were in the facility."

Grady shrugged. "I am a soldier. I protect and defend. I don't make small talk."

That startled a chuckle out of her that he wasn't expecting. This girl was something out of the ordinary but he couldn't put his finger on what was different about her.

"You seem to be doing well talking to me."

He looked down at her, raising his eyebrows. "You do have a point. I don't believe I've talked this much to anyone in the past six months. You're easy to talk to, Jaci 192."

She rewarded him with a bright smile. It touched that place inside him that sometimes yearned to feel, but never quite made it. The thought made him feel just a little empty. It was an uncomfortable observation and one of the many reasons he'd volunteered for this dangerous experiment. He wanted to know what was waiting in that empty place inside him. He wanted to experience the emotions he often watched on the faces of the Breeds he tracked. He wanted something...more than what he'd experienced of life so far.

"I hope then, you would consider me a friend, Grady Prime."

"That would be nice. I don't think I've ever had a friend who was not also a warrior before." The idea puzzled him and brought more of those odd sensations.

"You'll probably be facing some radical changes once you begin the experiment. I hope to be assigned to assist with some of the tech work but even if I'm not, I hope you'll remember to call me if you need someone to talk to. I'll pass no judgments and would be glad to assist you if I can."

He was surprised by her offer but also somewhat grateful for it. He didn't like scientists as a rule. They tended to look down on everyone who wasn't a scientist and warriors even more than most. He was comforted to know there would at least be someone there who was a friend. Even if he wasn't quite sure what made this woman tick.

"I'll remember, Jaci 192, and I thank you for your generous offer."

She shocked him further by reaching up on her tip-toes to

place a gentle kiss on his rough cheek. It did something inside him he didn't quite understand. It was a faint sensation, like the kinds of things he sometimes felt and attributed to his inferior Grady DNA, but this was a pleasant feeling, warm and almost friendly. It was something he'd never felt before and something he wanted very much to experience again.

The echo stayed with him long after she'd gone and made him all the more resolute to do this experiment. He wanted to feel. He wanted to experience those things he read on the faces of the Breeds he dealt with in his duties. Even if it were only the unpleasant feelings like fear and anger and rage, he wanted to experience them for himself at least once before he died.

He wasn't kidding himself. This experiment could very well mean the end of him. As a Grady, he was already considered on the lower end of the evolutionary ladder. He was more aggressive than was thought comfortable by the rest of the emotionless Alvian people. The High Council only allowed more Gradys to be bred because they needed them as soldiers, protectors for their own precious skins. Grady Prime had no illusions about why he existed.

Just as he had no illusions about what the experiment might do to him. If he reverted to the overly aggressive Alvian male of generations past, the High Council might well deem him too violent to be allowed to live. He could easily be put down for the safety of the rest of them because of his skills. But he knew—also because of his special skills—he could probably find a way to escape whoever they sent after him. He could easily disappear into the Waste to live out his life until madness eventually claimed him.

He wasn't as stupid as the High Council thought. He fully realized that if he did gain emotion through this experiment it might well mean his life would end in madness the way so many of his ancient predecessors' had ended. It was a soldier's curse, he well knew, for he was a student of history. He had read the ancient texts, accounts of battles to the last man and desperate struggles of brother against brother. He had read them and studied them, always seeking to understand the deep emotion that drove those long ago men, but he just couldn't grasp it all.

At times he felt...something...as he read the texts, but it was elusive. He prayed to the ancestors that after this experiment it would be elusive no more. He would die gladly to gain that understanding.

§

Jaci fell asleep almost as soon as her head hit the pillow. It had been a long day and her memories of the dream she'd had the night before had crept into her thoughts all through it at odd moments. She wondered if being with two men at once would be just like in her dream or something quite different. She didn't want it to be just any two men. She wanted it to be *her* two men. Michael and David.

Just the thought of them made her shiver, though in reality they'd never shared much more than a few kisses. Still, she hungered for their touch and their understanding. The emotions they felt showed in their eyes in a way she'd never seen in a male of her race...until today. Davin had looked at his mate with love and unmistakable lust. She recognized it now. Blood of the Founders! She *felt* it now.

While she slept the dream came again. One moment she was on her knees in her best tunic, accepting the Ribbon of Accolades of the High Council for her brilliance, and the next she was surrounded by her two men. Michael and David stood on either side of her. She was still on her knees, accepting the award medallion around her bowed neck.

When she lifted her head, they were there, smiling down at her. The crowd receded, but they were still there, watching in the background. The thought of it made her jump with excitement she barely recognized. She hadn't known she was an exhibitionist, but apparently all bets were off in the dreamstate.

David smiled over at his cousin. "I think I like this dream."

Michael nodded. "I definitely like the idea of our Jaci on her knees before us." He shifted his gaze to her. "Can you think of anything you might want to try from that position, sweetheart?"

He winked and she felt fire rush through her veins at the ideas forming in her mind. She smiled up at him and was satisfied with the wicked light in his eyes.

"I can think of a thing or two." She reached for his waistband with single-minded intensity. "But you've got too many clothes on."

"Easily remedied." Michael held up his hand and snapped his fingers and suddenly they were all naked.

"How'd you do that?"

He winked once more. "Magic."

She got distracted by the huge cock waving hard and long in front of her face. "Mmm, I like that kind of magic."

"Me too, sweetheart. Me too." He stifled a gasp as she put her hand around him, her hot palm moving up and down in a natural rhythm.

"Something tells me she's done this before." David stepped closer to her, his hard cock brushing her hair.

She moved back and took David in her other hand, moving just as expertly on him as she continued to work Michael. Her smile stretched from ear to ear but her concentration was near total on her task.

"What about it, Jaci?" Michael reached down to run his hand through her hair, holding her head and tilting it up so she would meet his eyes. "Have you given a lot of hand jobs?"

She was confused for a moment. She'd never used that term for stroking a male to completion but she guessed she must have heard the humans use the phrase somewhere. How else could she incorporate such a foreign phrase into her dream?

"I have given pleasure many times in this manner as part of my duty."

"I don't think I want to hear this." David's voice was a low grumble at her side.

"Servicing the elite for sample collection used to be one of my duties. I would take them in my hands or mouth or body, as they wished, in order to collect the necessary samples for the geneticists."

"I definitely didn't want to hear that," David grumbled again.

Michael's hand tightened in her hair. "Did you ever do two at once?"

"Two?" She was shocked by the possessive tone of her dream men, but perhaps her psyche saw deeper into their true natures than her conscious mind did. "No, I've never been with two males at one time."

"Did you ever want to?"

She shook her head. "No. Not until you. Only with you."

Michael stroked her hair, removing his hand. "Good. From now on, you'll only be with us. Your days of servicing other men are over. Do you understand?"

"Yes, I understand, but what if my duties—?"

David tugged her head up to meet his smoldering eyes.

"You will find another way. You're a smart girl, Jaci. You'll find a way to get out of such duties."

Their possessive words made her body yearn. She had to remind herself it was only a dream. Slowly, she nodded. What could it hurt to agree to the impossible in a dream? She couldn't forgo her duties any more than she could resist these two heavenly men, but she didn't want to anger them. It's not that she wanted to service other men, but if the Maras ordered her to do so, she had to do as she was told. She knew she wouldn't enjoy it. That last time with Grady Prime had been the first and last time she would enjoy sex with any male other than Michael and David. She knew that deep down in her awakening heart.

"I'll find a way," she whispered as David's hand relaxed in her hair. "I promise."

"Good. Now, suck my cock. I've waited a long time to feel your lips around me."

Jaci complied, leaning forward to take him in her mouth. His taste exploded on her tongue as she moved into the rhythm of sucking and withdrawing, using all her skills to pleasure him. She made an effort to keep her hand moving rhythmically on Michael as well, and she looked up briefly to find him watching her suck his cousin's cock with avid eyes.

"Look at me, sweetheart." David's hands tangled in her hair, angling her face up so she could meet his eyes. She smiled, humming deep in her throat as he gasped. "God, you're beautiful. Suck hard now, sweet. Make me come." She followed his orders to the letter and within moments he was jetting his sperm into her mouth. "Swallow it all, honey. Drink me down."

He tasted divine. She'd never been permitted to swallow any male's seed before. The many times she'd done this, it had been for scientific collection, not for enjoyment. She was definitely enjoying this. As was he, she could tell. He groaned as he finished in her mouth, then ordered her to lick him clean. She did so with pleasure, her hand tightening on Michael's ready cock waiting for the same treatment.

When David finally let her up, he didn't let go of her head. Instead he swiveled her face to Michael, directing her movement as she took his cousin in deep.

"She's got a talented mouth, Mike," he told the other man. "She'll blow your mind."

"Let her go, Dave. I want this all to myself for now."

She felt David's hands leave her and Michael's replace them in her hair, guiding her movements. He wanted it harder and slightly faster than David had and she was more than willing to comply. She also let him direct her as he held her still and pumped himself into her mouth hard, deep and fast.

"Suck me, baby. Use that hot tongue." His words were low rumbles of sound that made her pussy ache to be filled. "Get behind her, Dave. Rub her tits."

David's warm body knelt behind her and his talented hands started tugging on her nipples in the way she'd already come to love. She moaned as he pulled especially hard.

"I'm coming!" Michael warned, but she wanted it all. She wanted his pleasure, his heat, his sperm in her mouth. A moment later, she got it all. He came in great waves, tasting slightly different from his cousin, but just as satisfying.

David moved one hand down her body, rubbing her clit as she struggled to swallow the jets of come, playing her body as if it were a musical instrument. Within moments she was coming hard and fast against his hands.

She must've blacked out then because the next thing she knew, it was morning and her alarm sounded. She had to get up and go through the routine of her work day. But the dream lingered, as did the faint echo of their taste on her tongue.

Chapter Five

Jaci was fit to burst by the middle of the morning. Her dreams were getting hotter. She couldn't wait to see Michael and David, but wait she must until her normal routine brought her to their cell, lest she bring suspicion upon herself. The crystal Callie had given her was burning a hole in her pocket. She was eager and at the same time hesitant to perform the next test.

She wanted desperately to know she wasn't alone, but she also wasn't sure if she was ready for a mate. Particularly if that mate was being held prisoner by her superiors and there might never be any way to consummate the bond. Still, she had to know. The uncertainty was driving her nuts.

By the time her tasks took her to the cells she was practically squirming in her shoes. She had so much she wanted to tell her men—her friends—she reminded herself. She was already thinking of them in a most scandalous way, but she couldn't deny the attraction she felt for both of them.

Never before had she wanted so badly to initiate sexual intimacy with a male. She had performed her duties when assigned to sample collection, but never with the kind of enthusiasm she felt now, driving her temperature higher and her excitement level off the charts. She wanted sex. Badly. As she never had before.

She'd never engaged in non-work-related sexual activity. There were no casual bed partners in her life. There never had been. She was almost fastidious in that respect. She had never wanted a lover and never taken one, even out of boredom, but she wanted both of these handsome human males and she wanted them now. She wondered with one part of her mind that was still functioning on a more objective level if this mad desire was only produced by her changing DNA, or if it had more to do with the men themselves. Would she feel this sizzling attraction for any of the other males she came into contact with?

She could answer that with a firm no. She'd had a chance to bed Grady Prime, arguably one of the most handsome, fit and highly respected Alvian males in the city, if not on the entire planet, and she'd not felt anything like this spark of desire. She'd enjoyed servicing Grady Prime, but that was more a physical enjoyment, what she believed she'd gain from Michael and/or David was more of an emotional satisfaction. They made her feel alive with just a smile, and their hugs satisfied something deep within her soul she'd never felt before.

Their kisses were like water to a woman dying of thirst and she could only speculate on what taking either one of them inside her body would feel like—not just physically, but on that emotional plane she was just coming to understand. She wanted them with a soul-deep ache that was beginning to consume every one of her waking moments.

She walked into their cell and went straight for the monitor, trying not to let her eagerness show in the last few moments the monitor would follow her movements. She shut it off and turned to face them and suddenly she wanted nothing more than to be in their arms.

She ran to them and Michael caught her in what felt like mid-air, David closing in behind to cocoon her in their warmth and what felt suspiciously to her untried emotions like love. She sobbed as she sought Michael's mouth with her own. He kissed her long and hard but he kept his wits about him, pulling back after slaking the very beginnings of her thirst to look down into her dazed eyes.

"We had a long conversation with Harry last night. Where's the crystal, sweetheart?"

She'd almost forgotten! She fumbled in her pocket for a moment and came up with the crystal on her palm. She thought it might be softly glowing, but she couldn't be sure through the tears in her eyes.

Michael nodded over her shoulder to David and he moved off, taking the crystal with him. He placed it on the table beside them as he leaned back to watch, and then Michael's lips were on hers again and she was lost to coherent thought as the Hum increased and her skin felt aflame.

She heard David laughing in the background and moved back to see what he was so happy about when the blinding light of the crystal caught her eye. Michael and she had passed the second test! The crystal was glowing fiercely as she disentangled herself to check it, but the light faded as she let go of Michael.

But David was not deterred. With a deft move he took her hand and swung her into his arms, swooping down to capture her lips with his own while Michael watched. He took a long time, seducing her with his firm mouth, his masculine scent and his strong hands, but she came to her senses before too long and opened her eyes to see the bright light spilling about them.

David had passed the second test too! She smiled up into his eyes as *she* began kissing him. She'd never taken the lead before with any male and she felt powerful and seductive as he groaned and took the kiss deeper. She explored his mouth with her tongue and plastered herself against his hard body, enjoying the angles and planes of his chest, his narrow hips, his hard thighs and especially the harness between them as it nestled into her softness.

She felt him pulling at her clothing and before she knew it, they were both bare from the waist up, joined together in an almost carnal Embrace. She realized what he was doing the moment before she opened her dazzled eyes to encounter a shining, brilliant yellow light emanating from the crystal. They had Embraced, and David was definitely compatible with her in every way. He was her mate!

She started to laugh with pure joy as she pulled slightly back away from him.

"You must have had one hell of a conversation with Hara."

David smiled as he released her, much to her surprise, but she felt only a moment of awkwardness when he passed her to Michael who also had taken off his shirt to show her a powerful, masculine chest, lightly dusted with hair and hard muscled. His shoulders were strong and wide and she couldn't help but caress them as he cupped her bare breasts, pinching her tight nipples in a way that made her gasp.

He chuckled as he pulled her into the valley of his thighs. He was already hard, long and powerful as he pressed his hips against hers, finding his place between, even through the layers of cloth that separated them.

"I haven't touched a woman in far too long, sweetheart. You are beautiful and soft and feminine. You take my breath away."

His whispered words brushed past her ear as he pulled her in closer, snuggling her tight for a moment before bending low to press his lips to hers. He pressed his tongue inside and began to make love to her mouth. He licked and bit at her mouth in a seductive series of caresses that had her mewling in delight even as she clawed his shoulders for more.

"That's done it," she heard David's triumphant voice as if from afar, "she's definitely ours."

Michael groaned as he pulled back, but he couldn't seem to let her go. He continued to rub against her, his palms squeezing her breasts in a way that made her want to scream. He looked down at her and lifted her nipples, lowering his head to take one in his mouth. She'd never had a man suck her nipple before—except in recent dreams—and it produced a feeling inside her that was hard to describe. Wicked pleasure wrapped itself around her senses, stilling time and turning her veins to rivers of heated lava.

Her eyes closed, only to shoot open again when Michael shifted slightly and a second mouth closed over her other nipple. She looked down to see both David and Michael sucking on her body, her temperature rising and her skin crying out for satisfaction as the men rubbed against her.

Somewhere in the back of her mind she realized they had almost no time left. She reached down and found their hard cocks, so full and engorged she knew it would take little stimulation to get them to spill their seed. She plunged her fingers inside two pairs of pants, a tight fit with such large erections already taking up so much room, but she managed to get her hands wrapped around them both and started a gentle rhythm.

Michael pulled away, dipping his hand into her pants and spearing one long, thick, male finger up inside her. David reached around behind her to gently caress the pucker of her ass, which made her jump. No one had ever tried to enter there. Just the thought of such a thing made her both nervous and oddly hot.

He gentled her, getting her used to his touch and soon

pushed inside to the first knuckle, gently moving in and out as Michael speared two fingers now, into her dripping pussy. She came with a cry, clenching her fists around them as they spurted in near unison into her hands.

Nothing sounded in the room for long moments but heavy, heated breathing as they leaned against each other for support. None of them, it seemed, could stand on their own. Finally, Michael straightened.

"I think our ten minutes was up a long time ago."

"Oh, no!" Jaci straightened, hastily pulling her hands from their clothing and making use of the sink in one corner of the room. She quickly straightened her own clothes, turning back to look over her men, and stopped dead.

They were watching her with possessive eyes.

"You're ours now, sweetheart." Michael talked slowly, deliberately, as he buttoned his shirt.

"As we are yours." David fastened his own clothing as they walked toward her. "Harry filled us in on this resonance mate thing last night, but even without the proof of your people, we knew you were meant to be part of our lives almost from the first time we saw you."

"We've been dreaming with you for more than a year, Jaci, but only since your accident have I been able to enter your dreams and make you remember them."

"Enter my dreams?" She was shocked as she remembered the dreams that had felt so real and made her so hot.

Michael nodded slowly. "It is one of my gifts. I can dreamwalk. I've been in your dreams the past few nights, sweetheart, and I brought Dave with me. What you dreamed, we dreamed as well. It was real. Or at least as real as a dream can be. But the words we spoke were real and the feelings were our feelings."

"We love you," David said simply and she felt her heart fill near to bursting.

"I love you too." She sounded as if she were only just realizing what her emotions meant, but it was true. She loved them. Both. Endlessly.

"We know," Michael said with a satisfied smile. "We were only waiting for you to realize it."

"Better get a move on," Harry's voice sounded in the men's minds, *"they just noticed the monitor was off."*

Mike and Dave sprang into action, moving her to the monitor and giving her one last kiss before settling across the chamber in poses of boredom.

"Time to go, sweetheart, Harry just warned us that they noticed the monitor's down again."

"But I want to say so much more—"

"Tonight," Mike promised, "we'll walk in our dreams together. Tell us then."

With one last anguished look, she turned back and switched on the monitor. Dave hated to see their time together end, but it couldn't be helped. He watched her bustle around the room doing her routine tasks. She'd given them both an echo of the pleasure they could experience together but he feared, given their situation, they'd never have a chance to make love fully.

"Something's gotta give, Mike. We need her and she needs us."

"I hear you, cousin. We'll find a way."

"I may have a solution," Harry said.

"You listening in on us, kid? You must be one helluva telepath to do that when we were talking privately."

They could actually feel his shrug in their minds, proving the point. *"Sorry for the intrusion but I was keeping an eye on you guys after I realized the monitor was down."*

"Shit," Dave said with a certain amount of respect, *"you some kind of voyeur? You're too young for that, Harry. Get your own girl."*

"No, I figured you'd want some privacy for whatever you three got up to when the monitor went down. I learned fast to vamoose both physically and mentally when my dad and uncles closeted themselves with my step-mom. My Uncle Mick has a wicked slap down in his arsenal of telepathic tricks. I got whipped a time or two when I was a kid testing my reach."

"Caught an eyeful too, I bet" Mike added with a mental chuckle. *"Thanks for the warning. We would've been toast if they'd come down to check on her. You saved our asses again, Harry. We owe you."*

"No problem. But I've been talking your problem over with my family. You did the tests right? What's the verdict?"

"Happy to report that she is mate to both of us. Just as we hoped. Damn kid, that crystal shone like I've never seen before. Didn't know quartz could do that." Mike's tone was both awed and full of satisfaction.

"Wait 'til you get inside her."

"Shit, kid. I thought you said you weren't watching. How do you know we didn't do the deed already?"

"Not enough time," Harry answered a bit smugly. *"The monitors were only down for about fifteen minutes. I don't think either of you are that quick on the trigger."*

Male laughter all around was the answer to that little observation.

"Plus, judging by my sister's experience, the crystals in the

city would probably have been affected much more profoundly. As it was, there was a mild surge in power and a glow that I saw because I was looking for it, but I doubt the techs caught it." Harry added after a short pause, *"Which brings me to the possible solution to your immediate problem."*

They spent the rest of the hour talking over various possibilities, formulating a plan. It was still very tentative and depended on a lot of variables, but at least there was a chance. Sure, it was a slim chance, but they needed something to give them hope right now. Even a slim chance at a modicum of freedom to claim and take their mate was better than nothing at all.

Just before the dinner hour Harry tracked down Jaci 192. As he'd told her he would, he made a show of thanking her for her gentle and expert treatment of his sister and her unborn child. They talked a bit and Harry pretended their small talk about his sister's pregnancy was so fascinating, he wanted to continue it over dinner. Just that simply he'd arranged for her to have dinner with his uncle. He explained his prior commitment to his uncle took precedence but he was certain the other man wouldn't mind her lovely company.

Jaci found herself ensconced in Caleb's private apartment, which was much more luxurious than her own small quarters. Harry and his Breed uncle, Caleb O'Hara, whom she had met once before, made her feel comfortable. Not only was the apartment upper level, but the food he was served was of gourmet quality. Caleb O'Hara also had the unheard of ability to shut down all monitoring while he visited with his nephew and had already done so before they arrived on his doorstep.

Caleb was a big man who exuded confidence, quiet strength and a deep knowledge that was just a bit unnerving.

His eyes were pale green and had a piercing quality. She felt pinned by his gaze and it made her feel just slightly uncomfortable. It was clear from his expression that he already knew about her accident and her problems. He welcomed her to his 'apartment' that was as much of a cell as the ones beneath the city, even if it had windows and a view of the forest beyond the city's shield.

"Even I didn't foresee your little mishap, Jaci, but what I've seen since it happened bodes well for both our races. Before you got that drug into your system, I couldn't tell if the experiment was going to work or not. I'm happy to report yours is just the first of many changes coming to your race, and these changes will ultimately prove to be your people's salvation."

"You're not just saying that to make me feel better, are you?" She found she was at ease enough with these two men to speak her mind.

Both men laughed as they ate their dinner. She dug in to the gourmet food and enjoyed the various flavors as well. The company was good too, if quite different than any company she'd ever thought of herself keeping before she'd had her accident.

"No, honey. I only speak truth about my visions. They're hard enough to interpret without adding lies into the mix. I'm not a complicated man."

Harry chuckled. "I think Mama Jane would differ with you on that."

Caleb sat back and seemed to reflect. "Damn, I miss her."

"She's your resonance mate, right?" Jaci asked softly.

Caleb nodded. "She was my wife back in the old world. I married her right after her daddy died and took her into my heart and my home. I've loved her since she was just a child and the day she married me was the happiest day of my life."

His gaze turned inward for a moment before it cleared. "We learned about your people's resonance mate business only recently, since Davin made off with our little girl."

Jaci thought about her own resonance mates, sitting in a cell below the city and she wondered if they'd ever have a chance to be as happy. The love shining in this man's eyes was a sight to behold and she wished she had the freedom to share her own love with her men.

"I've met Callie. She seems very happy," she said softly.

"And you're wondering if you'll ever be happy with your fellas, aren't you?" Caleb's voice was kind, almost fatherly as he watched her with those haunting green eyes.

"It just seems so impossible. So unfair. Why would I find them and resonate with them if we can't be together?"

"There are ancient Alvian laws about resonance mates, you know. Davin resorted to them when the High Council wanted to break up his relationship with Callie because she was human. Apparently, once proven, no one can come between true mates for any reason. Resonance mating is the strongest bond in Alvian law or society, but it's so rare these days, few remember the ancient laws." Harry's voice was strong, giving her hope. "Still, the law *is* on your side, should you ever be in a position to reveal the nature of your relationship with Dave and Mike."

"I didn't realize that. I've never paid much attention to the laws of mating. I never had much interest in the idea before now."

"Emotions will do that to you every time." Caleb winked and smiled, putting her at ease.

Harry smiled too. "You and your mates had the crystals humming this afternoon. I called my sister and had her prepared to take the blame, but you'll need to be more careful until we come up with a solution for you three. I talked for a bit with Mike and Dave before I went to meet you and we came up with a plan. With Davin's help, we might be able to get you all tested and reassigned to his staff in the southern engineering facility."

"But I have no crystal gift."

Harry corrected her. "You *had* no crystal gift. I'd be willing to lay odds that now your emotions have been awakened, you'll discover all kinds of changes. Davin and I have been theorizing that emotion is an essential part of crystal ability and as the emotion was bred out of the Alvian race, so was the ability to manipulate crystal. The trait has been growing rarer with each generation when descriptions of generations past say it was a common trait most people had."

"What you say makes sense, but how would I explain a sudden appearance of crystal ability, if I do have it? I was tested at age thirteen, as we all are and it was not there. They would grow suspicious and want to know why it just suddenly appeared."

"Good point." Harry seemed to consider for a moment. "But they've never tested Mike or Dave. If we can get them transferred to Davin, we could probably come up with some other way to get you transferred there as well."

"Maybe Callie could request her?" Caleb added helpfully.

"Good one, Dad. Callie could ask for her to help with the baby. She's already established that she likes you, so it wouldn't be too out of the ordinary."

Jaci felt the rising, bubbling sensation in the pit of her stomach she knew now was hope. These men, these special men, would help her and her mates find a way to be together. She felt it in her bones and her heart was near to bursting with the wonder of such friendship, freely given. She didn't deserve it, but her mates deserved a free life and she would do anything she had to do in order to help them achieve it.

Suddenly it was all too much and she felt tears leaking from her eyes. She tried desperately to hide it, but both men saw her loss of control. A moment later she felt herself being lifted and turned, and then there was a solid male shoulder under her leaking eyes. Caleb had gathered her close and was rubbing her back as if she were a baby.

"You've had a lot happen to you in a very short time, honey. You're entitled to cry, so go right ahead." His deep, rumbly voice above her head made her feel safe and secure. It was an amazing feeling that only added to the alien emotions overrunning her control.

"But I'm getting you all wet," she protested, trying to draw away. Caleb shushed her softly and tucked her head under his chin.

"Think of me as a surrogate father. My Callie is about your age, I figure, and it's too long since I've been able to hold my children close to me. I'm missing a lot of their growing up, stuck here in this city playing at being a lab rat."

"I'm so sorry." She hiccupped, trying desperately to stop the tears but it seemed beyond her at the moment.

"Shh, honey. It's not your fault and it's only temporary." He rocked her slightly as she continued to cry, but eventually she calmed and he let her go gently, setting her back in her chair. He wasn't through caring for her. He leaned forward and dabbed at her wet face with a clean napkin, drying her eyes and making her laugh at his antics. "That's better. All cried out. Now, do you feel better?"

Oddly, she discovered she did.

"Yes. Now that you mention it. I don't know what came over me. I've never cried like that before the accident."

"But you've never had emotions before either, have you?"

Harry's quiet voice reminded her that he was still sitting at the table, slowly finishing his dinner.

"I guess not. It's hard to get used to." She sighed and reached for her glass, downing half the cool water in one long sip.

"You won't be the last Alvian to have to deal with new emotions. You are but the first of many and the time may come when you can help your brethren learn to cope the way you are learning to cope. Your mate David can be of help there too, I think, with his healing gifts and his background in psychiatry." Caleb's voice rang with authority.

"Is that something you've foreseen?" She was still in awe of the idea this man could actually see the future.

Caleb nodded calmly. "Like I said when we first met, you were a surprise, but now that events have begun to unfold, the future is starting to come clearer." He settled back and took a sip of his wine. "I see possibilities, Jaci, and I don't see every little thing that's going to happen. Sometimes I get bombarded with a series of visions and they won't let me rest until I've seen them through. Other times—most times—I don't see anything in particular, only random events."

"That is so fascinating. I bet you have people asking you all the time what's in store for them."

"No, actually, it has the opposite effect—at least on humans. They fear what I have to say more often than not. Back in the old world, I tried to warn some of my friends what was coming but they refused to listen. I only managed to convince my immediate family, my wife and brothers, that we had to move up to the Rockies and set up our own little survivalist world up there. Thank God they believed me."

"We've met once before you know. Back when you first came here, Mara 12 asked me to set you up with a recording device."

Caleb leaned back and smiled. "I remember you now. Shy little thing who didn't get my humor. You'll be glad to know I've made good use of that device. I don't think Mara and her group have a clue what my precognitive visions mean on the whole, but I bet they're tracking my percentage of correct predictions."

She nodded with a grin. "You're running about ninety-five percent with a five percent margin of error. The techs take turns checking your stats."

"You hear that, Harry?" Caleb grinned at his step-son. "Five percent margin of error. Makes me damn near perfect, I'd say. And that's just the visions I've given them to play with."

Jaci looked at him out of the corner of her eye. "I don't mean to be rude, but there is some speculation that you don't tell us everything."

Caleb laughed outright at that. "Damn straight I don't tell your scientists everything! What would be the use of that? Half my visions tell me the way of life they've dictated for ten generations of your kind is about to fall by the wayside and you, my friend, are just the beginning of the fall. I doubt Mara would welcome that news."

Jaci gasped, thinking through the implications of his words. "She might very well change her plans for the experiment should she guess what upheaval will be wrought by her actions."

Harry caught her attention. "I see you understand why it's important not to say anything just yet."

"Jaci, honey, I'm going to tell you straight out that things are changing for your people. It may seem difficult at first, but believe me, this change can only bring good for your kind as well as my own. Your people will die out in another few generations unless something radical happens."

Her eyes widened. "Grafting human DNA with our own to return emotion is pretty radical."

Caleb nodded solemnly. "You begin to understand."

"I've done extensive research into the ancient texts of the Alvian race," Harry told her quietly, "and I see the reason the scientists intervened in the first place. Your race was much more violent than humans ever were. I'm not saying humans didn't have some bloody battles and absolutely heinous behavior in our distant past, but by the time of the cataclysm, most of my human ancestors had evolved into more peaceful beings who used diplomacy and negotiation first before force of arms were ever considered. I concluded that humans and human-Alvian Breeds have strong emotion, but much less aggression than pure Alvians had."

"Mixing human and Alvian DNA also produced strong psychic abilities in subsequent generations," Caleb reminded them. "We don't really know if pure humans had the psychic abilities and the mix with Alvian DNA brought it out or if it's the other way around, but either way, it doesn't really matter. What does matter is that together the DNA of our two races produces an emotional—but not overly violent—and gifted being. The next evolution for both our races."

Harry sat forward. "Alvians stopped evolving about ten generations ago when the geneticists started tinkering with the genetic code. While their goal was admirable, the results got progressively more destructive as our ancestors became so apathetic, they couldn't really comprehend the damage that had been done. Think about it, Jaci, few Alvians have children the old-fashioned way anymore. It's considered eccentric to do so. Alvians allow geneticists to have sole control over the next generation when there is no need for it to be so any longer. Natural selection is gone. The next generation is exactly like the one before except they are even more disengaged from their fellow man. A few more generations like this and it will all be over for the Alvian race."

"I never even realized..." Jaci said softly, her mind whirling with the dreadful possibilities.

Caleb sat back from the table, finished with his meal. "But you begin to see now that what happened to you is a step forward. With emotions, your people will realize what they've done to the human survivors is wrong. They will also see that human DNA is the only thing that can restore what they've lost."

"Humans must live free, Jaci. It's the goal I've dedicated my life to," Harry said, pulling her attention with his low, powerful voice. "I want to save both my peoples from destruction. I want them both to live in peace, side by side."

"I want that too, Hara. I want David and Michael, and my other human friends, to live free. And I want my colleagues to understand what we've done to them and to their world. Our apathy led us to destroy an entire civilization without a shred of guilt."

Caleb stood. "When you put it that way, it sure sounds bad, but you're right, Jaci. Only a few days with emotions and already you realize it. I wonder what will happen when more of your people take the treatment. It'll be interesting to watch, that's for sure."

Harry stood too, picking up a small crystal from a side table and bringing it to Jaci. "This is an untraceable, undetectable data crystal that your friends can access in their viewer without anyone knowing, courtesy of Davin. The only thing is, they have to be careful not to be seen putting it in or out of the viewer. But it's worth the risk."

"Why? What's on it?"

"The first book of Caleb," Harry said with a mischievous

grin while Caleb snorted.

"There's information on there the folks down in the pens should know. I've recorded some of my farseeing visions and a few more immediate things that pertain to specific people down there, I think they should know about."

"Give it to Mike and Dave tomorrow. They have a viewer and strong telepathy. They can disseminate it on their own from there."

"I'll see they get it."

Their time was over but she didn't want to leave the atmosphere of friendly comradeship she'd never experienced before. She felt comfortable with these two new friends and she wanted to stay, but knew she couldn't. Spending too long with them would raise eyebrows, particularly with the monitors switched off. She had to get going and she made her excuses and a show of thanks as Harry quite deliberately switched the monitors back on, winking at her just before he pressed his thumb to the control.

She went straight back to her evening routine with practiced apathy the only expression on her face. When Lita 498 asked her about her dinner companions she calmly described the atmosphere and food, skipping all emotional content, editing her words carefully. They worked companionably until it was time to sleep and she went tiredly to her quarters. It had been a long, eventful day and she was eager to dream.

Chapter Six

This time she knew the dream was, at least in part, real. When she finally reached the dreamstate, she found herself walking down familiar corridors until she came to Michael and David's cell. But they weren't imprisoned inside. This time, they met her at the arch that led to their cell—outside the arch. She thought that was significant, perhaps symbolizing the fact they were now free, at least in the dream.

"You're right, sweetheart. Your love frees us." Michael walked toward her, wrapping her tightly in his arms.

"This feels so real, yet it's still just a dream, right?" She had to try to understand this alternate reality.

"What we say is real," Mike said softly, kissing her cheeks. "We play on the field of the mind, so what we do feels real while we're here, but when you wake up, you'll still be alone in your apartment."

"And we'll still be in that cell, unable to step through the arch," David added, stepping up close behind.

Jaci remembered her dinner conversation with the O'Haras.

"Maybe not for too much longer. Hara has a plan." Her tone was excited but the men soothed her with their caressing hands.

"We know, sweetheart. We had a long chat with Harry

tonight and he gave us a few pointers on how to pass the test his brother-in-law will be giving us."

David turned her within their embrace so he could claim her lips in a long, lingering kiss. Here in their shared dream, they had all night to spend together, not just the rushed moments when the monitor was down for maintenance. She shivered in their arms, wishing this could be as real as it felt.

"I must admit, I'm curious to meet an Alvian who has always felt emotion." Michael continued speaking while he kissed her neck from behind. "This Davin character sounds like quite a guy."

She wanted to respond but could only moan as David removed her nightdress and four big, masculine hands started massaging her skin all over. Michael's hand delved between her legs, making her gasp while David played with her breasts. She knew they would make love and this time, even if it was still only a dream, she knew her men were experiencing it as she was. It was real enough for now, she thought with a pang.

David released her and Michael pulled back as well, leading her by the hand to a magnificent bed she knew he'd conjured in their minds for her. The plush round bed was big enough to fit three comfortably and was hung in gold silk draperies. Golden nightstands held crystal pitchers of wine and other glowing liquids, golden plates held ripe fruits to tempt the palette.

They deposited her in the middle of the sumptuous bed and stood back, just looking at her.

"Aren't you both a little far away?" Jaci squirmed, uncomfortable under their eyes.

Michael sat on the edge of the bed and picked up a tray laden with a native fruit she especially liked. Peaches, they were called. And they'd been peeled and sliced, ready for eating. Michael picked up a slice dripping with sweet nectar and held it to her lips.

"I want to take this slow, Jaci. I can hold the dream and extend it for hours, unless something makes me lose concentration."

Dave snickered as he sat on the other side of the bed. "Yeah, like a really intense orgasm. That will send him to sleep and we'll lose the dreamstate. So let's hold off on that—for a while at least. Mike and I agreed. We never get a chance to really talk to you, sweetheart."

Jaci sat up against the silken pillows. "Talk about what?"

Dave brushed her hair back from her face, his touch so gentle, it gave her goose bumps.

"About your hopes, your fears, your desires for the future. Anything, Jaci. Anything that will tell us more about you than the obvious."

"The obvious?" She was dazed by the look in his eyes as he leaned in and placed a sweet kiss on her temple.

"Yeah," Mike moved closer, picking up the thread of the conversation as Dave moved back. "We already know you're sharp as a tack, tall, blonde, gorgeous and afraid of your new emotions." Mike leaned toward her and repeated the soft kiss to her other temple. "We don't want you to be afraid, Jaci."

"I can assure you, I don't like the feeling either."

Soft chuckles from the men invited her to join in and she realized they'd already made her feel better. Just by being there.

"Fear is useful, in its proper place," David said. "But there are so many flavors of emotion you've yet to experience. We want to show you all the shades of pleasure, desire, love and tenderness."

"I'd like that. And I like talking, but I feel odd being the only one naked here. I like looking at you too, you know."

"I like a woman who knows what she wants and asks for it." Dave's approval made her feel ten feet tall.

Mike stood up, reaching for the catches on his clothing. "I could do this instantaneously, of course, but I think we'll all enjoy it more the old fashioned way."

"A little Chip n' D for our damsel?" Dave asked his cousin. "Do you think she'd enjoy that?"

"Most definitely." Mike's gaze held hers as he licked his lips. A funny flutter went through her womb.

"What's a chipendee? That word isn't in the linguistic databases."

"Funny what they left out, isn't it?" Dave asked his cousin conversationally.

"It's slang, honey. Way back when, there used to be a chain of clubs where men would do strip shows for crowds of women." Mike laughed. "I don't think we're up to the caliber of those bodybuilder types, and we'd never have done this for money, but we can put on a little show for you, Jaci, though I'm not much of a showman. I'd do damn near anything for you."

She could tell by the flush high on his cheekbones that he was embarrassed and her heart went out to him. "I don't need a show, Michael. I just need you."

"Damn. And here I wanted to take this slow." Michael ripped the buttons off his shirt and they bounced away with tiny clicking sounds as he shrugged out of the shirt.

David laughed, drawing her eyes. "And he said he wasn't a showman. Nice sound effects, Dreamwalker." David unbuttoned the cuffs on his shirt and moved on to the buttons marching down his chest, but Jaci wanted to help.

She got to her knees and took over the job of unbuttoning the crisp white shirt, enjoying the discovery of his hard male chest. When she was half-way down, she began placing nibbling kisses on his skin for each button she released, until she was at his waistband, the two sides of the shirt bunched up in her fists as she tried to push it away.

David took hold of her shoulders and dragged her up to meet his hot mouth in a kiss that lit a fire in her belly. But then he placed her back on the bed, away from him.

"I think she likes the sophisticated act better than your caveman display, Mike." David winked at his cousin, a teasing light in his eyes, but Jaci didn't want Michael to feel slighted. She turned to him.

"Oh, no. I liked the display of strength, Michael. Truly I did. And I'd like to see more."

"More?" Mike raised one eyebrow in suspicion. "Then you're going to have to come over here and show me how much you liked it. I need some convincing."

"Is that what they're calling it nowadays?" David quipped.

"Keep out of this, Fred Astaire. We'll see who she likes better, the barbarian or the businessman."

Jaci chewed her lip, creeping worry making her hesitant. "What if I like them both?" She didn't want to make either one of the men feel less than the other. Truth be told, she didn't care which side of their personalities they chose to show her. She knew deep down, without knowing exactly how she knew, that she would love every facet of each of the men. Both had the capacity for danger that Michael was flirting with, and the caring soul of the poet that David often displayed.

"It's only a game, sweetheart," David reassured her. "Don't worry."

Michael stepped closer. "I keep forgetting how new this all is for you, Jaci. I'm sorry. Dave and I stopped competing against each other when we were toddlers. We've been partners in crime ever since. We only play at one-upmanship from time to time, but it's not serious. Telepaths as close as we are couldn't hide it from each other if we were serious about one feeling superior to the other. Our friendship never would have lasted this long if we didn't respect and understand each other completely. As you'll come to understand us—in time."

"I hope we have the time."

Both men moved to surround her, one on each side. "Don't worry, sweetheart. We'll get through this. All of us. Together." David pressed kisses to her temple as Michael rubbed her back. "Have faith."

"Screw going slow," Mike snapped his fingers and everyone was naked. The men were already aroused and Jaci's temperature spiked with desire.

"Your skin is so hot, sweetheart," David observed as he slid his palms down her body. "I love the way you feel. How you warm the cold places deep inside me."

"Alvian body temperature is slightly higher than human."

"So our lady is hot blooded?" Michael leaned in and sucked one of her nipples into his mouth. David followed suit on the other side as incredible sensations sparked through her body.

A moan sounded and she realized dimly it came from her own throat.

Michael pulled back, his teeth grazing her nipple as he let it go with a last gentle tug. "Tall, blonde, smart and stacked. How did we get so lucky, Dave?"

"Stacked? What does that mean?"

David moved back and cupped both of her breasts in his hands. "It means you have gorgeous, big breasts we both enjoy." He stared at her breasts as he spoke, as if dazed. She noted Michael's eyes were drawn to the way David massaged her nipples as well, and the sensations his hands produced were sent straight to her womb. Still, one part of her mind observed, wanting to understand.

"So larger than average breasts are a good thing?"

"As far as we're concerned, that would be a great big yes." Michael slid one hand down the curve of her hip, his eyes still trained on her body. "It was one of the first things that I noticed about you when you became our caretaker. I used to dream about getting my hands on you."

"I'm glad." Lust was something that didn't exist in most Alvians. Only the warrior lines were said to actually need sex, and lower ranked workers were usually employed to service them. She was reminded of her single run-in with Grady Prime. She'd truly enjoyed the sensations he'd aroused in her body, but with the added emotional component she had with Michael and David, the pleasure was exponentially increased. She'd never service another man. Those days were over. But she would make love with her mates. Gladly.

She leaned forward, offering better access to the breasts they liked so much. She was thrilled by the idea they liked her body. She began to feel a sensation she could only attribute to pride. It was a good feeling. And so was whatever David was doing to her nipples. He made them more sensitive than they'd ever been, and she wanted more.

But the men were too good at holding back. She needed to rile them. She wanted to see them breathing as heavily as she was. She reached for them both at the same time, their throbbing cocks within easy distance as she leaned forward. Mike jolted in her grasp as she slid her fist around him. David just purred and edged closer.

"Oh, baby." Michael groaned as she stroked him. "Yeah, just like that." He stroked lower on her body, insinuating one broad hand between her thighs as she spread her legs to make room for his questing fingers. It was her turn to groan when he dipped inside her sheath, touching deep.

"I need..." Her thought processes drifted as pleasure crested in her body.

"What, baby? Tell us what you need," Michael crooned in her ear, his hot breath on her neck making her shiver.

"I need you inside me. I need you both inside me."

"You go first, Dave." Michael spoke to his cousin, but his gaze stayed on her. "I'll hold the dream as long as I can."

A wide grin broke over David's handsome features. "Good man."

He lifted her as Michael moved back and made room. She was positioned on the bed, her legs spread wide as the cousins watched her with appreciative eyes. David moved between her legs, holding her gaze for a long moment.

"You know I love you." He took a moment to touch her face, kiss her lips sweetly as he seemed to savor the moment. Jaci was glad. She wanted to bask in the emotion she read in his eyes, though she didn't understand all of it yet, still, something inside her yearned and was fulfilled by their tenderness.

"I love you too," she said, hoping to return some of what he gave her in that gentle moment out of time.

He pressed inward, invading her body with small movements, claiming her with care. Jaci loved every small pulse, every secret sensation. She'd never felt like this before, even if it was only a dream.

"Oh!" She cried out as he seated himself fully within her, his gaze still locked on hers. Then he began to move. First slow and gentle, he rapidly moved to sharp, almost jolting digs inside her body. She loved the loss of control she could read in his expression. She loved the power of his muscular body. She loved him.

"I'm sorry, babe. I can't make it last this time. I want you too much," he panted near her ear, but she was close to an explosion of the senses from which she might never revive. She could only nod and spur him on with small movements of her hips. "Come for me, Jaci. Come with me now!"

Together they crested the highest wave she'd ever climbed, drowning in pleasure as he held her. They flew up and over, then down the other side, and all the while, he was with her, protecting her, loving her. Jaci understood then what it was to be cherished.

She felt replete when he lifted away with a final lingering kiss, but then she saw Michael, standing there, watching them. The expression on his face stole her breath. It was hot, hungry and somehow noble. She realized he'd held off his own pleasure to allow them that moment out of time while he used his amazing psychic gift to keep them all here in the dreamstate. She decided it was his turn to fly, even if it meant she'd lose this spectacular dream. She'd have the memory of it when she woke. One perfect memory to hold against the uncertain future. Now she wanted to give the same to Michael.

"Come here, Michael." That was all she had to say.

In the blink of an eye, the elegant golden bedroom was gone, replaced by black silk and red satin. She looked around with interest.

"What's this?" She offered Michael an uncertain smile.

"In the old world, this kind of décor was pure sin. I've dreamed of your pale skin against this kind of backdrop for weeks now. I hope you don't mind." A flush stained Michael's cheekbones.

"Mind?" She sat up, holding out one hand to him. "I want

whatever you want, Michael. I don't know much about your culture's sexual practices, but I'm willing to learn." She looked around again and realized David was gone from the dream. "Where's David?"

"You blew his mind, cupcake. He's gone too deep into sleep to stay here with us in the dream realm. Do you mind if it's just us?"

"No, I don't mind." She caught his hand and drew him forward, onto the bed. "Show me what you want, Michael. Teach me what you like."

"Oh, baby. Another time and place, I'd enjoy giving you detailed instructions, but right now I'm so hot for you, it's going to be hard and fast. I have no finesse left."

"If you ask me if I mind again, I may have to penalize you," she teased him and was heartened when he laughed.

Michael climbed over her. "As tempting as that sounds, we'll have to hold it for later. When we can be together outside of dreams."

He positioned himself and sank into her, filling her emphatically with his wide, hard cock.

"Oh, Michael, do you think that day will ever come?"

He stilled and propped himself up on his elbows so he could look into her eyes. "I have to believe it, Jaci. I can't live without you. Somehow, we'll find a way. Believe that."

"I want to believe, but I'm scared."

He surged forward, making her gasp. "Then believe this. I love you. Nothing on Earth will keep me from you now that I've finally found you. I know Dave feels the same. When we work together, there's nothing we can't do. Believe in us, baby."

He punctuated his words with hard thrusts of his hips, distracting her. But his message was clear. She had to believe.

She had to. These men—and their love—were the only things that mattered in her life anymore. All the years she'd lived to this point were gone in the blink of an eye. Irrelevant.

"Oh, Michael!" He moved so forcefully, she thought she felt the Earth itself move beneath their straining bodies. He moved almost violently within her, but she felt no pain, no apprehension. What she did feel was a reawakening of the amazing pleasure David had given her—just as intense, but slightly different in flavor.

As she rose with Michael, her senses were flooded with his masculine scent, his hardness, his almost animalistic need, all focused on her. It was a heady feeling and one that drove her closer to the edge. With short, sharp digs, he set her on fire so that she cried out on every deep pulsing thrust.

"Michael!" She screamed his name as she came, feeling him tense a moment later and spurt within her.

She blacked out for a time and hours later, when she woke, it was with a smile on her face.

Out of the dream and back in their cell, the cousins spoke telepathically as they lay in their lonely beds.

"It's no good, Dave. I'm afraid for her. She's so unprepared to deal with her new emotions. If her people find out, she's toast."

"We just have to help her as best we can and have faith that there are other people involved now who have more power than we do. Harry will keep an eye out for her. He promised."

"I know, but I'm not entirely sure about the kid yet. I mean, he's one of them."

"I hear you, cousin. But he's also half human and was raised by humans. I think his loyalties are on our side."

"I hope you're right."

"Me too, cuz. Me too."

Jaci blushed as she walked into Mike and Dave's cell the next day. Memories of the night before were clear in her sparkling eyes. Michael loved the flush of excitement he knew their shared dreams had put in her cheeks. She was so breathtakingly beautiful.

A tall woman, she was still shorter than he and his cousin. She fit between them as if she were made to do so. She had a body that didn't quit and a sharp mind that both men liked. In fact, she was perfect for them.

She shut off the monitor and walked straight into Dave's arms. Well, he'd been standing closer. Mike would be sure to be right next to the damn monitor next time. He wanted the kiss she was giving to his cousin. Tomorrow it would be his turn to go first.

"How are you, sweetheart?" Dave asked her when he let her up for air.

"Still scared, but doing better. I believe the emotions are starting to integrate better inside my mind and I'm better able to hide my reactions the longer I practice at it."

Dave laid his hands on her temples and Mike felt the slight surge of energy that always accompanied the use of Dave's mindhealing power. He gave her a small jolt of healing energy, but she stepped back.

"Don't do it, David. I don't want you to be weakened on my account. I'm feeling much better. I assure you."

"Please, sweetheart. Let me do this for you. I want to give you every chance of succeeding and this is the only thing I can really do for you while I'm stuck down here in this cell."

Her face reflected her compassion. She was such a beautiful woman, inside and out, even if her emotions had only been awakened a short time before. She'd always been nice, but now that her inner core was free, she was blossoming into a kind, sympathetic and considerate woman.

She hesitated and Dave moved closer to her. "Let me give this to you. Just a touch to be sure you're in balance."

"Only a small amount, David. I'm serious. I don't want you drained from helping me. I can handle things much better now, thanks to your earlier help."

Dave took that as permission and touched her temples. Once again, Mike felt the pop of his cousin's energy—a much larger blast this time. Dave was giving her a lot more of his energy than she realized. Good thing he was such a deft touch with that rare power he wielded.

Dave finished the burst of treatment with a kiss, probably to distract Jaci. He pulled back and sought Mike's eyes. Mike knew it was his turn to distract their woman while Dave took a moment to recover.

Mike stepped up behind her, whirling her around into his arms. He dipped his head, enjoying her dazed expression as he claimed the kiss he'd wanted since the moment she walked into the room. He was vaguely aware of Dave sinking down into a chair. Mike knew he'd need a minute to regain his balance after shooting so much of his power into Jaci's healing, so he let the kiss go on until they were both breathing hard.

When he pulled back, he still didn't let her go. A glance over her shoulder told him Dave was still sitting, but looking a lot less pale. Another few seconds should see him back on his feet.

"You have something for us, Jaci? That data crystal Caleb

gave you?"

"Oh!" She pulled one hand from around his neck and released the catch of her shirt. "I put it in here."

"Never thought I'd wish I were a data crystal. What a nice hiding place." His teasing words elicited a small smile as she put two fingers into her cleavage.

Alvian women didn't wear bras, per se, but they did have a formfitting garment that served the same purpose. Jaci pulled the crystal out from between her breasts and handed it to him. It was warm from her body, and he couldn't resist lowering his mouth to place a few nibbling kisses on her cleavage before she closed up shop.

He hated to see her creamy flesh covered up, but the clock was ticking. They only had a few more moments before the cameras would have to be switched back on.

"You should pop that into the viewer now while the monitor is off. Don't let them see you putting it in or taking it out. You're not supposed to have any crystals at all, but Hara assured me this one was undetectable without physical inspection. He got it from Chief Engineer Davin himself and there is no better crystallographer on the planet."

Jaci followed him over to the viewer station and watched as he opened the crystal port and inserted the untraceable storage device Caleb had sent. He actually heard her sigh of relief as the crystal went into the machine and was hidden from view.

"We'll take a look at this tonight, Jaci. Thanks for bringing it."

"I want to help you." She clutched at his hand, swiveling her attention between him and Dave. "Anything I can do, I'll do."

"I know, sweetheart." He pulled her into hug, rubbing her shoulders to comfort her. "You've already done more than you'll ever know, just by being you."

"It's not enough. It won't be enough until you're free to walk out of this prison."

"Amen to that." Dave walked up to them, touching her shoulder and drawing her attention. "We're almost out of time for today."

"I know. I wish we had more time. There's never enough time with you both."

Mike and Dave surrounded her with their warmth, enclosing her in a hug shared by all three.

"It is what it is, sweetheart. For now, we just have to deal with it." Mike stepped back and let Dave take her in his arms.

"We all have to believe that the day will come—soon—when we can be together. Believe in it and it will happen, Jaci, my love." Dave kissed her while Mike did the small chores Jaci usually did to keep their cell habitable.

"Who knows?" Mike tried to raise their spirits. "Maybe your precognitive friend Caleb O'Hara will have some good news for us once we get a look at that crystal."

Dave drew back, giving another small pulse of energy to Jaci that she seemed unaware of, though it seemed to help her regain composure. Mike leaned in and gave her peck on the cheek, handing her the small items he'd collected for her while she'd been in Dave's arms. All she'd have to do is switch the monitor back on and she could leave without anyone in the city above being the wiser about the emotional upheavals taking place inside the cell and its inhabitants.

"We love you, Jaci. Just keep doing what you have to do to survive and like my cousin says, just believe in that love. Our people have a saying—love conquers all. And with love, we'll conquer this situation. Maybe not today or tomorrow, but sometime soon we'll be able to be together."

Chapter Seven

Dave lay down on his bed, weary from giving Jaci so much of his energy in such short, intense bursts. He had to give her a boost to balance the turmoil in her mind—the new chemicals and synapses firing through her brain as emotions came on line. It was imperative she be able to handle the confusion of all the changes happening to her as smoothly as possible to avoid detection.

He lived in fear of her being caught by her people. She'd said they might kill her and would most certainly imprison her. Dave couldn't let that happen. If a little fatigue was the price to pay for helping her keep it together enough to pass in her emotionless society, so be it. He'd rest up today and be ready to give her another treatment tomorrow. In the meantime, his cousin was busy at the viewer, reading the information Caleb had sent. He talked telepathically to Dave when he found interesting tidbits to pass on.

"Listen to this one, Dave. Caleb wrote that 'People of many talents will gather around a blond giant named for Hickok, who is an angel in disguise.'"

"Hickock? Like Wild Bill Hickock?"

"Beats the hell outa me. Caleb goes on to say, 'Former enemy, he'll become the father of the resistance. Tell those who manage to escape to seek him out in the high places.'"

"So there'll be an escape?"

"He says 'Escape is possible, but not until two love days from now.' I guess he didn't want to give dates the aliens would be able to easily track down. There's a lot of that kind of thing in here. Stuff humans would understand, but probably not the aliens."

"Probably a wise move. But 'love days'? You think he means Valentine's Day—February fourteenth?"

"My thought exactly."

"We'd better keep track of the calendar. We let that slip in the past few months." Dave observed.

"Get this. 'By twos and threes, captives will be given the chance to move south. Take it. Go south when offered and if you can't get south, bide your time. The day will come. And when it does, seek refuge in the high places with our angel. By then, he'll be ready to step into the role he'll play for our future. Learn from him. Listen to him. And be ready to follow his lead when the time comes. Remember my boy too. He'll help, though it won't seem so. When the time comes, remember.'"

"So 'his boy' Harry's got a bigger role to play. No surprise there." Dave mused.

"This Wild Bill Hickok-angel guy sounds like he could be one of the aliens."

"You mean that bit about being a former enemy? Could be. But maybe he was a jihadist or something. We are still in North America and Caleb's frame of reference is American."

"Yeah, you've got a point, but how about that 'blond giant' bit? To me that sounds like one of the Alvians. Not many Jihad Jamals fit that description."

"Okay. I'll give you that one. But it seems improbable."

"Stranger things have happened. Like our very own blonde

bombshell."

"Got me there, cuz."

Mike read more of the Book of Caleb—a title it had been given as a joke, but seemed like it fit too well not to stick—but Dave slid into sleep, unable to keep his eyes open after the draining healing a few hours before.

§

Sinclair Prime had a camp, of sorts, up in the high country overlooking the protected valley that housed the O'Hara ranch. They didn't know he was here. Not yet. If all went well, they'd never know he'd appointed himself guardian spirit of their hidden valley. He owed them. They'd welcomed him when his own people would have ended his life without a second thought and absolutely no regret.

The first being to test Mara 12's new and improved gene therapy cocktail, he'd been unprepared for the emotions that nearly overtook him. Then he'd been sent out on one final mission—one final assassination in a long career of quick, deadly work. It had been too much. Sinclair Prime couldn't bring himself to kill Chief Engineer Davin and had only winged him, knowingly giving his own life as forfeit. But Davin, and especially the astounding woman who was his resonance mate, had surprised him.

Not only had they forgiven him, but they'd offered him sanctuary and a chance to start anew. As far as the Alvians were concerned, he'd escaped, never to be seen again. Mara 12 and the High Council had no idea he'd been transported by Davin himself to the O'Hara ranch, high in the mountains of the northern continent.

Sinclair liked the wild terrain and the brisk weather. He loved snow and the lush land up here where humans—and those with emotions—could roam free. He owed Davin, Callie and Rick his life. Literally. He figured a good way to begin to repay their astounding kindness was by keeping an eye on their relatives on the ranch down below.

There were children on the ranch who needed protecting. Sure, the humans were doing all right on their own and Justin O'Hara had some skills even Sinclair envied, but Sinclair had the high ground. As a sniper and assassin, the high ground was where he operated best and felt most comfortable.

He also had one other, top secret genetic modification that made him more comfortable up here than anywhere else on the planet, and he was finally free to use it as *he* wanted. Not as his masters directed. Sinclair was through being a puppet dancing when his strings were pulled. He answered to no man and lived what remained of his life according to *his* will and yes, his emotions.

Sinclair Prime, the top assassin for the Council, was no more. He did his best to pass for human these days, when it was absolutely necessary to have contact with the others living in this wild place. It had been Rick St. John who'd given Sinclair his new name, though it had started as a joke. Rick had decided, for no apparent reason, to call him Bill. And so Bill Sinclair had been born.

A hunter he'd met on a game trail across the ridgeline two days before asked him if he was the one folks were calling Wild Bill. Sinclair had no idea what such a moniker meant among humans, but only shrugged and let the hunter think whatever he liked.

Only a long time later, when the man was gone and the moonless night provided cover, did the man now known as Bill, take off his shirt and let his wings unfurl.

§

The whole city was buzzing with the news. Chief Engineer Davin was coming for a visit. The talented throwback was often the subject of gossip, and rarely left his engineering facility these days unless there was some major problem. The talk of his mating had spread through the Alvian population, and raised eyebrows. Many had watched the news feeds of his startling appearance before the High Council during the last big power outage. People were curious about him and intrigued that he had found a resonance mate among the Breeds.

That he was bringing his mate with him was even more interesting and many Alvians found themselves loitering on the path from the main shuttleport in order to catch a glimpse of the oddest of all Alvians. He stood out among his people for many reasons. First, he was a throwback, an aberration born with emotions unlike the vast majority of their race. Second, he was the most talented crystallographer in generations and had already accomplished engineering feats on this new planet that were legendary. Third, he had recently defied the High Council with a dramatic display of anger, pride and outrage that hadn't been seen in those hallowed chambers in generations. That he'd not only stood up to the Council, but stood up to them and won only added to his aura.

If all that weren't enough, he'd confirmed his theory that Breeds could have the crystal gift. His legend had only increased when he claimed his mate in a raw crystal cavern, causing explosions on the power grid the likes of which had never been seen as they together overloaded the system with their joining. His Breed assistant's healing of the fractured

Council Crystal was something spoken of in whispers.

Little was known about the private life of Chief Engineer Davin, but rumors ran wild about the fact that assistant, a Breed by the name of Rick St. John, now shared quarters with Davin and his Breed mate. Speculation was rife about this Breed male's position in the household but Davin was saying nothing on the matter and so far Alvians had been too polite to ask him about it outright.

The three who disembarked from the small shuttle walked confidently down the halls of the northern city, destination firmly in mind. Ostensibly they were there to visit with Callie's uncle, but each of them knew they were on a mission of mercy to help two human men and their poor, confused, Alvian resonance mate. They felt the stares of the people who tried to look as if they belonged loitering around the halls trying to catch a glimpse of them, but paid them no mind.

Well, that wasn't entirely true. Rick St. John seemed to get a kick out of the Alvian curiosity seekers trying to figure out who he was. He chuckled as he held Callie's left hand, Davin holding her right as they walked together as equals down the wide corridors.

Before too long they arrived at their destination, a large apartment on the upper level where Caleb O'Hara was housed. They didn't even have to knock. Caleb had the door open and whisked them inside, wrapping his niece in a huge bear hug as he welcomed them all.

After a lengthy visit, Davin and Rick left Callie with her uncle and took a tour of the city. Davin led them eventually to the cells where he looked in on various prisoners. At this point Rick made a great show of recognizing Michael and David, stopping for a chat and introducing them to Davin. All of this was watched with mild interest on the monitors, though the Alvian scientists could have no way of knowing this meeting had been carefully choreographed for their benefit.

Rick caught up on old times with his supposed long-lost buddies and told them he'd been tested for crystal talent. The subject rolled around to Davin, who conveniently pulled a few crystals from his pocket and placed them before the two men just for laughs. To his apparent shock, they had a great deal of crystal gift.

While Davin had been prepared to fake the results of the test if necessary, he was more than a little surprised when both of the men turned out to have a high degree of very real crystal talent. It would make what he had to do easier. The crystal gift took precedence over all other experiments. There were too few Alvian crystallographers to run the ever-expanding power grids that were coming online each day. Suitable candidates among the Breeds were learning at a rapid pace and were already doing some of the day to day tasks quite well. But he always needed more gifted people.

Suddenly his mission of mercy turned into a something slightly different. These two men would be more than welcome in his training program given their scores on his little test. They wrapped up their visit with a promise to be in touch and Davin sidestepped over to the very next cell. He had one more small task to perform.

He knocked politely on Ruth's door.

Ruth settled her fussing daughter into the cradle and stood in front of it as the two strange men lowered the shield and entered her cell. She tried not to show her fear as they moved within the small cell. She could see that one was Alvian, but one was human, and they both held their hands up, palms open in a gesture of peace. She didn't relax though. Her daughter needed her. She was the only thing that stood between her precious baby and the Alvian experiments that could come at any time. She lived in fear of what they might do.

"Be at ease. You are Ruth?" the Alvian man asked in a calm voice. "I am called Davin. Caleb O'Hara asked me to check on you and your daughter."

"Caleb O'Hara? The precog?"

The one called Davin nodded respectfully. "The very one. I mated with his niece Callie not long ago and together with Rick—" he gestured slowly toward the other man, "—we've set up a training program for humans who have the crystal gift."

"I don't know what that is," she admitted, still suspicious. Davin smiled and wonder of wonders, it was a real smile. It lit his eyes from within and radiated out from his handsome face. "You're different from the others," she found herself saying. "Who are you? What are you?"

The human he'd called Rick laughed hard at that and turned to her. "He's a throwback, ma'am. He was born with emotions, unlike the rest of his kind. He's not a bad guy once you get to know him, but believe me when I say, we mean you no harm. This is strictly a social call. We told Caleb we were taking a tour of the city and he asked that we check on you and your daughter."

The baby was still fussing, her cries pulling at her mother's attention even as she weighed the men's words. She turned swiftly and picked up her baby, rocking her to try to quiet her.

"Ma'am." Rick stepped forward slowly. "I have a bit of the healing gift. Is there anything I can do to help your baby?"

Ruth looked deep into his eyes and made a decision. She stepped forward hesitantly.

"She's been fussy all day and I think she's running a

temperature."

Rick moved his hand to hover near the baby's forehead. He looked to Ruth first, before touching the baby. "May I?"

Ruth nodded swiftly, holding the baby while Rick put his hand on her chubby cheek. She watched carefully as he closed his eyes and concentrated. She thought she saw an ever-so-slight glow from his fingertips where they touched, light as a butterfly, on her daughter's chubby cheek.

After a few moments he opened his eyes and moved back. The baby quieted and nestled against her mother, dozing happily and no longer fussy.

"Just a minor ear infection. It hadn't really set in yet so it was easy to get rid of. Be careful to keep water out of her ears and she should be fine."

Rick moved a few feet back to his position near the door, dragging just a little, she could easily see. He was a true healer, then. She'd seen how they gave of their own energy when they healed another person once, long ago, and she remembered it well.

"Thank you, Mister...um...."

"Rick St. John," he introduced himself, leaning forward to shake her hand politely. "Caleb really did send us down here. He told us he'd sent you a note when you were pregnant and he was wondering how you're doing."

"You can tell him that I'm doing well and I can never thank him enough for sharing what he knew with me in that note. Please tell him how grateful I am. I owe him."

"We'll tell him, ma'am. We'll be going back up to see him before we leave the city."

"You can come and go as you please?" She was shocked that Rick, a human, could have such free run of the Alvian city.

Rick nodded, kindness in his eyes. "It wasn't always that way for me, so I know how you must feel. But I'm part of Davin's group in the Southern Engineering Facility. We work with the Alvians, training, learning and helping maintain the technology that runs their cities. In return, we have a certain amount of freedom."

Ruth felt tears gather in her eyes. "I'm truly happy to hear that, and happy for you Mr. St. John. It gives me hope to know at least some of us are finding our way out of imprisonment."

Davin chose that moment to step forward, his hand outstretched with three crystals. Ruth had no idea what he wanted her to do with them, but it was pretty clear he was handing them to her. She moved forward and took them from his hand. Immediately they began to glow and she jumped.

"What are they?"

Davin looked at Rick, who broke into a broad grin.

"They just might be your ticket out of here, ma'am. Would you be interested in learning how to work with crystals?"

She looked more closely at the purple, white and yellow crystals in her hand. "These are beautiful. Amethyst, citrine and quartz, right?" Davin's eyes narrowed and she felt the need to explain. "I used to make jewelry back in the old days. I owned a small boutique. I did special orders and some metalsmithing too. Folks came from all over to buy my pieces and I made a good living. I worked with faceted stones of all kinds, so I got to know them pretty well. But I never did anything with raw crystals like these. Never saw them glow like this before either." She handed them back to Davin, who took them gingerly. They glowed for a short time longer and then dimmed as he put them back in his pocket.

"I think if you had worked more with raw crystals, you would have encountered the glow long ago. You are almost certainly a natural conductor. It's a rare gift, Ruth, and one that is much sought after in my engineering facility. Would you like to join us there and learn to use your gift?"

Ruth's heart jumped in her chest, but then she looked down at her baby.

"Only if I can bring my daughter. I won't leave her behind, no matter what."

"Of course," Davin was quick to reassure her. "I'm not heartless enough to separate a mother from her child." With a pointed look to the monitor she knew was in the corner, she realized he was making a point that was more than likely lost on the emotionless techs who were watching the cells from the city above. "I will talk with the scientist in charge of your area and see what I can do. If you are told to move in the next day or two, don't worry. I will be asking for two others—your next door neighbors, as a matter of fact—so if you end up on a ship with them, you'll be heading for the southern facility. I will see you there."

Davin turned on his heel and strode out the door but Rick took a moment to smile at her. She felt reassured by his human face and his easygoing manner. That he'd also healed her little girl meant a lot as well. Suddenly things were looking up for them both.

"I'm glad you'll both be joining us. We have a small but friendly group of trainees and Davin is a good teacher. I think you'll enjoy your new life."

"Thank you. Thank Davin as well, and please thank Caleb. Once again he's interceded in my life for the better. He's an angel."

Ruth realized as Rick left and the door shield powered up once more that Caleb O'Hara truly was her guardian angel. She'd never even met the man but he'd done so much good for her and her little girl. She included him in her prayers that night as she had from the day she'd received the note telling her that she would see Sam, her baby's father, again one day. She lived for that day and her heart had hope. All thanks to Caleb O'Hara.

§

Mara 12 was not pleased to learn that Davin had been randomly testing her subjects and even less thrilled to hear that three of them had proven to have very strong crystal gifts—one of them a natural conductor, which was rare indeed. There was no help for it. She had to relinquish custody of them to him. Crystal technology ran everything and crystallographers were growing rarer and rarer. Since his last, dramatic appearance before the High Council, Davin could pretty much request anyone who showed the crystal gift be transferred to his control.

"I realize you are probably in the midst of observations of these people and I don't wish to inconvenience you any more than necessary," Davin was saying as he sat before her in her office. "Therefore, I would have no objection to hosting one of your techs as well. This way, your tech can continue the observations and send you the data for your continued study."

Mara was surprised by his reasonableness. She'd thought because of their past dealings and the fact that he was a throwback, he'd be completely contrary. But he seemed to understand the value of her work and was willing to allow her to continue her study of the subjects, if only from afar. It wasn't ideal, but it was better than nothing.

"In fact, I was going to ask you, even before this development, for the services of one of your techs. I believe she is designated Jaci 192. It seems she was recently sent to check my mate's health and my mate took a liking to her. I am concerned about my mate's pregnancy and would feel better if we had a tech available to relay data about her pregnancy to the natalogists here in the city. My mate, being human, has a preference for Jaci 192 whom she has already met and found agreeable." Davin sounded entirely reasonable to Mara, which she definitely hadn't expected from a throwback. "So if perhaps you could spare the tech and reassign her to the southern facility, you could use her to continue the observations of the three Breeds I'm requesting as well as my mate's pregnancy."

Mara sat back in her desk chair, thinking through his proposal. It seemed to make perfect sense and she silently congratulated the throwback for being able to reason things through calmly and rationally. She'd expected a lot of fist thumping and heated words, but instead he was almost as sane as a normal Alvian. Intriguing. Perhaps finding his resonance mate had a calming effect on his expected aggressive tendencies, she thought, and perhaps closer evaluation was in order. All the more reason to reassign one of her techs, and if he wanted Jaci 192, well, she was high enough in the hierarchy to be trusted to do the job well without direct everyday supervision, but low enough to not be missed. Mara nodded with satisfaction.

"I will reassign Jaci 192 to your command effective next quarter. She is in the midst of preparation for a very important clinical trial that will commence soon and I would rather have her see that to its injection phase than bring in someone new at this crucial stage. However, once the experiment is initiated, she can be easily replaced. Is that sufficient?"

Davin stood, his expression calm, surprising her yet again. "Very good. I will look forward to adding her to my staff, along with the three adult Breeds and the infant."

"You want the infant too? I would prefer to have it here."

"Regretfully, the mother will not cooperate without her child and she is the most important of my finds. She is a natural conductor. Her gift is too rare to let go, so the infant must come with her."

Mara sighed. She would never understand these Breeds and their silly attachments to their young. "Very well. You may have the infant as well."

Davin strode to the door. "Thank you, Mara 12. I wish you well in your experiments."

§

Ruth was in tears when Jaci's duties finally brought her to the woman's small cell. Jaci quickly shut down the monitor for the daily maintenance routine, careful not to let any of her feelings show while those upstairs could still see. She went immediately to the other woman, dreading what might have caused her such an emotional breakdown.

"Ruth, what is it?"

"Oh, Jaci! It's the most wonderful thing!" Ruth grasped Jaci's hand and laughed outright when she saw her confused face. "We're getting out of here! Two men came to visit me earlier. The Alvian's name was Davin and his human friend was named Rick St. John. Davin put an amethyst, a citrine and a quartz crystal in my hand and they glowed and now I'm going with Samantha to something called the Southern Engineering Facility."

Jaci felt her stomach clench and her heart expand. Ruth was getting out so maybe Davin had succeeded with her men too. She felt tears she didn't understand.

"That is great! But why are we crying?"

Ruth laughed and sobbed with her friend. "Tears of joy, my friend, that's what these are."

Jaci was pulled in for a quick hug as Ruth stood to pick up her baby who was awakened by their laughter. "Little Samantha is going with me. I told them I wouldn't go without her and they still want me. I'm so relieved."

"I'm very happy for you both," Jaci said, feeling bubbles of joy bursting in her chest, in the vicinity of her heart as she watched the mother and child, happier than she'd ever seen them.

"Oh!" Ruth whirled with a smile. "Dave and Mike are probably going too. Davin said he would be requesting them. Lita showed up just before you did to tell me to pack, so if the guys are going too they probably already know for sure."

Jaci wiped her eyes and schooled her features, hastening through the rest of her duties and heading straight for the monitor. Before she switched it back on, she turned to her friend.

"I'll miss you both, Ruth, but I'm happy for you. Truly. Davin is a good man and I think you'll do well with his group. I won't be able to say goodbye when you go so please accept my wishes for a safe journey and a good, happy life ahead."

Ruth cuddled her daughter and nodded. "You've been a good friend, Jaci, even when you didn't quite understand what my funny moods were all about. You were kind even before your accident and that's more than can be said for many of your people. I liked you then, but now, I hope you won't mind if I say I consider you a true friend." Ruth's eyes started to flow again and this time Jaci thought she could tell they were happy tears. "I'll miss you too and I can only hope and pray that someday our paths will cross again."

Jaci swallowed hard against the tears that threatened. "That's my wish as well, Ruth. I've never had a close friend before, but I always liked you, even before I could sympathize with you. I am honored more than I can say that you would call me friend. I don't deserve it."

Jaci couldn't spend any more time. The monitors had to go back on and she had to be in control of her emotions. Swiftly, she turned and composing herself, switched the monitor back on as if nothing of import had happened. Ruth was still cuddling her laughing child and Jaci took her leave, showing only a mild fondness that was allowable for an unemotional Alvian. Inside, she agonized over whether she would ever see her newfound friend again. She was happy for Ruth and Samantha, but still feared for herself.

Steadfastly, she made her way next door and nearly stopped dead at the sight of her men packing their few belongings. As calmly as she could, she made her way to the monitor and switched it off, then turned and launched herself into the nearest pair of outstretched arms. Kisses rained down all over her head and neck and she reveled in the sensation of feeling her mates in the flesh.

The Hum surrounded her and imbued her with energy. Sexual energy that had no real outlet, as rushed as they had to be in this, and all their encounters.

"You're really going then?" she asked when they let her up for a moment of air.

Dave nodded down at her. "Lita came just before you with the word to pack and two carryalls. We're being shuttled down there tonight. God, I'm going to miss you!"

"But I'll love you in our dreams, sweetheart. Every night, I'll bring us all together. I promise." Mike kissed her neck, biting softly so as not to leave a telltale mark.

"Will your abilities work over such a distance?" She couldn't see his expression but she felt the hesitance in him. Turning, she took his face in her hands. "It doesn't matter. I will dream of you anyway, even if you can't dreamwalk to me from such a distance. I'll know you would if you could."

"I'll do everything in my power to be with you, Jaci. That I promise you."

"And don't forget Davin. He's working behind the scenes to get you reassigned," Dave reminded them softly. "Personally, I think if anyone can do it, he can."

"You liked him then? That's good, because he's in charge of the engineering facility. You'll have to work with him a lot, I think."

"He seems like a good guy, for an Alvian." David laughed at his joke. "Damndest thing I ever saw. An Alvian with feelings and a human friend he treats like an equal. It's going to take some getting used to."

"I'll let you in on a little secret. Rick *is* Davin's equal, at least in their relationship with Callie. They are both her resonance mates."

"No shit?" David seemed to think that over. "I had no idea such an arrangement could work. I didn't think an Alvian would willingly share his true mate with a human."

Mike drew his cousin's attention with a low whistle. "Says a lot about Davin though, doesn't it? I think I'm going to like this guy."

She couldn't bear it. They were leaving. She was overjoyed for them, but she felt a gaping hole begin to form somewhere near her heart. She clutched at them both, pulling them close, surrounding herself in their warmth as if she'd never see them again.

Perhaps she wouldn't. The thought sent a shiver of fear

straight through her. Anything could happen. Her secret could be discovered, or Mara 12 could just simply refuse to let her go for another reason. Worse, she feared that her mates would forget her in their newfound freedom and that thought brought the greatest pain.

"What's this?" David asked softly, gently touching her tears. "Don't cry, sweetheart, it will all work out. You have to believe."

"I'm afraid I'll never see you again. I'm afraid you'll forget me." Her voice was a mere whisper of fear.

"Never gonna happen." Mike's arms tightened around her, sure and strong. "We love you too much." He bent to kiss her then and it felt even better than it did in their shared dreams.

"I love you too." She tried desperately to get her new emotions under control. "I don't want to mess this up for you. I've got to turn the monitor back on."

Dave turned her and swept her close, hugging her for a long, long moment before he kissed her soundly. She felt the tingle of his healing energy passing into her and suddenly she felt more in control though her heart was still breaking.

"Remember that we love you," he said softly, pulling back to stare down into her eyes, "and love conquers all."

Chapter Eight

That night, she waited and waited, but the dreams never came. She woke in the morning with tears streaking down her face. Her mates were gone and more than likely the distance from the northern city to the southern engineering facility was too great for Mike's dreamwalking gift to bridge.

Jaci went about her duties with what felt like a lead weight wrapped around her heart. When she got to the cells, she found the living arrangements had been reshuffled and some of the folks who had shared more crowded cells were now given Ruth and the cousins' old chambers. She serviced the monitors and observed the new residents as she'd been trained to do, made her reports and sought her dinner while her heart twinged with a pain so deep, she thought she just might die from it.

But escape would not come so easily. She went to sleep that night after putting in some time preparing the life-changing experiment a few of her people were scheduled to begin in just a few days. How she wished she could warn them what was in store as their emotions began to take control. How she wished she could come forward and tell the truth, but knew she could not.

When she woke the next morning after another dreamless sleep, she felt just as despondent as the day before and could barely find the energy to get out of bed and start her day.

§

Bill Sinclair made his way out of the small town on the other side of the mountain from the O'Hara's protected valley. He went there once in a while to trade the pelts of animals he caught and ate for other kinds of foodstuffs, and also to gather information. The people seemed to accept him for human, though more than one had asked him if he was something called Scandinavian. Bill shrugged and nodded, preferring not to speak much. Alvian voices were more mellifluous than human. It was one of the few things that could give him away, but the humans in the small encampment they called a town seemed to accept him.

He didn't have any psychic ability. They all seemed to have one kind of mental power or another, but many were loners, so they let him be. He guessed they thought he was keeping quiet about whatever he could do, preferring to give him a wide berth after one big, drunken fool made the mistake of challenging him to a fight. Bill had put the man down without breaking a sweat. Since then, the rest of them had looked on him with respect and more than a bit of caution.

This had been a good trip. He came away with a sack of beans, a small wheel of cheese, and some other edibles he wouldn't otherwise have access to. He'd supplemented his mostly meat diet with whatever he could, but to get the really good stuff—the stuff grown on the O'Hara ranch and a few other plots of land scattered throughout the mountains—he had to barter.

Bill was over the first ridge, on a circuitous route that would lead him eventually to his small camp up in the high ground when he smelled smoke. It wasn't all that unusual, since others preferred to live out in the woods, but most were careful about campfires, fearing discovery by Alvian patrols. The quantity of smoke grew as he moved on, growing to alarming proportions. Bill feared it might be signs of a forest fire. Out here, that could be a major problem.

He made his way more quickly now, though he kept to his stealthy ways. If it was a forest fire, he needed to know where it was and how big before he decided which way to move. If it wasn't a forest fire, he needed to know exactly what—and who—it was.

Before long, he came upon a small lean-to. Sure enough, it had caught on fire from an untended campfire. Scouting quickly, Bill advanced into the deserted camp, using two buckets of water that were placed near the lean-to to douse the worst of the flames. The rest he kicked out with dirt.

Only then did he see the arm sticking out of the dilapidated structure that had somehow kept its shape, even while burning. Bill had caught the blaze before it could truly get out of control, but whoever was inside would be in bad shape from the smoke, if not from other injuries that stopped the man from tending the fire in the first place.

Bill dragged the body out, discovering a man in his middle years, dirty and smelling of disease to his sensitive Alvian nose. Some kind of infection had weakened the man to the point that he'd been unable to properly keep watch over his campfire, though he'd laid in supplies—the buckets of water—before succumbing to whatever bug had laid him low. He was only slightly burned, but he was unconscious and his lungs wheezed as he tried to draw breath. Who was he?

Bill set him against a tree while he searched through the man's few possessions. There was a small book near where he'd lain and Bill took a cursory glance through it. Inside, he found the blank pages had been filled in with hand-drawn images of a woman, drawn with such intense emotion, they leapt off the page. Whoever this man was, he'd loved this woman deeply. Turning pages, Bill found diary entries that detailed this man's escape from the northern city and subsequent life on the run.

He'd been a prisoner, then. Instantly, Bill's newfound heart went out to the man. He pocketed the book and looked around for a few sturdy branches. He fashioned a frame he could pull behind him, knowing he'd have to break cover and bring this man to the one place he knew he could find help...the O'Hara ranch.

Bill saw the tripwire and leaned down to deliberately make it trigger. He then sat down to wait.

Before long, Justin O'Hara showed up, as Bill had known he would. The two warriors eyed each other with wary respect.

"Sinclair Prime, isn't it? Though you look like a mountain man now." Justin held a shotgun perched against his hip, pointing upwards, but still ready. "What brings you here?"

Bill stood and moved aside to reveal his burden. "I found this man in a burning lean-to not far from here. He's human. An escaped prisoner from the northern city, judging by this." Bill brought out the book and threw it to Justin, who caught it single-handedly. "That's rare enough I thought he might be worth saving. He's very ill and a little crispy. I thought maybe your brother could take a look at him."

Justin's eyes narrowed. "I'll get him. If this man is infectious, I don't want to bring disease near the children."

"A wise precaution." Bill nodded and turned to go. "I'll leave him in your hands."

"Wait." The single word made him pause and turn back. "I didn't know you were still in the area." Measuring eyes made Bill feel uncomfortable.

"You weren't meant to know." Bill sighed, knowing he had to come clean, at least in part. This warrior was as tenacious as he was himself. "I've been watching over your valley from above. I like this land and I owe your family. I figured this was as good a place to be as any other."

Justin eased back, his shoulders going from tense to guarded, only a slight improvement. "You have the high ground?"

Bill liked Justin's quick grasp of the situation. Here was a soldier who understood tactics. He'd missed that in his isolation. Missed talking with others who shared his avocation. "Always. I always seek the high ground."

Justin actually smiled and Bill found his own lips quirking up, though he'd had precious little practice at the expression since he'd gained emotions.

"What have we here?" Mick O'Hara moved up from the lower slope behind some trees, having come at his brother's telepathic call, no doubt. These brothers had strong psychic powers. Bill had to remember they could communicate over great distances, unlike most human telepaths. "Sinclair Prime, as I live and breathe."

His former name made him flinch. "Call me Bill. That Alvian Prime is dead."

"Are you sure about that?" Justin asked, a challenge in his tone.

"Absolutely certain," Bill replied, holding the other soldier's gaze. "He's better left dead. He wasn't a good man."

Mick O'Hara examined the man and all three carried him back to a small outbuilding on the ranch where they'd once housed Sinclair as a prisoner. He remembered the small room with fondness, though his future had been uncertain in those early days. But this was also the place he'd talked with the female empaths of this family—Jane and her daughter Callie—who had helped him so much in those difficult times. They were truly special women.

"He had pneumonia even before the smoke inhalation," Mick said after a thorough examination of the still-unconscious patient. "I can bring out some breathing apparatus, but we're running low on oxygen. I was saving it for emergencies."

"I think this qualifies," Justin observed.

"If you are concerned you will not have sufficient supplies for your family, perhaps I can be of some assistance." Sinclair wasn't sure they'd take his help, but he owed this family. "I know where most of the Alvian supply stations are. I've been making a crude map of them in case I ever needed anything, but have so far left them alone. However, I do know the basic resupply stations have compressed oxygen canisters I could get easily, should you need them."

"Are you sure?" Justin asked. "I don't want to bring down the Alvian army on our heads over a few canisters of O-2."

Sinclair considered his response. "If I liberated a few tanks tonight, you could refill your tanks from them and I could return them tomorrow, leaving the valves slightly open. It would look like careless handling caused leakage. As long as nobody needs oxygen between tonight and tomorrow—which is highly unlikely anyway—you should be in the clear."

"It's a sound plan," Justin agreed. "I'll go with you, if you don't mind. I'd like to get a look at one of these resupply stations. We didn't know they had anything like that out here."

"It's standard operation when they're flying patrols in an area. They put in a few way stations so patrols can stay out longer."

"Good." Mick stood. "I'll get our tanks and start treating this guy. With some care, he should pull through. You guys go do your ninja thing."

Justin was a good soldier. Sinclair was impressed by his stealth and the way he moved in the wilderness. Here was a soldier who had trained hard and well. Sinclair respected that and the man who had been both tough and compassionate, when needed.

This man had once held Sinclair's life in his hands. Sinclair wouldn't be alive except for his leniency and willingness to give a reformed assassin with newly awakened emotions a chance. They watched a small two-man patrol ship packing up as they prepared to leave the resupply station. Crouching in the underbrush, they watched from afar, waiting for the Alvians to leave.

"I miss this."

"I hear ya, brother."

Sinclair hadn't realized he'd spoken aloud, but was glad he did when the quiet comment elicited a grin of comradeship from Justin O'Hara.

"My real job was a solitary one," Sinclair went on, testing the conversational waters. "But I had battalions under my command and a special team of operatives whom I trained with for covert work. They were my brothers. I miss them, though I'm sure they can't even begin to understand how to miss me."

Justin chewed the end of a weed stalk. "It's lonely being a hermit, eh?"

"I thought I understood being solitary, but it's very different with emotions. I've never before *felt* alone, but now I find it very disturbing. And I miss the action, but I don't miss the killing. It was good to have a job, to be useful. Now I just take up space and oxygen."

"That's not entirely true." Justin turned to face him. "You watch over the ranch. That's something I, personally, consider very important. Of course, I wish I'd *known* you were up there."

Sinclair went further out on the limb he'd scaled. "I wasn't sure you'd want me around, but I owe a debt to your family I can never repay. It's a debt of honor and of blood. For my kind, there are no greater obligations."

"I understand honor, Bill."

Sinclair liked hearing the name he'd adopted. He didn't feel like an Alvian Prime anymore. No, more and more, he was becoming the wild man, Bill Sinclair.

"I thought you might." Sinclair nodded toward the ship they were watching. "They'll move soon. See the hatch the taller one just closed? They're finished recharging."

Justin got ready to move. "Just for the record, I'm glad you've got the high ground and I don't think anyone would mind if you checked in with us at the ranch from time to time. I saw the sacks of supplies you had. You don't have to trade in town if you don't want to. We'll supply you direct, now that we know you're there. You run a risk, going into town. Those folks could string you up without a second thought if they knew you were Alvian."

"They could." Sinclair accepted that fact. "But so far, they seem to think I'm something called Scandinavian."

Justin shook with laughter. "Damn, I'm sorry. That just

took me by surprise." Justin's eyes were trained on the ship, still being packed up by two very slow moving soldiers. "Come to think of it, you do look a bit like a Viking, especially if your hair was longer. But you still don't have any psychic abilities. A couple of telepaths could run circles around you, even with all your training. And there are other powers that could stop you in your tracks."

"Like what?"

"Try and move your left arm." Justin turned away from the ship to watch him again, a grin on his face. Sinclair tried to lift his arm, but found his left arm pinned down by...something. There was no sign of any kind of physical impediment, but suddenly his arm was totally immobile.

"Shards! What is that?"

"Telekinesis. I can move things—and stop things—with my mind. And I'm not the only one out there, so be wary in your dealings with humans. A big enough group, with the right mix of abilities could kill you. Stop struggling, I'm going to release you now."

Sinclair felt the weight lift and his arm was free to move again. It had been a most enlightening—and frightening—demonstration. A minute later, while Sinclair was still rubbing his arm, the ship moved off. Finally.

When Sinclair and Justin got back to the ranch, Justin stayed outside the small outbuilding, as Mick had directed, sending Sinclair in to let Mick know they were back. The patient was doing much better. He was awake and responding well, Mick said, to the mixture of Alvian and human medicines he'd administered.

"I hear you saved my life." The man took a moment away

from his oxygen mask to speak in a raspy voice. "Thank you."

"I'm glad I was in time," Sinclair said, uncomfortable with the man's gratitude.

"Don't talk, Sam." Mick reapplied the oxygen mask. The man he'd called Sam was visibly tired and his eyes closed as Mick stepped back from the bed. "Just rest."

Mick signaled Sinclair to be quiet as he went outside with him. Justin was already across the field, heading back toward the main house. He waved to his brother, the two no doubt speaking telepathically as Sinclair watched.

"Jane's back at the house," Mick said as Sinclair assisted him in refilling the ranch's depleted oxygen tanks, which he'd lined up outside. "I don't want her exposed to Sam. He's contagious, but the good news is, with your Alvian constitution, you can't catch the bug. Justin and I will take precautions. I'm going to keep him away from Sam and do the doctoring myself."

"I will do it, Mick. Your family needs you and if I cannot catch the disease, it only makes sense."

Mick stopped and looked at him, as if considering his words. "I'm not too proud to admit I could use your help. Doctoring pneumonia like this takes more than one person and if I get too run down, I could easily catch the bug myself."

"Then I must help you."

"You're a good man, Bill." Mick went back to filling canisters, a small smile on his face.

The words touched Sinclair deeply, but he didn't feel like a good man. There was too much ugliness in his past he still had to make up for. Perhaps in time, he might yet live up to the sentiment he'd read in Mick O'Hara's eyes.

After a few days, Sam took a turn for the better. A week after Sinclair had dragged him to the O'Hara ranch, he was mobile and well on the mend. Sinclair had aided Mick in caring for the man at the height of his illness, but now he felt superfluous.

"I should go now," he said to Mick as they watched the sun set. Jane had sent out a delicious dinner the three men had eaten together in the small outbuilding. Sam, still weak, had fallen asleep right after the meal, leaving Mick and Sinclair to enjoy the quiet evening air as they sat outside in the dusky light.

"You could," Mick agreed noncommittally.

"I can't stay here. My people still monitor you. I've seen their patrols going over your land, even when you were unaware of it. If they saw me here..."

"That's a tough break, because we like having you around. If it weren't for the children, we'd ask you to stay, regardless of the risk."

Sinclair turned to look at him, surprised by the statement. He could see that Mick meant it too, though he was still learning to read facial expressions.

"I am deeply honored." Sinclair felt a lump rise in his throat that he didn't understand. He swallowed around it. "I will continue my watch from above, with your indulgence." He bowed his head in a very Alvian show of respect.

"I like that idea and I know Justin approves, but Jane worries for you living in such cold environs. She wants to send along some provisions for you—blankets and such. She also wants to arrange to stock you with food and perishables. Maybe set up a regular check-in. Justin thought it was a good idea too, and he sent along this." Mick reached into his pocket and pulled out a very small crystal. It looked like a short-range communication device.

But of course. They had access to Chief Engineer Davin's talent. This family had more resources than his people gave them credit for. Mick flipped the glittering crystal through the air to Sinclair.

"Completely untraceable and short-range. In fact, it can only communicate with our devices. Not that we don't trust you, but we don't want anyone getting a message out if you should lose it somehow."

"A wise precaution. I will report in when I see anything amiss."

Mick waved his comment away. "You can straighten that stuff out with Justin before you leave. What I wanted to know is if you'll take Sam with you?"

"What?"

"Well, Sam's an escaped prisoner. Just like you. If he's seen here, it'll bring down the Alvians, same as seeing you. We need to stash him somewhere and he's not entirely well enough to live on his own yet. I thought maybe you could take him with you up into the mountains, maybe show him how to survive up there, if he needs any advice."

"I..." Sinclair didn't know what to say. "I'll think about it."

"Good." Mick stood and began walking toward his office. Sinclair had taken night shift while Sam was so sick, with Mick sleeping in his office, away from the possibility of contaminating anyone in his family. They'd keep it up until they were certain all risk was gone. "I'll see you in the morning."

"So what's your deal? I know you're not a telepath 'cause you don't even twitch when I send you a mental scream." Sam asked as he ate lunch the next day. Sinclair had been dreading this line of questioning, knowing his lack of psychic ability marked him as alien, like nothing else. "I'm telepathic and a touch telekinetic myself."

Sinclair suspected from his tone that Sam wasn't telling him everything, but that was his prerogative, after all. Sinclair shrugged. He'd known this moment was coming since Sam had woken up and still didn't know quite how to deal with it. "I have no special abilities."

"No?" Sam chewed, looking at him oddly as Sinclair shifted uncomfortably. "Not even a little foresight? A lot of folks have that. It's what saved their lives." Sam swallowed and stared some more. "So what did you do in the old world?"

Again, Sinclair hesitated, but didn't know what to say. "Nothing."

Sam put down his sandwich and set the plate aside. "You one of them, aren't you? Son of a bitch."

Sinclair sighed with regret. "I was born Alvian, but I'm not like them anymore."

"Like hell you aren't." Sam seemed to study him. "What the fuck are you doing way out here, living like a hermit? Are you a fucking mole?"

"I don't know what that means, but I live out here because I'm a fugitive, like you. If the Alvian patrols find me, I'll be shot on sight." Sinclair stood, pacing the small room in frustration.

"Why?"

Sinclair turned to him, surprised to see he really wanted to know.

"Because I feel." Sinclair slumped into a chair against the wall. "I volunteered for an experiment and they made me...*feel.* I'm not Alvian anymore. I'm more like you."

"You'll never be human, pal."

"I know. And I regret that more than you'll ever know."

Sam swore and looked away. "Why did you help me?"

"Why?" Sinclair surged to his feet and picked up the small book he'd found with Sam, opening it to a page he'd looked at over and over again. He handed it to the other man. "Because of her."

When Sinclair left the ranch a few days later, Sam went with him. The men had reached an understanding in the days since their confrontation and an uneasy sort of friendship. Both were fugitives, hiding from the Alvian patrols. They found they had more in common than either one was comfortable with, but were smart enough to realize they had a better chance of survival together than apart.

Jane O'Hara sent them off with all kinds of food and supplies and when they made camp, for the first time in months, both were reasonably warm and well fed because of the supplies Jane had provided. The cave Sinclair had found was big enough for two and Sam shared in the chores, though he was still weak from the illness. After a few days, they fell into a routine and after a while, they even became friends.

Chapter Nine

Jaci was despondent after two weeks with no word from David or Michael. Not even dreams. She missed them more than she'd ever thought possible and trudged through her daily chores with no danger of smiling. She was simply too sad.

She had to be careful to school her expression. Sadness was easier to channel into the usual apathetic Alvian mask than happiness had been, but it still required effort. So far, she'd been able to avoid detection, but there had been a few close calls. Lita 498 questioned her about her sluggishness and Jaci had to fabricate a digestive disorder that kept her awake in order to explain her condition. A trip to the infirmary for mediation she didn't need had made her aware of how difficult it was becoming to keep up her charade.

She fell asleep with a heavy heart, having given up hope of Michael reaching her from such a long distance. And just when she'd given up, he appeared.

Michael sauntered through her dream as if he belonged there, sweeping her into his arms in a strong, reassuring hug.

"Jaci, my love. I'm sorry it's taken me so long to figure out how to reach you." He showered her face with kisses as she laughed with pure joy.

"Michael! Oh, Michael!" She hugged him hard, as happy as she'd ever been just to see him, even if it was only in a dream.

"How did you do it? Can you stay for a while? Where are you? Are you nearby?"

He soothed her with gentle hands on her shoulders, guiding her to sit on a stone bench he'd conjured in the garden of her dream. "I'm in Davin's engineering facility. We've been working for two weeks on using raw crystals to boost my natural dreamwalking ability. I finally figured out how to tap into the crystal earlier today and was waiting for you to dream so I could come check on you. Barring any complications—which I don't think are likely—I should be able to reach you every night now."

"How is David?"

"Jealous as hell that I couldn't take him along tonight, but I wanted to be sure I reached you so you wouldn't worry. I'll try to bring him tomorrow. Now that I've got the hang of it, I don't think it'll be too difficult."

"Is Davin treating you well? How are you both doing?" She couldn't stop touching him, wanting to know everything all at once.

"We're good. Great, in fact. We live above ground in a beautiful apartment with windows overlooking the rainforest and no locks on the doors. Davin's a great guy. He's teaching us all kinds of stuff about the crystals and Rick and Callie are really nice folks. They send their greetings, by the way. They knew I was going to try to reach you tonight. Damn, baby, it's so good to see you!"

He pulled her in for a kiss and Jaci felt his love, deep and true, resonating in her heart. When he pulled back, tears were in her eyes on the dreamplane as she did her best to memorize his beloved face.

"I've missed you so much."

"I've missed you too." He kissed her again, and for a

moment they were both lost in sensation, but there was much to be said and precious little time in which to say it. Michael pulled back. "Look, I'm still learning how to boost my natural abilities using crystal power, so I'm not sure how long I can maintain this dreamwalk yet. If I disappear suddenly, don't worry. We're safe with Davin. I mean that. Really safe. He's got more power than even Mara 12. This crystallography program is sanctioned by the High Council itself. Davin's got a lot of clout with those guys."

"Mara 12 took some of her assistants with her to the last Council session at which he appeared and news of those goings on filtered down through the staff. I heard about how he outmaneuvered Mara 12 to get approval for his expansion of the crystallography program and other concessions. It was all over the news feeds too, though not in as much detail. That man seems to have nerves of steel and his assistant is supposed to be some kind of miracle worker for what he did to repair the Council Crystal."

"Rick?" Michael nodded. "Yeah, he's pretty amazing. He's been working with David privately because they both have a similar kind of ability. Rick's a healer too—of the body, not the mind. David is making amazing progress with this crystal stuff, working with Rick. Apparently the healing talents give them both some really neat abilities to work with fractured crystal. Ruth's doing well too. She's got another kind of special crystal talent. She asked me to say hello to you, Jaci. She misses you, but she's happier than I've ever seen her. Callie helps Ruth with the baby. She says she's practicing for when her baby is born."

"I didn't think of that, but it must be nice for Callie to have the baby around. Little Samantha was always a good-tempered child. I liked her."

Michael tugged her into his arms again. "Maybe one day, we'll have children of our own, Jaci. Ever thought of that?"

She hadn't and the shock must've shown in her expression as Michael chuckled. "I never considered reproduction. I'm not high-level enough to merit sample collection in the normal course of things. And now...well, there's no way they can know how my DNA has been altered. I would never be allowed to reproduce."

"Maybe not the Alvian way, but you can certainly do it the old-fashioned way with me and Dave. Wouldn't you like to have a baby? I don't mean right away, but sometime in the future, maybe?"

Shock warred with wonder inside her. "I've never even considered it, but...I think I like the idea. It would have to be in secret though. The Maras would never let me pass on the changes in my DNA randomly. I fear we will not be free to pursue this idea for many years." She was surprised at the depth of grief that thought caused her.

"That's okay, sweetheart." Michael squeezed her in comfort. "We have many years ahead of us yet to deal with all of this. Who knows what tomorrow will bring? Things could change drastically for us all in less time than you think."

She grew suspicious at the hint of knowledge in his tone. "Why do you say that?"

"Let's just say I know a few precogs and they seem to think that change—big change—is coming for your people and mine."

"I'm afraid, Michael." The feeling of fear was nearly overwhelming.

"Don't be, sweetheart." His arms felt safe when nothing else did. "Change is hard, but these changes will work out for the better according to the Oracle."

"Who is the Oracle?"

"Can't you guess?"

"Caleb O'Hara? Is that what they're calling him?"

"It started as sort of a code name to keep his identity protected should the book of prophecies he gave us be discovered by your people. We didn't know it would stick, but that's what folks are calling him now. At least, that's how they're referring to his prophecies. Just a few of us know who the Oracle really is. It's our small way of protecting him." Michael shrugged. "I have to say, he's the most powerful foreseer I've ever heard about. He wrote things into that book of visions he gave us that are amazingly detailed and incredibly accurate."

"He has a near perfect record of accuracy according to the visions he's given us to study. Ninety-five percent with a five percent error margin."

"I believe it. Some of what he wrote has already come to pass and he's spot on. Some of what he's foreseen for our immediate futures is...difficult, but we can get through it, Jaci. Be sure of that. We humans have a saying—after the darkness comes the dawn. Remember that. When things seem bleakest, remember, they will get better. Believe in that and believe in our love."

"Did Caleb..." She gathered her courage. "Did he say anything about me in that book?"

Michael looked uncomfortable. "Not directly, which is what makes this so hard. He wrote down a vision that may or may not pertain to you. Dave and I have studied it and we can't be sure."

"What did it say?"

"'An alien girl will discover her heart's desire, but will go down in flames and be reborn like the phoenix. An angel and hermit will come to her aid and by so doing, will rekindle the embers of revolution. Together, they will begin something bigger than the sum of its parts. Out of the fires of fear will the flame of liberty be reborn.'"

Jaci tried to understand the words, but didn't comprehend most of the references. "It sounds dangerous."

Michael hugged her again. "It could be, but the good part is that in the end, something important will be reborn. If this alien girl is you, you're destined to have hard times ahead, but we'll all come out of it stronger and ready to reclaim some of what we humans have lost. Our society before the cataclysm—or at least the country in which Dave and I lived—was founded on the idea of liberty for all people. The imagery Caleb used sounds a lot like the imagery of the founding of our country, the United States. Our anthem talked of 'the rocket's red glare, bombs bursting in air'—fire and flames preceding a great victory over oppression and tyranny that lasted for hundreds of years and spawned the most successful democratic republic in our planet's history."

"I have much to learn of your people's past, Michael." Suddenly she felt very ignorant. It wasn't a comfortable feeling.

He stroked her hair. "We have years to tell you about the way we used to live and hopefully, we'll have a chance to rebuild some of what we lost. If Caleb's to be believed, wheels have already been set in motion that might bring about promising things for our future. But we all have our parts to play. His words are cautionary. He instructs us to bide our time and watch for the signs. Revolution is coming. We have to be ready for it. And if you're the alien girl he prophesied, you might be the start of it."

"That's a lot of responsibility, Michael." Her words shivered through hesitant lips. "I don't think I can handle that kind of thing."

"And no one is asking you to, Jaci, my love. Things will

happen as they must. You may not be the alien girl Caleb wrote about. It may be some other girl in another city somewhere. But if things do turn out to be difficult in the near future, I want you to remember that prophecy and know that after the dark comes the dawn. Remember that, Jaci. And remember that no matter what, Dave and I will always love you and come to you if you're in trouble."

"Oh, Michael." She threw her arms around his neck and kissed him with all the fear and desperation that had built up at hearing his dire words. "I love you so much." Tears fell from her eyes on the dreamplane as Michael held her close, crooning in her ear and trying to still her sobs of fear.

His image flickered a bit when she finally drew away and she could see he was growing tired. She'd never questioned what his dreamwalking ability might cost him in the way of energy, but the thought crossed her mind now.

"Come on, Jaci, no more tears. We're together now, and tomorrow night, I'll bring Dave along too."

She clutched at his shirt. "Only if it doesn't tire you too much. I don't want you risking your health just to visit my dreams. It's enough to know that you haven't forgotten me. Enough to hope that you'll come to my dreams again, when it won't weaken you."

"I love that you're concerned for me, Jaci, but don't worry. The crystal gives me a big energy boost, focusing my natural abilities so they're stronger than ever before. And we've missed you as much as you've missed us. Probably more. We want to be with you, Jaci, to hold you for real, but for now...if this is all we have, we're going to treasure our dreams. I can't deny myself the pleasure of holding you, even if it isn't real. Nor can I deny Dave the same. He's closer to me than a brother and he loves you as much as I do."

"You're a good man, Michael. Tell David I miss him and love him…as much as I love you." She reached upward then, sealing her words with a tender kiss that soon turned passionate.

Michael's hands roamed down her body, one cupping a breast, the other insinuating itself between her legs. In the dream, she was suddenly bare. In the blink of an eye he had her naked in his arms. Jaci didn't object. The only thing she could have objected to—if she'd been coherent enough to speak after his drugging kisses—was that he still had his pants on.

She ran her hands over his chest, tangling in the sparse covering of hair, so different from Alvian males. She felt the delicious dips and valleys of muscle that spoke of his solid strength, his steadfastness and his sureness. There was nothing remotely soft about Michael and she loved everything about him, from his hard, muscular chest to his calloused hands and thick, pulsating cock. She'd felt it in person just the one time, but she would never forget how broad and hard he was, how ready he was to pleasure her.

She reached between them to cup him through the soft slacks he still wore in the dream. But Michael had other ideas.

His hand between her legs stroked and enflamed as he sank into her, urging her legs apart with a gentle nudge of his foot. She spread for him, allowing greater access to his roaming fingers as they began to fill her, stroking in and out.

"You've feel so good, Jaci. I can't wait until I get inside you for real. I'll make you come so hard, you'll never forget."

"I can never forget you, Michael. In dreams or in reality." She gasped as he found that one special spot inside that made her senses soar. He stroked her higher, holding her gaze throughout, with deep male satisfaction in his eyes as he made her dance to his tune.

"Come for me now, baby. Come on my hand and show me

how much you want this."

She came on command for him, shocked by her own behavior, but too sated to question why this man had such power over her responses. It didn't matter anyway. She trusted him. She loved him. Everything else would fall into place given those two amazing facts.

"You're so beautiful when you come for me." He soothed her as she came down from the height he'd pushed her to, kissing her temple and stroking her intimately.

"What about you, Michael?" Jaci made a lethargic attempt to cup him through the damnable pants he still wore in the dreamstate.

"No, love. This was for you." He pushed her hand away with gentle but firm motions. "I'll cherish this memory, Jaci. And I'll take you up on that offer someday. Don't forget, you owe me one." He winked and smiled, making her chuckle weakly in response. She felt so drowsy after that amazing climax, she had trouble keeping her eyes open.

Michael cradled her in his strong arms and before she knew it, she'd drifted off to sleep, safe and secure in her lover's embrace.

The very next night, two dreamwalkers joined Jaci on the dreamplane. As promised, Michael brought his cousin along on the vision quest into Jaci's dreams and she welcomed them both with open arms.

"I can't believe you're here with me," she said through tears of joy.

"We wouldn't be anywhere else," Michael said, his eyes making promises as David walked right up to her and swept her into his arms.

David stole her senses with a mind-numbing kiss.

It felt even more real than it had before. She could taste the sexy flavor of David as more than just the dreamy echoes she'd grown used to. She pulled back, gazing from David to Michael. "Something's different."

"It's the crystal boost," Michael said. "I've worked out how to use it even better than I did last night. You're dreaming in Technicolor now, babe." The smug smile on his face made her want to laugh, but he was very obviously proud of his achievement and she loved the new, more real-feeling texture of the dreamplane.

"It's amazing!"

"*You're* what's amazing, Jaci, my love," Dave kissed her nose and passed her off to Michael's waiting arms. He kissed her in welcome, the feel of him igniting her senses and her desire, but he pulled back before she could tug him closer.

"Before I totally lose my mind, I have to ask—did Mara reassign you yet? Did she even tell you about it?"

Jaci shook her head, confused. "I haven't had communications from Mara12 in several days and nothing about my duty assignment."

"Dammit!" Michael swore. "Davin got her to agree to send you down here weeks ago, and she hasn't told you yet. The cold-hearted bitch."

"When Davin asked for us and Ruth, he also asked to have you reassigned to his facility—ostensibly to monitor and assist Callie with the baby," David clarified. "Mara agreed, but demanded you stay up there until you'd finished preparations for some big experiment. You're supposed to be reassigned at the beginning of this next quarter."

"Shards! Is this true?" Jaci couldn't believe the good news.

"I was supposed to make sure you knew last night," Michael admitted. "I got a bit...distracted. I'm sorry, babe. I feel bad for leaving you in doubt for even one day when you could have been looking forward to moving down here with us. We've got big plans. Davin gave us a nice big suite—more of an apartment, really—where we can live together. As close to free as a human can be in this brave new world."

"This is fantastic news!" Jaci laughed and cried at the same time, as joyful as she'd ever been in her life. She was moving to be with her mates. They would be together, for real, very soon. Things were looking up, where before she'd been in abject despair of ever seeing them again.

"We definitely have to celebrate," Michael said, conjuring a glass bottle with some kind of fermented liquid inside. He poured elegant glasses of the substance and handed one to each of them, holding the crystal so that the glasses chimed together just once for each of them. "To us. Together. As it should be."

Jaci followed their lead and drank from the pale liquid that had bubbles rising within it. They popped and tickled her nose with innocent abandon as she tasted something she'd never experienced before. She wondered at Michael's ability to make her feel, see, taste and smell things she had no frame of reference for. He was truly gifted.

"What is this?" she asked, sipping more of the delicately fruity vintage.

"Champagne," David said. "One of the finest vintages ever produced in France. In Michael's dreamscapes we can experience the best of our old life any time we want. This bottle is a memory of the one we shared when we opened our business. We started as we meant to go on—with the best. This one bottle of champagne set us back our first month's profits, but it was worth it." A nostalgic smile lit David's handsome features. Jaci didn't always understand their references, but she wanted to learn. She wanted to know what their lives had been like before. She wanted to know all about her men, down to every last detail.

But she had a lifetime to learn. Or so she hoped.

"Remember those Japanese clients?" Michael asked his cousin with a grin.

"And the karaoke bar they insisted on visiting?" David rolled his eyes.

"Or the strip club they wanted to go to after?" Michael countered.

David's gaze lit on Jaci speculatively, his mouth quirking up in a sexy grin. "Now that's a memory I'd love to explore with our little seductress here. Do you know how to strip, Jaci?"

"Strip?"

"Take your clothes off in a teasing, tantalizing way. Dancing around to entice your man," Michael filled in, explaining the concept. "Some women in the old world used to work at strip clubs where they would entertain horny men by taking off their clothes, slowly, to music. Dancing around naked, shaking their...assets...for the crowd. We'd tip them generously. Give them money to dance over by our table and more for a job well done. It was kind of sleazy, but also kind of exciting, in its own way. I always thought it would be better if it was just my girl stripping for me. To have someone willing to do that just for me was a sort of a fantasy of mine."

"I'd be willing to try," Jaci said with a bit of shyness. "But I'm not sure I really understand what you want me to do."

A grin lit Michael's face. "Not to worry. How about I show you the way it was?"

As he spoke, the scene changed. They were in a dark room filled with tables and chairs. Men sat around the tables, with various kinds of drinks set before them. Smoke drifted into the air from a number of lit sticks that some of the men put to their lips every few minutes. More tendrils of smoke wound up into the air above, giving the entire room a smoky haze. Spotlights lit a stage and runway of sorts that had silvery poles anchored to both ceiling and floor at strategic places.

Pretty girls in skimpy outfits moved around the room, serving drinks and smiling at customers as they patted their bottoms and handed them money. Whether the money was in exchange for the drinks or the liberties the men took with the girl's bodies, Jaci wasn't certain.

Music started somewhere in the room, though Jaci could see no source of the strange, rhythmic beat. The sound was intense, electrifying and sultry.

"The floor show is about to start. Why don't we sit down and have a drink?" Michael asked as a table covered with a sparkling white tablecloth materialized in front of them. It had only two chairs so Jaci sat on David's lap, facing the stage, eager to see what would happen next.

"Do you remember her?" Michael asked his cousin as a leggy brunette with massive breasts slinked onto the stage. She made her way down the runway, gyrating all the way and stopped to pose right in front of their table. Conveniently, one of those poles was right behind her, so she used it to perform a number of acrobatic moves that Jaci had a hard time following.

"Yeah, I remember. She's the one who kept shaking her tits in your face. She sure liked you, cuz."

"I don't think I want to hear this," Jaci objected, looking at the image of the woman with hatred.

Instantly, the brunette disappeared from the stage and

Michael turned to Jaci, taking one of her hands. "She liked the money I kept throwing at her, but that's all it was, Jaci. And it was a long time ago."

He had a valid point. Anything any of them had done before meeting didn't really count and Jaci had no real right to feel jealousy, but yet there it was.

Michael stroked her cheek. "I like that you're proprietary. You can bet David and I feel the same way about you, now that you're ours. If another man even looks at you funny, we'd probably break his legs."

She laughed at his outrageous statement and the mood stabilized. David was making light patterns on her thigh with his fingers and she suddenly became aware of his hardness beneath her bottom. He was getting more excited by the moment. And so was she.

"So do you think you could do what she did? For us?" David surprised her by asking. The idea made her insides jump as David pushed her slowly off his lap so she stood before him in her night attire—a plain grey tunic and pants.

"I can't wear this. What was that girl wearing?" She'd never seen an outfit like the one the stripper had worn.

Michael smiled. "That was a bikini. The smallest one it's ever been my pleasure to observe, in fact, but they came in all different styles. Originally, it was designed as swimwear."

"Really?"

"Hey Mike," David leaned back in his chair, watching her with an amused but smoldering expression. "Why don't you let her model the different kinds of swimsuits for us? You can handle that, can't you?"

"You've got a creative mind, cuz." Michael turned his attention to her form, creating clothing for her out of the fabric of their dream. The first creation was a sleek, sleeveless body stocking that had hi-cut thigh holes. It was stretchy and shiny, of a fabric that felt slinky against her skin. "That's a typical one-piece," Michael informed her, motioning for her to spin around. Mirrors stood behind her now, in a three-paneled formation so she could see many angles of the suit in one glance. "Then there's the sporty racer-back style, the bare midriff style and the classic bikini." Colorful fabric in smaller and smaller proportions clothed her as he talked.

"And this was for swimming?" she asked, uncertain of the efficacy of such a volatile arrangement of fabric.

"And lying on the beach, looking beautiful. Getting tan and making grown men drool," David added with a mischievous chuckle. "And, baby, you have definitely got the body for it. You look good enough to eat."

"Then there's the string bikini, the hi-cut bikini and my personal favorite, the thong bikini." Michael's voice deepened as the outfits became skimpier and skimpier. More of her skin showed with each new version until she was wearing something almost exactly like the brunette had worn. "Spin around for me, babe," Michael instructed as the music started again in the background.

She did as he asked and wound up facing the stage again, Michael standing close behind her. His warm hands cupped her bare ass cheeks, one in each hand as he squeezed. His hot breath blew into her ear as he dipped his head.

"Will you dance for me?"

"I'm not sure if I can."

"Will you at least try? I'd give anything to see you move to the music for me. Tease me with glimpses of your beautiful body."

"I'll try."

"That's my girl."

Michael boosted her up onto the low stage, smiling broadly as she turned to face him and David, sitting back like a king to watch the entertainment. She only hoped she didn't look like a fool.

"Feel the beat of the music, sweetheart. Let it move you." Michael's words helped. "Close your eyes. Just listen."

Jaci liked human music. This particular melody, accompanied by driving rhythm and a low thrumming drum beat touched her deep inside, stirred something to life that had long lain dormant. Her hips began to sway, as she'd seen the other woman move. At first, she just tried to emulate some of her rhythmic movements, but after just a short while, the music grew louder and she felt invigorated. Inhibition disappeared. She didn't worry about looking foolish, she just let the music drive her motions.

A long, low wolf-whistle sounded and her eyes snapped open. Both Michael and David were grinning in that sinful way that made her squirm. She didn't know which of them had made that jarring noise, but she took it for the compliment she could clearly see on both of their faces.

"Turn for us, babe." Michael made a spinning motion with one finger and she complied. Feeling decidedly wicked, she bent from the waist, displaying the strip of fabric that just barely hid her bottom from them. A growling sound from behind her made her smile. They liked that.

As she swung her bottom from side to side, the stage suddenly disappeared, the illusion of the club fading to blackness beyond their immediate area. Michael was losing focus, or perhaps he just didn't care to have the strip club atmosphere anymore. Either way, she was pleased. All she wanted was her mates.

Two sets of masculine hands touched her skin, tweaking

her ass cheeks with exciting little pinches and sliding down over her legs. As she straightened from the deep bend, Michael was in front of her.

"You're a born temptress, Jaci."

She felt the thong being pulled down her legs from behind and knew it was David's hot breath on the backs of her thighs as he bent, following the skimpy fabric down. When he placed a sucking kiss on the tender skin behind her knee, both knees went weak and Michael had to catch her. He grinned at her reaction, then bent to kiss her as David licked his way up her thigh, multiplying the weakness in her limbs.

David stood behind her once more, his warm chest rubbing her back. Michael seemed to take that as his cue to move back. David untied the strings at her neck and between her shoulders while Michael peeled the tiny triangles of fabric from her breasts. He caught her freed flesh in his hands and rubbed her nipples between his fingers, making her squirm.

Bending, he kissed her there, sucking and drawing back so that she moaned in pleasure. But he kept moving back when she wanted more and soon he was sitting in the chair once more, watching her.

All that remained of the strip club atmosphere was the cloth covered table and two chairs. Michael occupied one as he watched David maneuver her around so Michael had a side view.

"Bend over, Jaci," David urged, his breath hot in her ear. "Lean on the table."

She complied, wondering what he would ask of her. She jumped when his fingers delved between her ass cheeks, teasing the pucker there. Suddenly a bottle of viscous liquid appeared on the table in front of her as Michael grinned.

David reached for her, his cock prodding her from behind.

He was naked and fully aroused and she wanted him. Badly.

"You think we should?" David was clearly talking to Michael, as Jaci tried to follow their meaning.

Michael nodded. "This is a dream, cuz. We can do anything we want here. And you know we both want this."

"But does she?"

Michael leaned forward to touch her face. "Do you want us both at the same time, Jaci?"

The very thought of having them both inside her at once tantalized. She'd seen some of the humans do it during experiments in the pens and she'd always wondered if the woman found such things enjoyable. Her mates would make anything enjoyable, she knew, and as Michael reminded them—this was a dream. Things could be tried in dreams that she wouldn't necessarily do in the real world, though she'd do just about anything for her mates.

"I want you...both," she managed to say as David applied some of the warm liquid from the bottle to her bottom.

Michael kissed her. "That's our girl. I promise you'll enjoy every second of this." He sat back to watch David prepare her and her focus shifted to the smooth feel of David's big fingers as he worked the lubrication into her flesh.

Michael was right, she did enjoy the foreign feel of his fingers as they worked their way inside her, little by little. It was a very different sort of stimulation, but it felt deliciously good. She enjoyed the new sensations for a few minutes before David took her to the next level.

He eased into her, his long cock finding its way inside with only minor difficulty. As Michael promised, it didn't hurt, though she imagined in the real world, there might be discomfort taking something so thick within her with so little preparation. But all thoughts of the real world were banished when he rested fully inside. She was bent over the table and Michael watched every motion as David began a slow, gentle rhythm.

Jaci began to pant and moan on every short thrust. Her internal heat grew, as did her moisture level. She was aching for Michael, wanting him where she was empty. David filled her in such a sensual way. She needed more.

"Michael!" His name was ripped from her throat as David sped his pace. But he stopped completely at her cry.

"I think she's ready," David said, his voice gruff behind her.

"I think you're right," Michael agreed. "But the question is, are we?" He winked at her as the table disappeared and she was suddenly resting on a soft cloud in the nothingness of the dreamplane, David behind her, his cock still tight within her body. He used his long legs to spread hers and open her for Michael.

"Now that's a pretty sight," Michael licked his lips before moving between her legs. Then he leaned forward to lick hers, his tongue delving into her mouth even as his cock found its home within her.

It was a tight fit with them both, but in the dream, it was perfect. Michael broke the kiss as he started to thrust and David resumed in a counter-rhythm to his cousin.

"You'd better move this along, Dave," Michael said. "I don't know how long I can hold the dream. We need to make her come."

"I hear you, cuz."

David bit down on her earlobe, licking her neck and sucking there as Michael watched. She loved them both so much. Her temperature rose once more as she neared total meltdown. Having them both with her—inside her—on the dreamplane was something she never could have imagined. It felt so good. So right.

She came with a blistering wave of heat that flooded her womb and flushed her skin as she shook with pleasure. "I love you!" The words were dragged from her lips as her eyes shut and passion took her in wave after wave of climax.

She felt David come not long after, then Michael before she floated away on a sea of bliss into a deep, peaceful sleep.

Chapter Ten

"Good morning, Grady Prime."

"Good morning, Jaci 192, it is good to see you again."

The big man strolled into the room and sat on the chair provided. It was Jaci's duty to go over the placement of the skinpatches that would administer the mutagenic agent for the big experiment. She was scheduled to meet with the ten participants in the study one by one all day long. As a result her normal duties were being taken over by another tech for the day, which was just as well because she hated going into Michael and David's cell and finding other people there. She missed them too badly.

She sat at the table across from Grady Prime and went over the proper procedures for placing the skinpatch and what precautions he should take before doing so. She would actually be putting the patches on all the other participants in the study, but Grady Prime's military position made it easier for him to begin his treatment as soon as he got off duty. Since the effects of this treatment were unpredictable—at least to the scientists who hadn't been through what she'd been through—they wanted the participants to have at least the first day free to absorb the agent away from the stresses of their usual jobs.

Whether or not they would remain in their current jobs was

up in the air. It all depended on what the treatment did to them. Part of the study in fact, was to see how these subjects coped with the day-to-day stresses of their jobs during this treatment. That's why participants had been chosen from a broad spectrum of the population.

"What kinds of symptoms can I expect?" Grady asked quietly, holding the wrapped skinpatch between his calloused fingers.

Jaci considered for a moment what to tell him. She actually liked this man and wanted to help him if she could, without giving herself away. It would be a fine line she had to walk, but for his sake, she would do it.

"At first you will probably feel no real change. It's expected that after the first twenty-four hours, feelings may begin to manifest. Faint at first, they will grow stronger and more amplified. Although my supervisors have not said this, I would recommend you spend some time at that point, analyzing your responses. It may also be of some benefit to consult the data banks for our ancient historical records and, forgive me if this sounds farfetched," she paused slightly, "but you might wish to observe some of the Breeds. I think you may find that you understand them better, once you have undergone some changes yourself."

Grady's eyes narrowed and he looked closely at her. "You seem to have given this some thought."

She knew she'd almost said too much, but she wanted to help him.

"I'm just a tech, but I was assigned this task quite some time ago. I have given much thought to the consequences of this experiment since I first learned of it, and you probably know I have close daily contact with the humans." She cringed, knowing she'd just misspoken. Only the humans called themselves that. Alvians called them Breeds. For her to call them by that name, meant that she had been spending a great deal of time among them—perhaps too much. But there was no way to call back her words now. Best to forge ahead, she thought.

"Part of my duty is to observe their reactions and I've tried to understand the emotional component that drives their behavior, as much as I can. It's quite difficult. Perhaps after administering the agent, you will gain a better understanding of what motivates them. That's all I'm suggesting."

Grady still looked suspicious, but he seemed willing to let it go for now.

§

"Mara 12, I believe there is something you should see." Mara's assistant entered her office with a small data crystal in hand.

"You've completed your assignment then?" Mara 12 put aside her data pad and looked up expectantly.

"Yes. It is as you suspected. Jaci 192 has been compromised."

"Did she do it intentionally?"

"No. From the visual record it appears as if a skinpatch adhered to her arm while she was preparing them."

"Sloppy work," Mara 12 commented.

"Yes. Though why she has not yet reported the incident is not clearly understood."

"She's well aware of the consequences of her mistake," Mara 12 said, reaching for the data crystal. "Have her brought to me at once. Ask Grady Prime to assist."

"You think she will resist?"

"I believe it is a possibility. She is, as you say, compromised. I have no reliable data yet on how she will react. We must assume the worst."

§

"Jaci 192," Harry said with a jovial smile as he stopped her in the hall, "how are you?" On another level, she heard his voice echo through her mind, though she'd never experienced telepathy before. *"Jaci, my mother sent Grady Prime to take you into custody. Do not go back to your quarters, unless you wish to become a prisoner. And don't react to my telepathy. They're monitoring everything, though it'll take Grady some time to get here. I've set up some roadblocks."*

"I am well, Hara. Thank you for asking. And yourself?" She nearly stuttered in fear, but knew she had to keep up the pretense of a normal, casual conversation between two acquaintances.

"I'm quite well, Jaci 192. I meant to ask you how your work progresses. Is all well there? *If you want to get out of here, there's a small atmospheric shuttle in Bay 12 with the access codes taped to the door. Head south for the engineering facility. Davin will see to it you're well hidden and safe."*

Harry's words in her mind were rushed, but she was relieved to learn he had a plan. She knew how to pilot a shuttle and she most definitely did not want to be caught, questioned, imprisoned and probably executed for her one mistake. She nodded almost imperceptibly at Harry. She understood and would do as he suggested.

"My work is very satisfying," she said as they resumed walking. They were heading in the general direction of the shuttles as it happened. "Thank you for asking."

They spoke a few more pleasantries until Harry left her at a branching corridor. With little hesitation, she took the branch that would lead her to the shuttle bays. Harry had also managed to let her know he would be delaying any pursuit long enough, hopefully, so she could get to Davin. Just how he would do that, she had no idea, but Harry had talents she could only guess at, so she had to have faith that he could do as he promised.

She made a beeline for the shuttle, popped the hatch and punched in the access codes that were so conveniently taped to the hull for her. Within moments, heart racing, she turned off the comm so she didn't have to listen to them threaten her anymore. She'd had enough of the threat of imprisonment and termination. What she really wanted was to be free.

It was either that, or die trying.

She was heading south and suddenly a huge grin split her face. Her mates were in Davin's custody and soon she would be too. They were waiting for her and for the first time in her life, she felt like she was heading home.

But it wasn't meant to be. She headed south, but she could see military ships sent to intercept her on the short range scanners. She had to veer off, uncertain of where to go, hoping they hadn't seen her.

Jaci had hammered the beacon soon after leaving Bay 12 so her people could not track her by it, and since then had not touched anything but propulsion controls, leaving the comsys powered down. Although they might guess she would head for the southern facility where her human friends had been transferred, they would not be able to find her easily in the dense jungle surrounding the facility.

Communications from the military craft came in a minute later, negating her hope. They'd not only seen her, they were on a course to intercept. Jaci was an adequate pilot, but her meager skill and this small civilian ship were no match for military patrol craft.

Where could she go?

Suddenly a thought came to her. She could try to lose the patrol in the mountains. She had a general idea of where the O'Haras lived and it wasn't too far. From her interactions with Harry and Caleb, she thought she might have a chance of getting help from the rest of the O'Hara clan. If she could just make it there.

§

The fire that erupted from her console burned her fingers, but that was the least of Jaci's worries as her small craft plummeted toward the trees. She'd managed to dodge the patrol ship and it had spun on a vector over the ridgeline, thankfully out of sight at the moment, but they'd gotten off a few shots in their mad scramble and more than one had hit Jaci's ship. It was going down. There was nothing she could do but to try to steer it to a more controlled crash, but she was definitely going to crash.

Jaci said a quick goodbye to her men in the privacy of her mind as the first tree branches buffeted the sides of her vessel, eliciting metallic pings, bangs and shrieks as she hurtled toward the earth below. She was thrown from side to side, the harness digging into her shoulders and thighs, but keeping her from hitting anything vital on the crunching shards of metal that were cascading all around.

She screamed as a thin sheet of jagged hull imploded and sliced into her upper arm. She screamed again as the craft bounced off a giant tree trunk and careened into another on its way down to the ground. She knew the crashing rebounds slowed her descent, but each bone-jarring thud sent her careening off into dizzying spins that threatened to pull her right out of the safety harness.

The noise was deafening. So much so that she could no longer hear her own screams, though she was certain she still pled for mercy from the horrific twists and turns of the crumpling metal.

When the clash of the hull made a swift and final boom on the pine needle-strewn floor of the forest, the very last thing Jaci noted was the blessed silence.

§

"Sweetheart, where are you?" Michael's voice came to her out of the mists of her unconscious.

"I'm here," she whispered into the darkness.

Moments later there was light and warmth as Michael's arms cradled her against his chest. David was there too, his hands on her head and his warmth at her back. She felt the worry in both of them, but was powerless to reassure them. Her head was swimming and even in the dreamstate, she felt pain radiating up her leg.

"This is a dream, right?" She asked just to be sure. Everything was fuzzy. "You're not really here?"

"I wish we were," David said next to her ear. "I would give anything to touch you. To heal you. What happened, Jaci? You're in pain. We can tell."

"Ship crashed."

"What ship?" Michael asked, cupping her cheeks as David soothed her with gentle hands sliding over her head, neck and back.

"Mara 12 found out about me. Hara warned me and gave me the codes to a transport. I was..." She gritted her teeth against the pain. "I was going to try to reach you, but a patrol spotted me. Shot at me. I got him back, though, before the crash."

"Where are you? Where did you crash, love?" Michael's voice was urgent, but the dream wavered.

"Tried to find the ranch. Thought the O'Haras could help."

"God! Jaci, stay with me. You're in the mountains by the O'Hara ranch? Is that right?"

She nodded, feeling David's dream hands slip away as she started toward wakefulness. She would rather have stayed with her mates, but the pain was pulling her away, back toward the daylight and the broken ship in which she lay.

"I love you," she whispered, but she wasn't sure if they could still hear her.

§

"Did you see where it landed?" Bill asked Sam as they sped through the woods near their campsite.

"Crashed would be a more accurate term," Sam said as he followed right behind. He was strong for a human, silent in the woods and skilled. All in all, Bill didn't mind having him for company now that they were hiding out together in his aerie.

"It didn't look like a patrol ship. More like a civilian transport."

"Either way, we can't let them find our camp." Sam's tone was grim. Bill knew they might have to kill whoever they found, if they weren't dead already. He hated it, but knew it for the truth. Still, he'd look for any other alternative before he added one more soul to the long list of those who haunted him.

They came upon the wreckage a moment later, approaching cautiously. The hull was still smoking, but it didn't look like fire was imminent. Bill could make out only one occupant, still strapped into the pilot's chair of the small craft. A female. And she looked familiar.

He approached cautiously, motioning Sam to stay back.

Terrified, water-filled eyes looked up at him when Bill stepped up to the destroyed ship. He'd never seen such emotion in an Alvian face before and it gave him pause.

"Sinclair Prime." His old name was a gasp of surprise and dread from the female he'd known briefly in that other life. He saw her thoughts reflected in her eyes. She knew him. Knew what he'd been. Knew there would be no mercy from the man who had been the Council's top assassin. "Please..." she whispered. "*Teaverda.*"

"What's that mean?" Sam stepped up behind him, jumping in where fools fear to tread, as usual. Any hope of keeping the woman in ignorance of Bill's new life evaporated in that moment.

Bill sighed. "She begs for a final request before I kill her."

Sam seemed surprised, which made Bill feel somewhat mollified. "But we can't kill her. She's *frightened.*"

That one observation changed everything. Bill looked back at the crying girl, realizing the truth of his friend's words. The Alvian woman was displaying very un-Alvian emotions. Perhaps Bill had been associating with humans too long. It had taken his brain longer to process the obvious clues that something wasn't quite right with the lab tech he'd known as Jaci.

"What is your *teaverda*, Jaci?" He stepped closer, noting the straps that held her immobile and the odd angle of her right leg. It was most likely broken.

"My...mates." Her voice trembled. "Please let them know what became of me. Let them know I...love them."

Bill stooped low to look directly into her eyes. "You feel love?"

Tears fell freely from her eyes as pain slashed over her features. "I do. I feel...so much, Sinclair Prime. I only wish you could understand."

He watched her reaction for a long moment. He knew what he had to do. Decision made, he reached for his knife, compressing his lips in a grim line as she gasped in fright, but he went on, cutting the restraints from her bruised body as gently and quickly as he could.

"You're running, aren't you?" he asked as he lifted her from the pilot's chair. Her arms automatically went around his shoulders, though her gaze was filled with confusion.

"Yes. The patrol is after me. I damaged their craft and it spun out over the next ridge, but I believe they will regain my trail soon."

"Then we'd better get the hell out of Dodge," Sam said from behind them.

"Anything in the ship to give away your identity or location?" Bill asked her as he carried her clear of the wreck.

"No. I smashed the beacon before I left the city limits. The ship is not mine and I had no luggage."

"Good girl," Bill said in approval. He jerked his head toward Sam. "Clear our tracks, friend, and we'll see about patching her up."

Bill was rewarded with a huge grin from his friend. Sam had a soft heart and something he called chivalry where females were concerned. They'd discussed women a lot while they sat around the campfire—one in particular. The angel-faced woman who haunted Bill's dreams and who Sam knew to be the love of his life. A fragile human prisoner named Ruth.

They reached a hidden cave only minutes later. Jaci was shocked to see supplies and bedding that made her conclude the men lived here. Her leg was throbbing so bad she almost lost consciousness several times. In fact, she did pass out when Sinclair Prime jerked her leg to straighten the broken bone.

When she woke, her leg was wrapped and splinted, still throbbing, but manageable. She was propped up on a soft pile of blankets and furs while the men ate. Something was very different here.

The Sinclair Prime she'd known as a young lab tech was not the same man she observed now, consorting with a human and living in secret in the woods. The men spoke in low tones, but she could hear soft laughter from time to time and see Sinclair Prime smile and even look wistful at different points in the conversation. This was not the Alvian Prime she had known. He didn't even look the same. His hair was long and wild, his face showing emotion the proper Prime had never known.

Sinclair looked over and saw that she was awake. He stood and came to her, his human companion not far behind.

"How are you?" he asked.

"My leg hurts and I feel bruised. It's what I expected."

"But I'm guessing I'm not at all what you expected, eh?" Sinclair Prime chuckled, making her gape at his humor. She'd known him for years and never had she seen him smile or laugh. "Things have changed for me, Jaci, as I'd be willing to bet, they have for you."

Mutely, she nodded.

"You're a bright girl, Jaci. Surely you knew what was in the skinpatch you gave me all those months ago?"

"The gene-altering agent." He'd been the first to receive the experimental treatment, she now recalled, but after she'd given him the patch and instructed him on its application, she'd never seen him again. "It worked on you."

"It did. As, I suspect, it worked on you too. What happened, Jaci? Did Mara 12 make you take the treatment? I always hated that bitch, even when I couldn't really feel hatred. She played with our lives like a child with its toys."

Jaci knew the moment of truth had arrived. It was time to come clean with this man—this soldier—who had always treated her well, even when he had no concept of emotion.

"Nothing so sinister, I'm afraid." She shook her head at her own stupidity. "I accidentally dosed myself when I was preparing a new batch of skinpatches. I didn't find it until the next day, after it had turned blue. It was stuck to my arm."

"How long ago?"

"A few weeks."

"And you've hidden your condition all this time?" He seemed impressed, which made her feel oddly better.

"I had help. Two of the human prisoners I tended were able to help me."

"Are they the mates you spoke of?" Sinclair's eyes narrowed

yet his expression seemed almost...hopeful?

"Yes. David and Michael. Both have been moved to Chief Engineer Davin's facility. Without them—" her voice cracked.

"I understand." Sinclair Prime's voice was soothing, the hand he put on her shoulder, comforting. After a moment, he moved his hand to her cheek, cocking his head as if listening. "It's a shame we don't Hum, Jaci. I always liked you best of all the girls they sent to me."

She was surprised and touched by his words. "You were kind to me, Sinclair Prime. It was no ordeal to be with you as it was with some of the Primes they sent me to."

"Hold on a minute," the human male stepped up behind where Sinclair knelt at her side, his face full of curiosity. "Do you two know each other in the Biblical sense?"

"I don't know what that means, but if you're asking if we've been intimate, we have." Jaci looked up at the man, puzzled by his words and his reaction. She didn't like talking about her past, but it was a fact she could not deny. She'd serviced more than a few Primes as part of her duties in the past. Sinclair Prime had been the nicest of them—until her encounter with Grady Prime—but she'd not talk about that. "I had five Primes assigned in the collection unit while I was stationed there. I was only there for a few months."

"How did you feel about it?" Sinclair Prime asked, shooting a look she couldn't decipher to his companion.

"At the time it was just another duty. Of the five Primes I was assigned, you were by far, the most agreeable. You made certain I had some pleasure of the experience every time, Sinclair Prime, and for that I am thankful."

Sinclair looked uncomfortable. "Please, Jaci, call me Bill. It's my name now. Sinclair Prime is dead."

"I don't understand."

"It's a long story, but to put it as succinctly as possible, I was ordered to assassinate Chief Engineer Davin just after I'd taken the dose. As my emotions began to surface, I found I couldn't kill him. I gave away my position and expected to be permanently sanctioned for my failure, but Davin and his new family took pity on me. I've been living in secret ever since. If the Alvians find me, I'll be executed. I know too much."

"And if the humans around here figure out he's an alien, he's just as dead," the human male added. "So we call him Bill and watch his back."

"You are a kind man," Jaci said as she looked over Sinclair's shoulder at his friend.

The man looked uncomfortable with her praise. "I owe him. Wild Bill here saved my life. The least I can do is help him fit in when we get around people."

"But we don't see many people. We live up here in the wilderness," said Sinclair Prime—no, she must think of him as *Bill.*

"You are fugitives," Jaci realized.

"Yes, ma'am." The human male grinned. "My name is Sam, by the way. And I hear him calling you Jaci. Pretty name."

"Thank you, Sam. And you, Bill." She looked at the man she'd known as Sinclair Prime and saw the relief on his face. She thought she felt the beginnings of friendship too.

"I envy your mates, Jaci, as I envy you for having found them." The sentiment touched her heart as Bill sat back, watching her. "Now we must decide what to do with you. It will be some time before your leg heals and our existence here is tentative at best. When they find the remains of your craft, they'll search the area."

"How do you know they haven't found it already?"

"We put up some telltales—human tech—that should alert us when the crash site is disturbed without tipping our hand to the patrols. We have a bit more time yet, but I'd prefer to be cleared out of here before they start searching the woods in earnest. This cave is well hidden, but if I found it, they could too."

"I understand," Jaci didn't like where this was heading. She was unable to walk and didn't like the idea of being left behind, but she understood their reasons for wanting to stay hidden.

"No, Jaci." Bill's tone made her look up at him. "I don't think you do. We have a place we may be able to take you. The trip will be hard with your leg the way it is, but it's something we must do if we all want to make it out of this safely. Do you trust me?"

She thought about that for a moment. The man she'd known as Sinclair Prime was highly skilled and secretive, though she knew he was a top soldier of some sort. He undoubtedly had the knowledge to keep them all as safe as possible. More than that, he'd always been kind to her. Since meeting up with him again, he'd shown her more compassion than she'd ever known from an Alvian and seemed to actually care what happened to her. He was the closest thing she had to a friend among Alvians, sad as that was to say, and she had little choice, injured as she was. She had to trust him.

"I trust you."

He actually looked relieved. "Good. We'll leave soon. Sam and I will need a few minutes to police the cave so it looks like nobody's been in here. We have hiding spots for our gear, but we'll pack what we need for the trek. It won't take long. Rest up while you can. We'll be carrying you down the mountain, but it'll be a bumpy ride no matter how careful we are."

"I understand." She didn't look forward to the pain as her

leg was jostled, but being found by the Alvian patrols would be infinitely worse.

"Good girl." Bill patted her head in approval as he stood.

Sam and he bustled around the cave, working well together as they hid their larger bits of equipment in ingenious places they'd devised throughout the dark cavern. Even when light was shone directly on the hiding spots, she couldn't make out any hint of their passage or what lay hidden beneath and behind the rock in secret compartments.

When Sam came to her a few minutes later, she was surprised. She'd assumed Bill would carry her, since it was well known that Alvians were generally stronger and had more endurance than humans. Some of her thoughts must have shown on her face because Sam grinned at her as he made ready to pick her up.

"Bill's better at reconnaissance than I'll ever be. I swear that man has eyes in the back of his head and sonar like a bat. We figured he'd be better off on point starting out until we're more certain of where your people are."

"They're no longer my people, Sam." She wanted that to be clear.

"Heard and understood, ma'am. I can appreciate that." He placed one arm around her and one under her bent knees. "This may hurt a bit and I'm sorry for it, but we have to get you out of here."

Jaci gritted her teeth and did her best not to make a sound as Sam stood with her in his arms. He was much stronger than she'd have credited. She felt the lean muscle of him through his clothing as she settled against his chest.

They'd left the cave far behind before the pain in her leg settled into a dull throb that spiked whenever she was jostled. But she was getting used to it, and she felt a certain amount of pride in the fact that she hadn't cried out once. She'd do nothing to jeopardize these men who were risking so much to help her. They could have just as easily left her to die in the wreckage or be found by the Alvians.

"I remember you now," Sam said in a low voice as they followed along behind Bill. The men had conferred a few minutes before, agreeing that the Alvians hadn't yet begun searching the mountainside. Perhaps she'd damaged their patrol craft more seriously than she'd thought. Her mind drifted in a fog of pain, but she tensed at Sam's words. "You delivered medical supplies to Ruth's cell when she was patching me up after..."

"After she was raped in that terrible experiment."

"That was torture, Jaci. Not an experiment."

She nodded. "I agree. Now. If that's any consolation." She held his gaze, as serious as her own. "I never understood what the Maras were trying to accomplish, but as a mere Jaci it wasn't my place to question them. I think now, I should have. Even if it ended my career. Someone should have demanded to know why they made your people suffer so."

"Thank you for that, at least." He was silent a long time as they headed down the mountain. "You weren't as bad as the others. You were kind when you could be, though you probably didn't realize it at the time."

"Even before I could feel, I liked serving in the pens. Not that I liked seeing your kind held prisoner, but I liked observing humans. They always fascinated me. And I thought...I thought I was friends with some of them. Ruth especially. She helped me when I had no one else to turn to."

Sam's arms tightened on her as his body tensed. "Can you tell me how she is? Where she is?"

"She is very well, Sam. Don't worry. A few weeks ago, she

was taken to Chief Engineer Davin's Southern Engineering Facility. She has a rare crystal gift and I've heard from my mates that she and little Samantha are doing very well indeed."

Sam stopped in his tracks, his face a mirror of shock. "Samantha?"

"I thought you knew," Jaci backtracked, though the agony of her leg was making it hard to think. "Ruth had a baby girl a few months ago. She is named Samantha, after her father. When you said you remembered me from Ruth's cell, I assumed you were the father. Is your name Samanth?" she tried experimentally. Jaci had limited knowledge of human names.

"Samuel." The man seemed to be in a state of shock as he continued to follow in Bill's tracks. "My name is Samuel. The feminine version of my name is Samantha. Ruth named her baby for me?"

"I believe so, if you were her lover. She once told me that her lover had escaped. She was happy for it, but she missed you."

"God!" It was a broken whisper torn from his being. "I miss her too." His gaze refocused on her. "You said she was safe? Ruth and my...daughter...are at Davin's?"

"They are. Both happy from what I've heard. Davin is a good man. He's been bringing humans to his facility a few at a time to train them in crystallography. They live above-ground in nice apartments and have many freedoms. They live there under his protection. My mates are there. That's how I know."

"You can communicate with your men? How?"

Jaci wasn't sure what to tell him, but decided on the truth. This man literally held her life in his hands. "One of my mates is a dreamwalker. I never know exactly when he'll come to me, but when I sleep, if he's dreamwalking, he'll come and we can talk. He's learned how to use crystal power to boost his own abilities so he can reach me over such long distances."

"My God." Sam seemed more than impressed by Michael's power. "If you talk to him again, would you ask him...?"

She thought she knew why he hesitated. "Ruth would want to know that you're alive and well. She pines for you, Sam. She loves you."

"Then ask him to let her know I'm all right. If there's any way—if there weren't a price on my head—I'd make my way to South America. I'd do anything to be with her. But I'm a wanted man. I killed an Alvian soldier to gain my freedom. They won't let me cruise back into one of their facilities like nothing happened."

"You're right." Jaci felt compassion for the man who so obviously wanted to be with his mate. "Maybe Davin can come up with something. The man has accomplished some amazing things on behalf of humankind."

"For now, it's enough to know that Ruth survived. And I have a daughter." A look of wonder passed over his handsome features. "I never thought I'd have a child. No matter who her father is, she's named for me and she's mine. My baby. Samantha."

"Ruth believes she is yours," Jaci had to tell him. "The Oracle, Caleb O'Hara, sent her a message before the baby was born, telling her so. I delivered it myself. Caleb foresaw that the baby was yours and wanted to let Ruth know so she would love it, as she loves you."

Tears gathered behind the strong man's eyes, but he didn't speak for a long moment. "Thank you," he finally rasped out, turning his attention back to the trail they followed downhill after Bill.

After they stopped for a short break, Bill carried her a portion of the way down the mountain. They paused one more time, in a copse of trees while Bill withdrew a communication crystal from one of his pockets. He left her sitting on a boulder while he moved off a short distance to speak quietly with someone over the crystal.

Jaci would have been concerned about the use of Alvian technology, but her leg hurt so badly by that point, she didn't much care. Bill could be calling the High Council itself, but all she wished for was a respite from the pain.

"We have to wait for the surveillance drone to pass, but then we'll make for the outbuilding we used before," Bill said to Sam as he rejoined them. "Mick will meet us there."

Sam carried her this time as they made their way carefully downward toward some objective only the men knew.

Chapter Eleven

"Release the female," a cold Alvian voice said from behind a nearby tree.

"Son of a bitch," Sam uttered as he lowered her to the ground. "How'd he get in front of us?" Jaci looked around and realized Bill was nowhere to be found. She hoped that was a good sign. "Sit tight, sweetheart." Sam left her sitting on a fallen log, with a thick boulder between her and the Alvian soldier.

"Step away from the female and have her stand," the voice commanded.

"She can't stand," Sam said, raising his hands and stepping back toward cover, though he wasn't quite there yet. "She has a broken leg."

A soldier dressed in light armor stepped out from behind the tree in front of them, a weapon grasped in one hand and trained on Sam. "Step away from her," the soldier ordered and Sam moved.

The soldier stepped closer, and the next thing she knew, Bill was diving out of the tree above, to land on the man's back. She heard the sickening crunch of bone as the man fell, lifeless to the forest floor. Sharp reports of projectiles being fired sounded through the forest. She looked up at Bill, her savior, but he'd spun away so fast, she could barely follow his progress. He ducked and twirled as Sam sprinted away, toward the new threat. A moment later, a muffled cry reached her ears and she knew the second soldier had met a similar fate when Sam stepped clear, the weapon now in his hand.

"That was close," he said as he stuffed the weapon in his pocket and bent to pick her up once more.

"Are there more of them?" she asked, looking around at the now threatening forest.

"Only two," Bill said shortly, beginning to scout ahead once again.

He stopped short and signaled Sam to stop as well. It seemed they were waiting, but for what, Jaci had no idea.

A moment later, two humans stepped clear of the surrounding trees and faced them.

"What brings you, Bill?" the taller of the men asked.

"This girl crashed her ship and broke her leg. She's on the run and…she feels."

Suddenly Jaci was the center of attention, the two newcomers looking her over with measuring eyes. The shorter of the two stepped forward. "Let me take a look at that leg."

Bill stood aside and let the man approach. He had a friendly face and a caring smile that set Jaci at ease, though she strained to hear what the taller man was saying to Bill.

"We saw them come into the woods and decided to hike up and see if we could help."

"As you see, we have the situation in hand, but we could probably use some help hiding the evidence until I can dispose of it far enough away from your property to alleviate suspicion," Bill replied.

"Can do, my friend. I've got a place to stick them until we can move them far enough away, but the sooner the better. There's lots of traffic on Alvian channels. They're looking for the girl."

Bill shrugged. "That was to be expected. She can never go back, Justin. She wasn't supposed to be part of this and now that they know about her, she'll never be free."

"Then we'll have to figure a way to help her." The tall man's tone was matter-of-fact, which surprised her. She never expected to find humans so willing to help her out of the mess she'd made of her life.

The second man moved her leg in a way that made her gasp and drew her attention.

"It's a clean break." He smiled at her. "I'll fix you up with a cast when we get to the ranch. I'm Mick O'Hara." He held out one hand for her to shake in the way she'd seen humans do. She returned the gesture.

"I am Jaci 192."

"Pleased to meet you, Jaci. I think you might know our brother, Caleb." Mick and Sam started down the mountain once more. She noted Bill and the other human had gone off together—probably to hide the bodies of the Alvian soldiers.

"You are the brothers of the Oracle, then."

Mick laughed. "Is that what they're calling him now?"

Jaci blushed. "It's what the humans call him. Unofficially, some Alvians refer to him as O'Hara Primus. It is the designation for progenitors. Since he is the leader of your line and your line is the progenitor of Hara, it is something a few of the techs on the project who know of his origins have begun to call him."

"Primus?" Mick laughed again. "Makes him sound like a gladiator." Jaci didn't understand the reference, but it seemed to amuse both men.

"Are you Hara's father?" she asked, curious.

But Mick shook his head. "Harry's my nephew. Justin is his father."

"The warrior who went off with Bill?"

"The very same."

That gave Jaci something to think about. Gossip about the O'Haras was rife within the tech community. One was rumored to be a doctor—undoubtedly that was Mick's role—and the other a warrior of great skill. It was interesting to her that Hara's father was the warrior and not the scientist. He seemed such a studious young man, but then, perhaps he had hidden depths. Most humans did, she was coming to understand.

When they reached the edge of the trees, Mick took out a very complex crystal. Not only were humans prohibited from having crystal technology, but this kind of advanced tech was out of their realm completely. Apparently these O'Haras had friends in high places.

Mick took a few readings, then turned to them. "The drone is gone for now. It's safe to get out from under the trees. You know the building, right, Sam? It's all ready. I just have to go back to my office for a few bits and pieces for the cast. I'll be back in a half hour. Make yourselves comfortable."

They walked as he spoke, coming out of the trees into a field planted with some sort of food crop. It was tall and gawky, planted in neat rows and nearly as tall as she was. She'd never seen the like.

After the neat rows ended, they came out into a clearing in which lay a small, wooden building. Sam took her inside while Mick moved past, toward the other buildings she could see in the distance.

They weren't inside long when Bill arrived.

"Justin's hiding the evidence and clearing the scene."

"Good man," Sam said, nodding as Bill closed the door behind him. "Mick went down to his office to get supplies."

"Then I need your help." Bill looked like he'd rather be anywhere else but asking for his friend's help at that moment.

"What is it?" Sam asked, moving closer to the other man while Jaci watched from where she was propped up on the bed, her leg held aloft by a number of pillows.

"I got hit during the fight. The projectile had a barb that I can't remove by myself," Bill admitted. That sounded serious to Jaci, who hadn't realized Bill was hit at all.

"Mick should see to it. I'm no doctor," Sam objected.

"It can't wait and you'll probably find out sooner or later."

"Find out what?"

Bill turned angrily. "Will you take the damned thing out or not?"

Bill eased forward. "All right, all right. Where'd you get hit?"

"Upper right shoulder." Bill shrugged and his collar dropped low, exposing the top of an angry red wound.

"I see it, but I need more exposure," Sam said, pulling at the cloak and shirt Bill still wore. Bill seemed oddly reluctant to let the shirt fall any lower, but Sam was able to maneuver enough to grasp the protruding end of the barb and work it out backwards with a minimum of fuss. He did it fast and clean, which was probably a mercy to Bill. Sam reached over to the small table and got the disinfectant, spraying a liberal dose on Bill's exposed shoulder. He pulled at the shirt to get to the rest of the wound and stopped short.

"Holy shit!" Sam's voice was low and filled with puzzled awe as he stepped back.

The shirt and cloak fell away as Bill struggled forward. A set of glorious golden wings came into view, folded compactly along the ridges of Bill's back.

"You're an Avarel," Jaci said in reverent tones.

"No, I'm not." Bill's words were adamant as he turned to face them. "I'm as Alvian as you, Jaci, but I was bred as an experiment."

"What's an Avarel?" Sam wanted to know.

"The Avarel were an advanced race of explorers who visited our worlds many generations ago," Jaci explained. "It was from observing them that we first realized our aggressive ways were destroying our own people. They taught us the way of peace and after they left, our leaders determined on the path that has led to our current emotionless existence."

"Somehow, I don't think that's what these people would have wanted," Sam said. "They sound like what we call angels in our mythology. Beings of light who had wings and brought messages from God—warnings, teachings and the like. Maybe your Avarel visited Earth in the distant past as well."

"It's likely," Bill admitted. "They were explorers. But your mythology makes it even more imperative that I hide my wings. I'm no divine messenger. I'm just a man. A reformed assassin. I have the blood of many on my hands, and on my conscience."

Jaci hadn't ever heard him speak so plainly about the past she'd only guessed at. Her heart went out to him. "They designed you with Avarel traits, didn't they? For what purpose? And how? Such tampering with the Alvian genetic code is forbidden."

Bill's expression turned grim. "Nothing is forbidden to the Council. The Avarel DNA sequence is just one of their secrets. I was created to be the hand of death. The assassin who can swoop in and kill before the target is even aware of his presence. And I was good at it too. My genetic codes are those of the hunter, not the prey."

"So you're saying you're a hawk, not a chickadee." Sam's lips lifted in a lopsided grin. "I get that. But that's a nifty set of wings you got there, my friend. How in the world do you manage to hide them?"

"They are smaller than full Avarel wings, they tell me." Bill curled one wing around to the front of his body, stroking the feathers in contemplation. "I assume real Avarels can fly for long distances, but I'm only good for sprints."

"Do you know if the wings breed true?" Jaci asked, fascinated by the idea.

"I was never meant to breed." Bill leveled his gaze on her, his face grim.

"Then why did they send me to collect your samples?" Even as she said the words, she realized the horrible truth.

"For experimentation." She could see the devastation in his eyes. "As far as I know, I've never had a viable offspring."

Jaci reached out to him, taking his hand in hers. "I'm sorry." He settled the cloak back over his shoulders, hiding his wings.

"Please don't speak of this to anyone," Bill asked without looking at either of them.

Mutely, Jaci looked to Sam and he nodded just once. "It's your secret to tell, Bill. I'll respect your wishes."

"As will I," Sam agreed.

Bill left the room without looking back.

Mick returned shortly thereafter and set her leg in a cast made of a sticky white substance and bandages. It was low-tech, but it would work. She complimented him on his skill and they spent some time discussing Jaci's former job. Mick had a level of understanding she hadn't expected from a human, though she'd known many of them were highly educated in various fields.

She didn't realize any of their medical practitioners would be so aware of genetics. She told Mick as much and he spoke of human research into genetics that had been ongoing at the time of the cataclysm. She was impressed that humans had progressed so far and not for the first time, she realized the heinous crime her people had committed when they'd sentenced most of this world's population to death.

"I'm sorry to be such a bother," she said as Mick cleaned up and prepared to leave. "I didn't know where to turn and I remembered how nice Callie and Harry were to me, but I didn't mean to bring more danger to your door."

"Don't worry, Jaci. I've been in communication with Harry and let him know what happened to you. He made sure I promised to help you. If he hadn't said you were already bonded to two human men, I'd wonder if he didn't have feelings for you himself."

"Hara and I don't Hum," she said simply.

"But you do Hum with the two men who are at Davin's? I think Harry said they were named Mike and Dave."

Jaci nodded, her heart pining for her mates. "Yes, I Hum with them. Hum and more. We are true mates. But I just don't see how we can ever be together." She felt tears start in her eyes, but refused to let them fall.

"Now, now. Don't worry about that yet. You need to concentrate on healing. The rest will fall into place as it's meant to be. I'm a big believer in fate, Jaci."

"With your brother Caleb's powers, I can understand that, but I just don't see this situation working out. I'm a fugitive now, just like Bill and Sam."

"True, but like Bill and Sam, you have friends, Jaci. We'll

all do what we can to help." He patted her shoulder in a paternal way and gathered the last of his equipment into the bag he'd brought with him. "Justin's bringing a meal up from the house. Surveillance will be stepped up once that patrol fails to check in and they realize you're still missing. Don't go outside."

"I won't. Please give my thanks to your family, Mick, and accept my appreciation for your kindness. I owe you all a great deal and I'm afraid I will never be in a position to pay you back."

Mick walked to the door. "Like I said, don't worry about any of that now. Concentrate on getting well. The rest will work out in time."

He gave her one last smile before departing and Jaci felt the weight of the long day settle over her like a blanket. She sank back against the mound of pillows they'd given her and promptly fell asleep.

§

"What's up with her?" Sam asked Bill in hushed tones as Jaci's head moved, in the throes of a dream.

"She dreams."

Sam watched her with envious eyes. "One of her mates is a dreamwalker. I bet she's with them now."

"Human mind powers never cease to amaze me," Bill observed. Both men watched Jaci's delicate form as a smile lifted the corners of her mouth, even in sleep. "There are those among you who can enter someone's dreams?"

"It's a rare thing," Sam admitted. "But I've heard of it before. Her mate's gift must be really strong to be able to reach her here. Jaci said he's been learning how to use crystals to boost his range."

"He's harnessed the power of the crystals? I know Mick's been looking into how crystal energy can enhance human mental abilities for some time. Looks like Jaci's mate has at last found the secret."

"Imagine that." Sam thought of the potential uses such a skill could have. Given enough crystals and the right talents, the human race could be a force to be reckoned with once again.

§

Warm arms enveloped her as Jaci floated into the dreamstate.

"Are you okay, love?" Michael asked, his voice full of concern. She opened her eyes to find him at her side as David held her in his arms, cradling her against his chest.

"I'm all right. My leg is broken, but Mick O'Hara put it in a cast. Messy and low-tech, but it'll do the job."

Her response startled a laugh from Michael as David's arms tightened around her. He hadn't spoken yet, his head bowed, his gaze drinking her in. Of the two cousins, he seemed the more affected by her narrow escape. She reached up to stroke his firm jaw.

"Thank God you made it to the O'Haras," Michael said.

"I had help. Sam and Bill found me in the wreckage and hid me, then carried me to the O'Hara ranch. Oh! Which reminds me. Please tell Ruth that Sam is all right. He didn't know about Samantha but he was deeply touched when I told him he had a daughter. He sends his love to Ruth and the baby."

"That's the Sam who found you? We knew him," Michael spoke since David seemed incapable of it at the moment. "He's a good man. But who's this Bill?"

She didn't know how much she could reveal, though she wanted to tell them everything. Still, she'd promised Bill she wouldn't speak of his secrets. "They call him Wild Bill. He's a recluse who lives up in the mountains. Sam partnered up with him, apparently. They're both on the run, but they are good men. The O'Haras know them."

"That's enough for me. We've already talked to Callie, Davin and Rick about how we can get to you. They think it's too dangerous right now and after checking the Alvian military communiqués, I have to concur. You're safe for now. They're searching the other side of the mountain and further afield. They don't believe you could have hiked over the ridge and down to the O'Haras without them knowing it. Apparently they're pretty cocky about the surveillance they have on the ranch."

"From what I gather, the O'Haras know exactly what's watching them and when."

"That doesn't surprise me one bit," Michael agreed as David shifted her in his arms. "Now, just how is your leg? Are you hurt anywhere else?"

"It's a clean break, Mick said. It should be fully repaired in a few weeks, even without Alvian medicine. We heal faster than you humans."

"Thank God for that." David spoke for the first time and she could see the evidence of tears behind his eyes. "It's probably best for you to stay at the ranch for now, until you're healed. We're working on a way to be together, but it relies heavily on Davin and the O'Haras."

"I don't see how, David. I'm a fugitive. You're still prisoners, even if Davin allows you more freedom than any other Alvian. I just don't see how we can be together." She began to cry, much to her dismay, but David held her close, cradling her against his chest as he bent over her. She felt so safe in his arms, so protected and loved. It was a feeling she didn't think she could live without. But she must. At least for the foreseeable future.

"Let us worry about that, sweetheart," Michael said, stroking her back with soothing hands. "We have more friends than we thought. If there's a way, we'll find it. We have to. We need you, Jaci."

"And I need you," she sobbed. "I need you both. So much."

David held her tight throughout the storm, sharing in her sadness as they touched, but only in dreams. At length, she regained a measure of composure, finding herself on a dreamy soft couch made out of clouds, seated between the two cousins. She took a closer look at Michael's face, appalled to find him looking haggard and worn. She reached out to cup his cheek.

"Have you been getting enough sleep? You look so tired."

A rueful grin passed over his lips before he turned them into her hand to place a gentle kiss on her palm.

"I've been dreamwalking pretty much non-stop since that first contact after you crashed. I didn't want to miss you, love. We were so worried."

"Michael, I don't want you to strain yourself on my account. All is well now. I'm among friends and safe for the moment. I want you and David to get some sleep." She tried to get stern with him, but it was hard to chastise him for something so sweet as worrying about her welfare.

Both men chuckled at her little tirade, David reaching out to turn her on the cloud couch. She moved willingly, though she could easily see from the nebulous setting that Michael's power over the dream was not total. Usually he conjured detailed settings with furniture and vibrant colors, scents and sounds. This dreamplane was filled with wisps of thought as if they floated among the clouds, only the illusion of fog supporting them. In a way, it was even more seductive than Michael's elaborate sets.

"Oh, we'll sleep very well, once we've made love to you," Michael assured her. She was glad to see the sparkle of mischief in his eye. It told her that he wasn't too tired to play a bit before he left her dream.

David stretched out below her, floating on the cloud, able to move her as if they were in zero-gravity. It was a novel experience, and one that she found strangely alluring. David's gaze still held shadows.

"I thought we'd lost you, Jaci." His words were stark, sounding as if they were ripped from his soul. "Don't ever do that to us again. I can't take it. I need you more than my next breath."

"As I need you." Tears threatened once more, but Michael intervened, distracting them all by doing away with their clothing in the blink of an eye. She turned to look up at him, hovering at her side.

"The time for sorrow is over. Now it's time to play." He winked and gave her a roguish grin.

"With you, it's always play time, cousin," David quipped.

"And with you it's all work. Work, worry and work. Face it. Without me around, you'd never have any fun at all."

It was good to hear their easy banter. It refocused her on the here and now instead of her worries about the uncertain future. Daring greatly, she took hold of David's forearms and sent them both tumbling around the cloud plane, Michael's laughter following in their wake.

"Now what was that for?" David asked as he grinned up at her.

"Just getting your attention. I could grow old waiting for you to get to the good part."

"The good part, eh?" David raised one eyebrow. "I think I like the sound of that. In fact, I know for certain that you have quite a number of good parts that I would like to pay more attention to."

"Such as?" She dared him with a saucy smile.

David slid below her, hovering near her bouncing breasts. He licked out, teasing her nipples with slippery suction as he circled with his tongue.

She couldn't help herself. She giggled.

"Oh, so you like that?" David teased as he moved lower, licking a line down to her navel and delving within. Her tummy contracted with pleasure and ticklishness, causing another carefree laugh to escape.

David hovered below her, going lower until his lips teased the apex of her thighs. When his tongue slid into the crevice that hid her clit, she moaned. But Michael was there to catch the involuntary sound with his mouth as he kissed her long and deep.

Michael's tongue played with hers while David's teased her most secret places. Strong hands spread her legs, making room for him to delve deeper, lick longer, tease her with his skill.

"Are you enjoying having Dave lick your pussy, sweetheart?" Michael's gaze was as hot as she'd ever seen it while he watched his cousin go down on her. She could only mutter a muffled agreement as David hit a particularly sensitive spot. A moment later, his fingers stretched her passage, adding to the delicious torture.

Michael repositioned her in the nothingness around them, situating her between the two men, sitting upright with her legs spread as wide as they would go. David had stopped tonguing her clit in order to pay more attention to her breast. A heartbeat later, Michael did the same.

Each had one hand roaming up her thigh and their mouth on one of her breasts. Jaci didn't think it could get any better, but then Michael's finger joined David's inside her. Both slid into her from opposite sides, the very extravagance of the act firing her senses. Not only did she have two men to please her, but they were both inside her. Together. The idea made her think of other things they could all do together, but she feared they'd have to wait until they could pursue those thoughts outside of her dreams, in the flesh.

Michael lifted his head from her nipple to kiss her neck as David did the same. Michael nipped her earlobe as he whispered words of desire that set her senses aflame. She felt her body temperature spike and knew it for a sure sign of sexual intensity. Alvian females were able to regulate their body temperature most of the time. It was critical in population control. Only high internal temperatures would allow the ovaries to expel an egg. In that way, Alvian women were able to control when they became pregnant.

But these two men drove Jaci beyond all control. When she was with them, she could barely think, much less practice the mental tricks that allowed her to regulate her body temperature. If she were with them outside of her dreams, she'd have to be extra cautious. More than likely, she'd be pregnant within a week if she were ever to be with them for real.

Suddenly that didn't seem like such a horrible thing. What could the Alvian hierarchy do to her for gestating without permission? They were already as upset with her as they could be. A little thing like getting pregnant would be a minor trifle compared to what she'd allowed to happen in one careless moment of lab work.

"Hey, Jaci, are you with us, babe?" Michael stroked her cheek with his lips, whispering to her as she let go of the troubling thoughts.

"I'm with you. Don't stop. Make me forget all our troubles."

"Happy to oblige, sweetheart." Michael placed nibbling kisses down her arm as he moved away.

David moved closer, sealing his lips to hers, taking and giving a kiss so filled with passion and promise, she couldn't think of anything besides him. It was just what she needed. He maneuvered her around on the dreamplane until she was straddling his body, her core throbbing for the hard cock positioned just out of her reach.

"Don't tease me, David. Please!"

He looked deep into her eyes. "You know this is forever, don't you? You know I'll never leave you. Our separation is only temporary. We will find a way to be together. I promise you. I can't live without you, Jaci."

"Oh, David!" He came into her then with a nearly violent shove that made her screech in pleasure on the dreamplane. He pumped into her with hard, desperate movements until she came with a keening cry, shuddering around him as he filled her with his seed. For a brief moment, she wished the seed was real, that the possibility of creating life was real. But it was not meant to be. Not yet.

Michael lifted her away from David after a few moments, when her body had cycled down from the amazing high she'd just experienced.

"I'm sorry, love, but it's got to be fast. I held out as long as I could so Dave could have you, but my strength is running low." So saying, Michael lay her down on a cloud and pushed into her from above. His face was a study in strain, but the satisfaction in his gaze as it met and held hers could not be denied. "God, you feel good, woman. Like a little slice of heaven here on Earth."

Jaci had barely had time to catch her breath before her desire rose once more to meet Michael's. He tantalized her, stroking deep within her, hitting that spot that made stars appear before her eyes. Within moments, she was gasping and grabbing at his shoulders as he thrust more forcefully within her.

Michael cried her name as he came with her, the abandon of their lovemaking sending her into a deep sleep almost at the same moment he winked out of existence on the dreamplane, sent back to his own body, thousands of miles away.

§

Over the following weeks, Jaci's leg healed as Mick monitored her progress. Michael and David visited her dreams every night until she finally made Michael promise to get some true rest between visits. They came every other night now, sometimes to make love, sometimes just to talk over their situation. They were growing closer with each visit, gaining knowledge about each other that they hadn't had time to share before.

Bill and Sam came and went, doing something to drive the Alvian patrols onto different tracks, away from the ranch. She didn't ask, but she knew from listening to their talk that they'd shifted the bodies of the Alvian patrolmen to the other side of the mountain, fouling the backtrail. They were doing everything they could to move suspicion from the O'Hara ranch and Jaci was grateful for it. She didn't want to bring Alvian wrath down on these good people.

Some of the children had come out to meet her. The older ones had brought meals prepared in the big house, under the watchful eye of their mother. Jane O'Hara visited regularly too, sharing talk and a cup of herbal tea with Jaci most evenings. She enjoyed the woman's company and her wisdom. Jane O'Hara had been through much in her life and had found a rocky path to happiness with the O'Hara brothers.

Jaci envied their happiness, though she knew the family was incomplete. Caleb O'Hara was kept in the city, under surveillance as the subject of intense study. When his years of the study were complete, he'd be exchanged for another brother. It would be decades before the family was once again whole. Decades during which the children would grow into adults and perhaps find mates of their own. Even the Alvian aging gene wouldn't keep them young forever. Their aging only slowed after puberty and the gene became fully engaged when they reached adulthood. By that time, each of the O'Hara brothers would have missed large chunks of their children's formative years.

Jaci and Jane often talked of these things and Jane's desires for humans to live free. Jaci told her what she knew of Mara's plans, giving the O'Haras as much information as possible. She also shared technical details with Mick about the Alvian genetic modification experiments already underway. She owed these people much and felt a camaraderie with them that she'd never felt with her Alvian brethren. She was so different from most Alvians now, she thought she might as well be human.

"I think it's time we took off that cast and see how your leg looks," Mick said one morning when he brought breakfast over from the big house. "Natural Alvian healing rates are much faster than human, so by my calculations, I think it would be safe to try it out today. What do you think?"

"I agree completely. In fact, if you hadn't suggested it, I would have requested removal of the cast today. It's been long enough by Alvian standards."

"Great. I'll bring over the tools after breakfast. In the meantime, enjoy this." He laid a platter of cooked eggs and meat in front of her that smelled divine. Jaci enjoyed the rich and tasty foods served on the ranch—so different from the bland sustenance offered in the city.

"Thank you, Mick. And please thank Jane for this lovely meal. I've never eaten so well as I have while being your guest."

Mick left her with a wink and a smile and Jaci enjoyed the delicious fare. About an hour later Mick arrived back at the outbuilding with a small saw and some other equipment he'd need to remove the plaster cast.

Jaci was fascinated by the process and eager to see the result of such simple, rustic medicine. When her leg was uncovered, it looked well enough, but it was weak compared to the other leg. A few exercises would fix that up, along with a few more days of careful maneuvering, but for the most part, she was healed.

"Looks good," Mick commented. "How does it feel?"

Jaci tested the newly-knit bone's limits. "Coming along nicely," she said finally. "A few more days and I'll be as good as new." She reached for his hand, clasping it in both of hers. "I can't thank you enough for all you've done, Mick."

He patted her shoulder. "Think nothing of it, Jaci. You're one of us now. We help each other. It's the only way to survive out here in the Waste."

"The Deity of my forefathers was watching over my path when it led me to you, and Bill and Sam. Your family and those men have helped me in ways I could never expect and I will hold you all dear in my heart for the rest of my days. I hope you won't mind if I think of you as a friend."

Mick's smile was the answer she'd hoped for. "You're definitely a friend of the family, Jaci. Rest easy on that count."

Jaci felt as if she'd just been given a tremendous gift. "Again you have my thanks. I will treasure your words and your friendship."

Bill broke the mood by entering the room. He threw off his cloak and collapsed into a sturdy wooden chair by the table.

"It looks like the patrols have given up and gone home," he reported.

"Are you certain?" Jaci worried that it might be some kind of trick, but she was no soldier.

Bill shrugged. "As certain as I can be at this point. They might've left a few men on the ground to follow any sign we missed, but it isn't likely. The ships have moved off. I'll keep monitoring the area around the ranch to see if this is just a ruse to smoke you out." He leaned back, surveying the room. "I see you took the cast off. How long before you're back to fighting form?"

"A few days," Mick answered for her. "It healed well, so now all she needs to do is strengthen the surrounding tissue and let the bone finish knitting completely."

"That's good." Bill nodded, his gaze focused inward.

"Something bothering you?" Jaci asked, watching his expression.

Bill shook his head, but his face remained troubled. "I'm not sure. It could be nothing, but I got a feeling in the woods just now..."

"Trouble?" Mick asked sharply.

"Nothing immediate. But it would pay to keep vigilant.

Something about the path bothered me, but I can't figure out what it was. I'll keep thinking about it. Maybe it was nothing, but maybe with time, the puzzle with come clear in my mind. I'll let you know."

"I'll tell Justin. He says he trusts your hunches more than most people's facts." Mick grinned and the ghost of a smile lit Bill's face for a brief moment.

"If they've truly gone, then Sam and I should go too." Bill's gaze moved pointedly to Jaci. "What we need to decide is where Jaci will go."

"She could stay here," Mick offered half-heartedly. Jaci knew her presence here on the ranch for any extended time would put the family in too much danger. It was fine while she was immobile, but she'd be unable to hide from the surveillance forever. Sooner or later she'd screw up and get them all in trouble.

"It's kind of you to offer, but that's not a good solution," she said, knowing she didn't need to go into detail about why it would never work. The men knew she was no covert operator. She was a lab tech—a sloppy one at that. If she'd been just a little more observant, she wouldn't be in this mess to begin with.

"Then you'll come with us," Bill said decisively as he stood.

She knew that wouldn't work either. "I'd only slow you down, Bill. You and Sam are experienced outdoorsmen. I'm a lab tech with no experience of the woods or living off the land. I'd be a hindrance."

"But what other choice do you have?" Mick asked with kindness in his tone.

Jaci stood, stretching and placing just a small amount of weight on her newly-healed leg. "I have a few more days yet before I can walk freely. Perhaps some other alternative will arise in that time. If not, I will go with Bill and Sam—for the time being. There's got to be someplace I can go."

Mick came over and patted her shoulder. His gaze was sympathetic. "My brother says everything happens for a reason and I tend to concur after all I've seen. I'll contact Caleb and see if he has any advice for you. I don't want to believe that your accident was just a fluke. I think there was a higher purpose. We just need to figure out what it is and where you need to be. Don't worry. Like you said, you have some time yet."

"Thank you, Mick. Unlike most of my fellow techs, I was always fascinated by your brother's writings. If he has any idea about my future, I'd love to hear it, though I'm convinced my own stupidity has doomed me. I just can't see how dosing myself in a moment of inattention could have any use whatsoever besides screwing up my life and destroying my career. Of course, I'd also never have realized Michael and David were my mates."

"Fate works in mysterious ways, Jaci. Having Caleb around has taught me that, if nothing else." Mick winked at her as he moved toward the door. "Let's see what he has to say first, before we make any drastic decisions."

§

Out in the forest, very near the treeline that circled the O'Hara ranch, Grady Prime knelt in the dirt, rubbing disturbed soil between his fingers. Something wasn't right here, but it was very hard to detect exactly what it was.

Still, something bothered him and he'd learned to always trust his instincts. It was part of the reason he'd risen so quickly to Prime of his line here on the new planet while so many of his comrades were more ready to take everything purely at face value. Grady Prime would not ignore his instincts this time. He'd stay while he sent the majority of his troops back to the city.

He liked being out in the woods and if nothing else, this exercise would give him a chance to work on his bush skills. He could also look in on the O'Hara ranch from a different vantage point—from above.

He liked the O'Haras. As much as any Alvian could actually *like* anyone. But being a soldier gave Grady just a bit more than his compatriots. He felt...echoes...of affection when he saw the O'Haras together, or viewed the littlest members of the family playing. He wouldn't mind a chance to observe them from afar. They intrigued him and were the main reason he was considering participating in Mara 12's latest experiment. They'd given him the skinpatch, but he'd have to be off duty to apply it. He could still change his mind. The skinpatch was back in the city, in his quarters, waiting for him to get back and take himself off the duty roster while the experiment ran its course. He wanted to have Jaci's disappearance tied up before it came to that.

So he'd stay. For a while at least. He'd watch and wait, and see what happened. Probably nothing would disturb his silent vigil, but vigilance was his calling.

Chapter Twelve

"Caleb says to sit tight," Mick reported back the next day on his conversation with his oldest brother. "Things are happening fast now, he says, and he's not altogether certain of your future, but it is a pivotal one, Jaci. Your accident wasn't without purpose. Take comfort—what comfort you can—in that, at least."

"I don't know if I should be glad or scared to death, being the subject of one of the Oracle's visions." Jaci stifled a laugh that was on the edge of hysterical. Without her mates nearby to stabilize her emotions, she was feeling decidedly ragged.

"Things were vaguer than usual for Caleb, but he did tell me that you'll have a role to play in the ultimate goal we all have for the human race."

Jaci wasn't sure how she felt about that either. "But I'm Alvian."

Mick waved one hand in her direction. "You're more human than alien now—like Davin's always been. I've gained some understanding of Alvian culture from him and I can say from my observations, you're not like them anymore, Jaci. You may look like them, but you're more human every day."

Tears formed behind her eyes. She was at a loss. And she felt lost. Who was she anymore? She had no idea.

"Look, I can tell you're having a rough time with all this."

Mick stood from the chair beside her bed. Her leg kept her mostly in the small bedroom set off from the rest of the building by wooden walls and a hand-made door. "Take some deep breaths. Rest a while. Find your center and don't sweat the small stuff. For now, your job is to heal and you're coming along nicely. The rest will sort itself out as time goes on."

"I wish I had your confidence." She tried to wipe her eyes surreptitiously, but Mick saw and pulled a clean handkerchief from his pocket. He gave it to her, making her meet his eyes before he handed it over.

"I know it's hard, but try not to worry. If even a small part of what Caleb glimpsed in your future comes to pass, it'll be a good thing for all of us." He left her then and she tried to take his advice. After a while, she dozed.

§

Michael and David came to her in dreams that night, as usual. It was her greatest pleasure and her greatest heartache. She wanted to be with them in the flesh, but if these interludes in dreams were all they had, she wouldn't trade them for anything. Still, her heart pined for them during the days when she was awake, separated from them by the reality of life.

They dared not communicate too often by crystal. They didn't want to take the chance of being found out by some random spy. Davin had been careful to shield all the crystals he gave the O'Haras, but he'd also warned them that since his mating, other crystallographers had been working on ways to crack his protections. The Alvians needed him, but didn't trust him—with good reason, Jaci realized. As a result, their conversations were limited outside of the hour or so every other night when Michael brought them all together on the dreamplane.

And when they were together in dreams, they didn't spend a lot of time talking. More often than not, passion was the topic and pleasure their only goal.

"Do you like to be watched, Jaci?" David kissed her stomach, his hand between her thighs on the dream bed Michael had conjured for them. She didn't know how to answer and her hesitation must have showed on her face. "Hey, Mike, I think our little vixen likes the idea of being observed."

"Really?" Michael hovered in the background, allowing David time with her while he held them all in the dream using his special gift. He leaned in, a twinkle in his eye that spoke of mischief. Of the two cousins, Michael was the more spontaneous, she'd learned, much to her delight.

"What do you think?" David moved back to look at his cousin.

"I say we give it a go."

Both cousins looked at her, a speculative gleam of excitement in their eyes. She didn't know what their cryptic words meant or what they intended, but she'd learned over the weeks to trust them when it came to pleasure. They knew how far to push her and just how hard. They were masters.

Michael shifted closer as the setting changed. The bed turned to a platform with restraints that wrapped around her arms and legs, posing her according to Michael's whim. The small room opened outward, the walls replaced with blackness that hinted at an audience she couldn't see as a spotlight interfered with her vision into the distance.

She was on a stage of sorts, bound in front of the two men she trusted and loved more than life and the illusion of others watching. The feeling was decidedly wicked.

"I think she likes it, Mike." David smiled at his cousin, watching her reactions with approval.

"I think you're right," Michael agreed as he moved to her side. David was standing near her waist on her right, Michael at her left. "But maybe we can step it up a notch." Michael tipped her chin up with one finger so she had no choice but to look into his dancing eyes. "Think of someone, Jaci."

"Someone?" She didn't understand.

"Someone you want to watch you come for us." Michael's expression practically steamed as her temperature spiked higher. Without conscious thought on her part, the image of Grady Prime appeared in her mind.

Both men jumped when the hulking mass of Grady Prime materialized in the dream. She'd forgotten how big he was—and how much the cousins hated him. Truth be told, she wasn't sure why he came to mind, but then she realized he'd been her last encounter of a sexual kind before the cousins, and of all the Alvian men she'd serviced, he'd been the only one to give her pleasure that even came close to her mates. Close, but not the same maddening rush her two men gave her with the simplest of touches.

"Son of a bitch!" David looked at the new arrival on the dreamplane with a mix of anger and disgust.

"Interesting choice, babe," Michael looked at her speculatively. "I was expecting an Alvian, but not this one." His eyes narrowed with suspicion. "Did you have sex with him?"

Caught, she couldn't lie to them. Mutely, she nodded. Michael looked at Grady Prime with even more hatred than before, if such a thing was possible. Michael turned his smoldering gaze back to her.

"Never again, Jaci." She felt the vibrating thrum of his warning through her whole being.

"No. Never," she agreed. "I don't want him."

"But you did," David accused. "You must have."

"I didn't," she protested. "It was an assigned duty. And it was only once. But it happened right after my accident and I felt..." She couldn't finish the thought as their eyes darkened.

"You enjoyed it?" Michael asked finally, shooting Grady Prime a speculative look.

"It was the first time I'd really enjoyed the act of sample collection."

"Sample collection?" David asked, shock and outrage warring in his tone. He stared into her eyes while he got control of his emotions. "Your people are barbarians, Jaci."

"I understand that now, David." Her voice was tempered with regret, but the situation was getting to her. She was restrained and naked on the small stage, a confused Alvian warrior off to one side watching everything. She noted that Michael had conjured restraints for Grady Prime, locking his wrists and ankles together so he couldn't move.

"You do realize we'll have to punish you." Michael's words shocked, but the look in his eyes promised nothing but pleasure. Unable to speak for the excitement rushing through her veins, Jaci looked up at him and nodded agreement.

"Good girl." David's voice purred over her senses, teasing, tantalizing as he flipped her over. The restraints allowed any movement the men directed, it seemed, but gave her no quarter when she tried to move her arms or legs. Convenient, considering that Michael controlled everything about the environment of the dream.

Masculine hands smoothed over her ass. She liked the feel of David's strong hands against her bare skin. He dipped lower, into the dark valley between her thighs, lingering a moment, stroking inside the wet lips.

Her legs were still together, but now the restraints moved, pulling her knees up and apart. David's large fingers spread her and exposed her most intimate area to Grady, who stood directly behind her. She couldn't see the Alvian warrior from this position, but she knew he was there. The very idea of it—even though this was only a dream—raised her temperature.

"I love the way you warm for me." David's fingers stroked rhythmically within her.

Her only response was an almost incoherent keening as he sent her higher. She needed relief and she needed it soon.

Thwak!

The sound of the swat made her jump almost as much as the sting on the fleshy cheek of her butt. She looked over her shoulder at Michael, and he grinned at her.

"You have the most perfect ass, Jaci. And your skin is so fine, it won't take much to turn it a lovely shade of pink."

"She likes it, Mike," David said, his fingers still within her. "You do understand the concept of spanking, don't you, Jaci? It's punishment, but as I think you've just discovered, it can be exciting under certain circumstances."

"I—" Jaci had a hard time speaking, but she knew they were waiting for her to answer. "I'm learning rapidly."

Michael tipped her head up to meet his gaze. "Is it okay, sweetheart?"

"She liked it, Mike," David didn't give her a chance to answer, though Michael kept watching her. "Take my word for it."

Still, Michael hesitated. "Honey?"

Since David's fingers were teasing her again, she could only nod. Michael smiled and the satisfaction gleaming from his eyes made her feel even better about her response. When his hand came down on her butt once more, this time on the other cheek, she felt better still.

The sensations racing through her epidermis would bear study, but they were so exciting, she found she couldn't concentrate on anything beyond the next delicious wave of sensation. The mix of pleasure and the sting of those loud smacks made her hotter than almost anything the cousins had tried with her before. These two men could surprise her and turn her on like no one and nothing before.

"That's just beautiful," Michael said and she looked back again to see him gazing down at her with a mix of lust and satisfaction.

"I'd say she's learned her lesson, cuz." David pulled his fingers from her pussy. She whimpered, wanting his touch back in the worst way. "And now it's time for her reward."

David lifted her upward with little effort on the dreamplane, bringing her face to face with Grady Prime. She gasped, seeing the heated look in the soldier's eyes. She'd almost forgotten he'd been watching, with a pussy-level view of her torment.

Grady Prime's jaw firmed and a tick near his eye indicated just how tense he was. She looked downward and noted the thick bulge she remembered from their one encounter. He was aroused. And she was naked, aroused and wanting. But not Grady Prime. Certainly, having him there—or the illusion of him, at least—elevated the experience, but the only men she wanted were her mates. And she wanted them now.

"Please." Her voice was just a whisper as she tried to focus on her men. Her body was Humming as they touched her, the vibration of sound and the blistering heat of her arousal sending her higher than she'd ever been before. Making her needier than she'd ever been before. But they wouldn't leave her wanting. Would they?

David moved her again as Michael stepped back. In their dreams, Michael always held back to let David make love to her first. He had to. Michael held the dream with his power. If he came first, the dream would dissolve, leaving his cousin unfulfilled.

They worked well together and especially when they made love to her, their teamwork was something she loved to indulge. After all, she benefited greatly from their sharing of minds.

David spread her out before him, flat on her back so he could look down into her face as he joined them together. His was a dominant personality and she loved the way he dominated their loveplay.

He came into her in a rush and his excitement matched hers. She was more than ready for him and the hard thrusts sent her spiraling upward with little effort.

"See him watching you? Wanting you?" David thrust heavily within her. "But he can't have you. He can only watch. And wish." David sped his strokes, raising her temperature yet again as her excitement rose higher. She cried out on every inward push of his strong body, clinging to him for strength as she came hard around him.

David came with her, thrusting one final time and holding, tight within her while his seed erupted in a hot, gushing torrent. His eyes closed as his head fell back in ecstasy. She loved making him look like that. She loved that they could drive each other to the brink of sanity.

David stepped back, disengaging from her body as he left her. A recliner formed behind him so he could collapse into it—one of the few times he was able to stay in the dream even after the tumult of climax. She looked to Michael, knowing he was holding this dreamplane together for all of them.

His grin was wicked as he turned the stage into a decadent

bed, wider than any that existed in the real world and twice as comfortable. He came to her, kneeling between her legs as David looked on with indulgence from the side of the room.

Grady Prime was still there too. Bound hand and foot.

"Let him go, Jaci," Michael kissed her cheek, nibbling down to her jaw.

"What do you mean?"

Michael flicked a look back to the Alvian soldier. "He's here because he's part of your imagination. Frankly, I'm surprised you held his image this long, but we don't need him. All we need is each other." He continued to kiss his way down her neck.

Jaci tried to locate the thought that was Grady Prime and realized she hadn't been thinking of him at all for quite some time.

"Uh, Michael..." She tugged at his hair to get his attention. "I'm not thinking of him. It must be one of you."

Michael left off sucking on her skin and looked up, his narrowed gaze going from her to Grady Prime to David.

"It's not me," David protested.

"Son of a bitch!" Michael leapt off the bed and turned to confront the Alvian warrior. He walked around the captive man as if inspecting him. "You know, Dave, I think he's really here."

For the first time, Jaci noted the way Grady Prime observed them, his calculating stare one she'd never received, but which was legend among the troops he led. Grady Prime was studying them. He didn't speak, but then his image was more transparent than Michael and David's, as if he weren't fully with them on the dreamplane. Jaci didn't know what that meant, but his presence here was troubling, to say the least.

"That means—" David began, but Michael cut him off.

"No shit. He's nearby." Worry crept into both of their expressions as Jaci sat up, clutching the bedding to her chest.

"Can you—?" David didn't even need to finish his thought, so aligned were the cousins.

"I'll escort him back and plant a few suggestions. Hopefully he won't remember any of this."

"You can do that?" Jaci asked, astounded anew by her mate's power.

Michael sent her a mischievous wink. "How do you think Dave and I handled dishonest competitors when we were in business? There's a reason we were as successful as we once were. Between Dave's smarts and my ability to make folks play fair, we were able to compete with the big corporate sharks and do rather well." She could see the pride Michael had in his long-ago achievements though she didn't understand all of what he talked about. "Don't worry. I'll take our voyeur back to his own mind and try to figure out what he's doing so close to you, sweetheart. Warn the others. Grady Prime is closer than any of you think." He turned back and gave her a kiss as David stood and did the same. "When I go with him, this dream will collapse. Know that we love you, sweetheart, and we'll be in touch. Try not to worry, but be vigilant."

"I will." She did her best not to cling to either of them, but the specter of Grady Prime watching—knowing now that it really was him—was enough to want to end this dream as soon as possible. "Be careful."

David gave her a hug. "You too."

With a last look, they left the dream and Jaci woke with a gasp, sitting up in bed, worry hitting her like a sledgehammer.

"What's wrong?" Bill was in the doorway to the small bedroom, disheveled from sleep but alert.

Tears gathered behind her eyes, but she gathered her

courage and faced him. "Grady Prime is nearby."

"How do you know?" Bill seemed skeptical and she couldn't blame him. Besides crystallography, Alvians had no special powers. Not like humans.

"He was in our dream. Michael and David said it was because he was near. Michael was going to follow Grady Prime back to his own dreamplane and try to convince him to forget the interlude, but my mates seemed to think he was closer than we realized."

A soft whistle sounded from over Bill's shoulder as Sam came into view. "That bastard is tenacious as a leech. We're going to have to be careful."

"That's what Michael and David said. They wanted me to warn everyone and I assume one of them—or maybe Davin—will be in touch as soon as they know anything. Michael seemed to think he might be able to tell us more after he visited Grady's dreamplane."

"That's one freaky talent he's got," Sam said with admiration even as his jaw firmed. "I'll make my way up to the house and let the O'Haras know. It should be dark enough to get there unseen if I'm careful. Besides, Grady's dreaming, right? So as of a few minutes ago at least, he was asleep."

"Good idea," Bill agreed.

By dawn, Davin had checked in with the O'Hara family on a secure crystal, filling them in on what Michael had found out. Sam reported back to the inhabitants of the small outbuilding when he came back with breakfast for them all.

"Grady Prime is in the woods near the Northeast perimeter of the ranch. Michael seems to think he's been there for a few weeks. Ever since the search teams gave up on finding you, Jaci. Looks like our old friend Grady never gave up."

Jaci couldn't really describe her feelings at the news. On the one hand, she was resentful that the soldier was still on her trail when all others had given up. Of course, that tenacity was part of what had made him rise to the level of Prime in the first place, so there was also a hint of admiration in her mix of emotion. In with that was a lot of fear, knowing how good at tracking Grady Prime truly was. His reputation was well earned and her mates knew firsthand how tenacious he could be.

Then there was a smidgen of flattery. The fact that he remained, personally, was good for her burgeoning ego. She knew from his own words that he liked her. Perhaps that was why he'd stayed when he sent all his men home.

"He will not give up," Bill said with a grim expression. "The only thing that would make him leave is an emergency elsewhere. Even then, he is Prime. He decides where he is needed. He probably is ordering his men from here. He has advanced technology not available to most Alvians. His crystals are some of the most complex in the system, allowing him to work from anywhere."

"Great." Sam's disgust was plain, his gaze accusatory. "And you know this how?"

To his credit, Bill held the other man's gaze as he divulged part of his past of which the human was no doubt unaware. "I was Prime," Bill said without detectable emotion. The man who had been Sinclair Prime had come a long way in controlling his emotions, Jaci realized with some envy.

Sam and Bill stared at each other for several long moments. "The Prime assassin, I'm guessing."

Jaci gasped.

Bill only nodded.

"And they chose you for the emotion experiment? Damn." Sam whistled between his teeth. "What were they thinking?

Give a stone killer emotions so he either turns into psycho who revels in his kills, or a regular guy who now has to live with the remorse of what he's done. I'm guessing the latter happened to you, Bill." Sam raised his coffee mug. "For what it's worth, I'm glad you didn't turn psycho. And you have my sympathy."

Bill seemed at a loss for words and the silence stretched as they continued their meal. Finally, Sam sat back and looked at them both.

"So what now? Grady's in the area. We need to get Jaci out of here. No offense, kid, but you're a lab tech. You don't stand a chance against someone with half Grady's skill."

"You'll get no argument from me," she agreed ruefully. "But where can I go? I dare not stay here. I don't want to bring down any more trouble on the O'Haras."

"But if you go anywhere by land, you'll leave a trail Grady can follow," Sam said. "We'll need help from the O'Haras to get you off the ranch. Maybe Davin can send a ship or something. If we take you out by air—"

"Grady Prime undoubtedly has a ship nearby at his disposal. He could easily follow another ship and probably would investigate any irregular flights in or out of this valley or the surrounding areas." Bill sat back as well, fingering his water glass with a thoughtful expression. "But there might be a way."

"I'd be interested to hear it." Sam challenged the other man.

"I can fly her out."

Silence greeted Bill's pronouncement as both Jaci and Sam regarded him with surprise.

"Can you carry her weight? I thought you said you were more of a sprinter," Sam asked.

"In my youth, trainers tested me for various abilities. I can carry her for short hops with periods of rest in between. If we pick our spots well and use the cover of darkness, the trail will be minimal."

"No shit." Sam sounded impressed. Jaci was too. The idea of flying with Bill, without a ship to support them, sent a nervous tingle through her midsection.

Bill sat forward, clearing a space on the small table in front of him. Using various utensils, he made a sort of map of the area. A knife was the ridge line, a fork the opposite mountain and a spoon the third ridge that created the triangular valley. A salt shaker was the ranch house, a small book of matches the outbuilding they were now in.

"If Grady stays along this side of the valley—" Bill pointed to the northeastern ridgeline, "—we can go out through here." He indicated the path, shielded by several outbuildings and planted fields that led away from Grady's last known position. "We can take horses this far, and you can return our mounts to the pasture with none the wiser." Bill nodded toward Sam as he fingered a path out beyond the ranch house and just up to the treeline to the southwest. "Even if Grady moves, we should be far enough from him if we move quickly and target a site directly opposite his last known location for our initial departure. I can probably get her as far as the ridge on the first flight. It's clear enough up there for me to land safely and the rocky slope won't hold tracks."

"If need be, I can lay some false trails elsewhere," Sam volunteered.

Jaci didn't like the sound of that. "I don't want you to put yourself at risk, Sam. Grady wants me back, but he'll take you in just as quickly. I'd feel terrible if you got caught because of me."

Sam's lips quirked up in a half-smile. "Thanks for that,

Jaci, but I want you to get away from here safely."

"I think we can do that, Sam." Bill ended that train of thought, though Jaci was still troubled. Yet, these men were the experts on this kind of thing. She had to trust their judgment.

"But where will we go?" Jaci was more than curious.

"I've been giving that a lot of thought over the past few days," Bill said. "There is a place you could go."

Jaci didn't dare get her hopes up too high, but she was feeling a strange mix of anxiety, relief and fear. "Where?" It was the only word she could get out past the lump in her throat, and it wasn't loud, but Bill seemed to hear her.

"A few days hike from here there's an old cave complex. It appears to have been a mine at one time and is solidly reinforced, with interior plumbing and even wiring that we might be able to get working again if we can rig some power. Davin or the O'Haras might be willing to get us a power crystal or two. If we can get that place up and running, we can hide there easily. Even if we can't restore power right away, it's a great place to hole up. There are multiple layers of security, which I guess is why some other group hasn't already taken up residence there. The place is big, with many large underground chambers. It can be easily defended and is impervious to surveillance of any kind due to the metal that permeates the living rock. I scoped it out months ago as a fall-back position. I think if we can get it up and running, we could perhaps provide a safe haven for ourselves and the O'Haras too—if they ever need it." His face grew very serious. "We owe them much."

"I see you've given this a great deal of thought," she said, feeling hope rise to crowd out the other emotions. "And I'm overwhelmed that you would allow me to join you."

"It is a wise move on many levels," Bill said, his expression guarded. "I need a base of operations, but the mine is too big to leave unguarded. If there are more of us, we can keep it more secure. One will always be inside and able to monitor for intruders. I didn't want to use it when it was just me alone for that very reason, but I'd been thinking of it more since Sam joined me. We both would benefit from a safe place to live that is out of the weather. Winter will be here soon."

"I think it's a good plan," Sam agreed.

"But is it safe for Sam to be alone in the woods, making his way on foot, knowing Grady Prime is out there, tracking?" Jaci asked, worried.

Bill nodded. "Far safer for him than you, Jaci. He knows how to hide his tracks and he has the advantage over Grady Prime, knowing where he is right now. It's a good start. All we need to do is get you out of here without Grady Prime knowing. Right now he may suspect you're still in the area, but he has no real evidence. It's key that we keep it that way during our escape."

"That's where I come in," Sam added. "And maybe the O'Haras can help a bit too. Justin could go out game hunting and stumble across Grady's path." A mischievous smile lit Sam's face.

"It's plausible. Though doubtful that Grady Prime will leave enough of a trail to be easily discovered. Still, Justin has skills. It wouldn't be out of character for him to follow any trace of a trail found near his homestead," Bill allowed. "And while you're playing in the woods, Jaci and I can begin work on the mine site so when you get there, we'll be able to hole up against the entire Alvian army, if necessary. It won't take much. The place is perfect for our use." Bill sat back once more, after rearranging the table so no evidence of their plans remained.

He stood to leave and Jaci followed suit, going over to give him a hug as she'd seen the O'Haras do countless times. She finally understood the meaning of platonic hugs to show affection and she felt it deeply at the moment for Bill.

"I can't thank you enough for all you've done." She squeezed him gently, feeling his surprise in the rigidity of his muscles. After a short but heartfelt hug, she let him go and moved back. "I may not be any good in the woods, but I do have technical skills. I know I can help get the power up and running. Aside from biotech, I did several courses in power distribution early in my career. I even worked in a grid station for a year while waiting for a spot to open on Mara's team."

Bill regarded her with approval. "You're full of surprises today. We can use those skills, Jaci. Now we just need to get a decent power source. I'll go over to the ranch house and have a talk with the O'Haras."

Chapter Thirteen

The O'Haras were able to supply them with a decent-sized crystal Davin had given Mick to power some medical equipment he'd been running off a generator before. Mick said he didn't mind using the generator again if they needed the diagnostic equipment during the time it would take for Davin to get them another crystal.

So they had a power source and Jaci had the skill to install it. Now they just had to escape the ranch unseen and make their way to the old mine.

They'd raised a few eyebrows when telling the O'Haras the bare bones of their plan. As far as the human family knew, Jaci and Bill were making their way on foot. The questions they didn't ask were more telling than those they did. The O'Haras seemed to realize that Bill wasn't being entirely forthright with them, but for whatever reason, they didn't pry. The O'Haras—most likely because of Caleb's abilities—often *knew* things without being told, but neither Jaci nor her companions were volunteering any information about Bill.

Jaci had never ridden a horse before, but Sam was an expert. He gave her a quick lesson and in no time they were trotting off over the ranch landscape, using the outbuildings, trees and fields of tall crops for cover. There was only a sliver of moon that night—not enough light to give them away. Or so they all hoped.

Justin had gone out into the woods earlier that day, ostensibly to go hunting game animals, but in reality he was pursuing prey of a different kind altogether. He'd picked up Grady Prime's faint trail in the afternoon and had reported back to his brother telepathically. Grady Prime had scouted further afield, but returned to camp on the northeastern edge of the ranch at dusk. He'd likely go out again that night, but he was probably too far away on the opposite side of the big property to catch them in the act.

All too soon Jaci's first horseback ride was over. She slid out of the saddle, surprised to feel her legs were somewhat rubbery, but the most nerve-wracking part was yet to come.

Flying.

She wasn't looking forward to it.

She'd flown many times in ships, but never without the warm reassurance of steel and circuitry between herself and the elements.

"God willing, I'll see you both in a few days," Sam said as he took the reins of all three horses in hand and tethered them to a nearby tree. Jaci knew the men had already discussed how and where Sam could find the old mine and Sam was an experienced woodsman. He'd be able to find it.

Jaci went to him and gave him a hug. "I can't thank you enough for all you've done. If we do not meet again, may light shine on your path for all your days." She didn't know why the ancient Alvian words came to mind, but they fit. Modern Alvians didn't believe in such superstitious wishes, but in the far past, there had been many sayings her ancestors had used for both greetings and leave-takings. She thought she understood now why such occasions had inspired both formal and heart-wrenching words.

"Thanks, Jaci," Sam said, returning her hug then stepping back. His smile didn't quite reach his eyes and his expression was kind. "You're a good kid. Wild Bill will take good care of you. Trust him."

"I do." She looked from one man to the other, noting that Bill had taken off both his jacket and shirt, rolling them up and storing them in a small sack she would carry. He began to stretch—both his muscles and his wings—and the sight made her speechless. His wings were a tawny golden color shot through with pale ivory and white. Even in the twilight darkness, she could see they were a thing of beauty.

From tip to tip, she'd estimate his wings to be twice as long as he was tall. How he hid them under his baggy clothes, she had no idea, but she'd never even suspected. Of course, now she could see his torso was quite a bit leaner than she'd expected, rippling with ropes of muscle. He was fitter than any man she'd ever seen. A true specimen. His body a work of art. And his wings, a thing of legend.

A low whistle reached her ears and she turned to see Sam watching just as intently.

"You'd better be careful, my friend." Sam walked up to Bill as he turned to face them. "Any human who sees you will think you're an angel come to earth."

"I'm no heavenly being."

"A fallen angel then." Sam grinned and Bill begrudgingly smiled in return.

"Just don't start calling me Lucifer."

"So you've been reading up. Good for you." Sam stuck out his hand and the two men exchanged a handshake. "I'll watch the backtrail for a while before I return the horses, just to be certain you made it out unseen."

"We'll see you in a few days."

Bill turned to Jaci and she knew her moment of truth had come. He must have seen her hesitation because his expression softened.

"There's nothing to be afraid of. I won't drop you and I can assure you, I'm very skilled at flight."

Jaci took a deep breath. "I'm sorry I'm such a coward." She firmed her spine and reached out to take the sack from his hand. She would hold it while they flew. In fact, she would tie it to her arm since it contained not only Bill's clothing, but also the all-important power crystal. They didn't want to drop it.

"You're not a coward, Jaci," Bill's voice was soft with understanding. "A coward would never have made it this far." So saying, he scooped her up into his arms and waited until she was settled comfortably. "All right?" he asked.

She nodded, her arms around his chest, under the soft feathers of his wings and the sack tied to her upper arm, resting on her middle. It would be awkward, but it would work.

"Let's go before I lose my nerve."

With a smile and a soft laugh, Bill leapt into the air.

The rush of air under his wings startled her at first, but the sensation of flight soon overcame the sheer intrigue of his wings. They were high above the trees in a matter of seconds. She dared not look below to see Sam and the horses, for fear they'd be little specks. She closed her eyes and concentrated on being as light and small as possible, though she knew the futility of wishing for things that were impossible.

"Are you all right?" Bill asked and Jaci could feel the humor in his voice.

"Don't talk. Concentrate on flying!" Her words were a terrified whisper.

"Don't worry. I won't drop you, Jaci. I've carried people aloft before."

That idea intrigued her since his mere existence was a closely held secret. "Trainers?"

"And targets," Bill's voice dipped into grim tones.

She preferred not to think about those he'd killed. She preferred he didn't think of them either, actually.

"How long?"

"Before we land?" His breathing was labored. "Momentarily."

"Really?" She peeked through clenched eyelids and felt tears stream over her temple as the wind blew into her face. The treetops were far below and the rocky ridge of the mountain loomed closer. Bill set them both down gently, landing on his feet as his wings softened the jolt of coming back to earth. She could see he was winded and felt the sweat of his exertions on his skin as he lowered her to her feet.

"I need to walk," he said, his breath coming in puffs. "Stay here and don't move around too much. Stick to bare rock if you can. Less tracks."

Jaci followed his orders to the letter as he stalked off across the bare rock slope at a lazy pace, working the muscles in his arms and stretching his wings. After a few minutes, he came back to her.

"Are you all right?" He was breathing more rhythmically now, but she was still concerned for his welfare.

"I'm fine. The first leg was the most difficult. From here on, we can go from peak to peak. It's more of a soaring start than a drive to gain altitude. It's not as tiring."

"If you say so." Jaci was amazed at the freedom his wings gave him, and despite the fact that she was still afraid, she found herself looking forward to the next leg of their journey.

"At this rate, we will be at the mine in a few hours. It'll be good to approach the site while it's still dark outside. Less need for our eyes to adjust to the interior gloom and less chance of being spotted in the area should anyone be nearby."

Jaci trusted his judgment. Bill had been a soldier Prime—one of the elites. He probably had skills she couldn't even dream of. She'd trust him with her life, and was in fact doing so with every inch they put between themselves and the O'Hara ranch.

"It must be so amazing to be able to fly, but I have no idea how you hid those wings for so long."

"Not all that difficult really. I was kept mostly in the field and my men..." A tight look came over his face as his words died off.

"What?"

"We'd better get going. We have a lot of sky to cover."

Jaci understood from his tone that he didn't want to discuss it further. She felt bad that she'd broken the mood of camaraderie they'd developed. Still, she thought she knew Bill well enough by now that their friendly banter would return.

Bill stepped close to her and she fought against stepping back. He was a handsome man, but he wasn't either of her mates. Being held in Bill's arms was no hardship, but it reminded her too much of all she'd never shared with Michael and David.

He lifted her into his arms and waited while she arranged the pack with the crystal and his shirt and coat. The crystal would be key when they arrived at the mine site.

"This flight will be longer. Can you handle it?"

"It takes getting used to, Bill, but I can do it. I have to."

"You're a trooper, Jaci. I never had much use for lab techs, but you're different."

Jaci smiled, glad to have his good opinion. "Thanks."

He leapt from the edge of the ridge and Jaci had to hold back a squeal of fright as they dipped low, plummeting a dozen feet before his wings unfurled completely. After that, it felt like they were sailing through the night sky, buffeted by wind currents that flowed under Bill's cupped wings.

After a while, Jaci started to notice the way he used his feathers to make the most of the wind and airflows that kept them aloft and going in the right direction. They soared far above the trees, probably indistinguishable from the ground as much more than a very large bird. Given lack of depth perception in a black sky, if anyone was out there in the forest and happened to see them, they'd probably be mistaken for an eagle of some sort. Such birds were often spotted above the forest and made the treetops their home.

It was beautiful in a scary way. Looking outward, Jaci could see the stars, appearing all that much closer given her distance from the ground. The sky was a cloudless black sea with white stars bobbing here and there. She was just starting to get over her fear when Bill brought them in for a landing on another rocky ridge.

On it went, repeating the cycle several more times before they landed for the final time. Each time, Jaci enjoyed the experience more, though Bill seemed to be tiring more with each short flight.

They were deep in the mountains now, in an area far removed from the Alvian city. Nobody lived out here except a few hermits. The small human villages were usually found in more hospitable areas.

Bill was noticeably tired, but still led her in a roundabout way to the mine entrance. It didn't look like much from the outside, which was part of its charm, but as soon as they'd gone a few yards inside, Bill halted their progress.

"Wait here." Bill left her sitting against the cave wall to one side of the entrance. She could still see the mouth of the tunnel, but not much else. Bill had scouted ahead far enough to reassure her that they were alone in the cylindrical cave.

He checked their backtrail, erasing the few signs of their passage while leaving an agreed-upon pile of rocks and twigs in a formation he'd discussed with Sam. The terrain was rocky. Jaci didn't see how Bill could discern any sort of trail, but he apparently did.

"We need to move slowly from here on out," Bill said as he rejoined her. "There could be animals or even people in here. With all the bare rock, prints are hard to come by and easy to mask, but it is a good sign that my markers were left undisturbed from the last time I was here."

"I didn't see any markers."

Bill only smiled. She saw the gleam of his teeth in the darkness and it sent a chill down her spine. He took the pack from the stone floor at her feet and dressed in his loose shirt and coat, hiding his wings under layers of cloth.

"I'll take point. You stay close behind me and hold the crystal." He handed the pack to her, now much less bulky and somewhat lighter. Jaci swung it over her back in a comfortable position as Bill led the way at a slow pace through the tunnel, winding downward for several yards before branching left.

An hour later, it felt like they'd covered every inch of the tunnel complex, but Jaci feared they'd only scratched the surface. They were both tired and in need of rest, assured that at least their immediate area was free from danger and would be long enough for them to rest.

Bill had a light of Alvian design he must've scrounged from her ship or some patrol outpost. He lit the area, chasing the shadows away, and Jaci got her first really good look at the rough-hewn tunnels.

"A bit farther on, these tunnels become blocked by heavy steel doors. Inside there is the complex of which I spoke. We'll rest for a few minutes and maybe eat something to regain a bit of energy, then tackle the first of the locked doorways."

"They're locked? Then how do you know...?"

"Who do you think locked them in the first place?" Again that mischievous grin shone in the dim light and this time Jaci could see the teasing sparkle in his eyes.

They ate some of the food from Jaci's pack, then set out once more, this time using Bill's light to lead the way. But when they rounded the corner before the last stretch of tunnel leading to the first door, Bill halted.

"There is light up ahead," he whispered, cautioning Jaci to stay back. Light this deep in the caverns could only mean one thing.

Someone was there before them.

Jaci peeked around Bill's broad back and saw the heavy steel door he'd mentioned was standing wide open and a dim light shone from within. If she strained her ears, Jaci could just hear the murmur of deep voices.

"Male voices, but not Alvian. Humans are inside."

"Good call," Bill confirmed. "Let me go take a look. You should be safe out here. I'll leave the light for you. If you need to move, we can rendezvous back where we stopped to rest. If I don't meet you there within an hour, make your way out and try to meet up with Sam. Can you do that?"

Swallowing her fear, Jaci nodded. Bill was as serious as

she'd ever seen him. She clutched his arm before letting him go. "Be careful."

The wait was interminable. It felt like hours had passed but it was really only minutes before Bill came back through the doorway, walking easily. Jaci took that to mean the threat had been either eliminated, or there was no threat to begin with. But the two males who followed behind Bill's tall form had her running to meet them.

"Michael! David!"

She was thrilled beyond words to see both her men.

She jumped into Michael's waiting arms. He covered her face in kisses as she clung to him.

"Thank God you're safe." Michael whispered his relief into her ear as he kissed her with a desperation she felt too.

David tugged her out of Mike's embrace, bending her back over his arm and planting a kiss on her, the likes of which she had never known. He simply took her breath away. Moving back, he let her rise but held her close to his long, muscular frame. Michael stepped up close behind.

"We missed you, honey. We won't ever let you be apart from us again."

She felt tears in her eyes, and thought she finally understood what tears of happiness felt like. She had come home, indeed. Home to these two men's strong arms. Anywhere they were, that was her home.

She was overwhelmed with joy to see them in the flesh. "Tell me I'm not dreaming."

David swatted her ass playfully as Michael took her fully into his arms. "Does that feel real enough for you?" She giggled as they laughed and surrounded her with their warmth and love.

"How did you get here? I'm so happy to see you both!"

"Davin had a long talk with Justin and Mick last night after dinner," Michael told her. "We left in a hurry to be here when you arrived. We figured you'd be a while yet, but Mick said to expect you sooner." A raised eyebrow indicated he'd let the subject lie for now but it would probably be revisited at some point, she knew. "Davin dropped us here with a load of supplies to get us started. It seems the Oracle had a say in our move. Caleb sent a message to Mick just after you set out and he passed it on to Davin. Caleb had a strong vision, showing us setting up this place and creating a sanctuary of sorts for folks who need to lay low."

"We only got here a little while ago," David added. "We took a look at the power grid, but we'll probably have to take it slow when we fire things up. There's a lot of hardware in this mountain that we may not want to awaken just yet."

"Why not?" Jaci walked between her men as they ushered her through the doorway into the interior of the complex. It wasn't a cave, as she had expected. No, this was a high-tech installation of some kind, complete with painted walls and a myriad of symbols, hatches, conduits and doorways all leading to another doorway that stood open at the end of the large tunnel.

They walked through and the sight that met her eyes robbed her of speech. The cavern was enormous, with entire buildings inside. Rough-hewn stone columns supported a domed ceiling far above and roadways with vehicles still parked on them wove between the buildings. It was a small city inside. And it was eerily empty.

"What is this place?"

"Near as we can figure, this isn't a mine, Jaci," Michael

said. "This is some kind of old NORAD site. NORAD was a protective military partnership between two of the countries that made up this continent. There are still missiles in the silos and everything. And the computer equipment is top notch. All we need is power and Davin supplied us with plenty. He's already arranged to send a replacement crystal to Mick, by the way. Some of the tunnels we saw in the short time we've been here had natural crystal formations in them. I think Dave and I can manage to mine a few power crystals locally in addition to what we brought with us."

"So you plan to stay?" Jaci turned to them, her heart in her throat.

"Anywhere you are—" David pulled her into his arms, "—that's where we want to be. Davin will cover for us. We've got it all worked out."

Bill needed to rest after his long flight. He looked haggard and he was noticeably tired—something seldom seen among Alvians—especially soldiers.

"What's wrong with your friend?" Michael raised one eyebrow suspiciously.

"He's just tired." Jaci didn't know what to say. Bill's secret was his to tell.

"And why is that?" David stepped right up to the Alvian warrior in challenge. "Look, we know there's something different about you, Bill. Now we find you here days earlier than you should be. Jaci's fine, but you're looking awfully rundown. What's up?"

Bill stared him down, a muscle ticking in his jaw, his flinty eyes tired but strong. "You have abilities beyond the realm of normal beings. Suffice to say that I do as well."

"If we're going to stay here together, we need to start trusting one another." Dave stood his ground. "I'm a mind healer. Mike's a dreamwalker. There's not much you can keep secret from him if he wants to find out. Don't you think it's better you tell us straight out than have Mike traipse through your dreams, looking at your memories?"

"I don't respond well to threats." Bill's jaw firmed and Jaci moved to stand between the men.

"Stop this right now." Jaci put one palm on each of their chests, pressing them apart but having little effect on the strong males. She gave up, instead taking David's hand in hers to get his attention.

David's gaze shifted to her. "How did you get here so fast, Jaci? What's he hiding?"

She shut her eyes, unwilling to lie to her mates, but likewise unwilling to betray her friend. "It is Bill's secret to tell. Not mine. But it cannot harm you. Believe me on that."

"Let us decide that, Jaci." Michael moved up next to David to stand with his cousin.

She turned to Bill, hoping he would settle this in a way that would let her be honest with her mates. She didn't like to hold secrets from them.

Bill's gaze showed his reluctance, but he gave in with a sigh. "I will bring no strife between mates," Bill grit out through clenched teeth. "Even now I can hear the Hum as she touches you."

Jaci lifted her hand from David's arm. "I'm sorry if it makes you uncomfortable."

Bill's head tilted to the side as if he were considering his words. "Not uncomfortable. Jealous, perhaps. Maybe even hopeful. If there are mates for you, perhaps in time, I will find one of my own."

Unspoken was the fear that if Bill didn't find a resonance mate to temper his emotions, he might well end in insanity like their ancient ancestors. Jaci nodded, acknowledging what they both knew. Bill turned his attention back to the cousins.

"I can fly."

Silence greeted his bold statement.

"No shit?" Michael finally asked. "Like levitation?"

"No." Bill shook his head. "I have wings."

The cousins just stared.

"It's true." Jaci tried to ease the awkward moment. "We flew here in stages. That's why he's so tired. He carried me over the treetops. It was amazing."

"Amazing," David echoed her words.

"Is this an Alvian thing? Or is this something special?" Mike's tone was more curious than upset.

"I was an experiment." Bill sighed, visibly weary. "Pure Alvians never had wings. It is something the geneticists wanted to try."

"And you were the guinea pig. You have my sympathy." David's dark eyes spoke of compassion and understanding.

"Mine too," Mike added. "But my envy as well. It must be pretty cool to be able to soar with the birds. Thank you for bringing Jaci here, to safety."

Bill's expression lightened. "You're welcome. She is a special person and seeing the feelings between you three gives me hope for my own future, but I need to rest now. The trip was not easy." He moved away and the cousins stepped back to let him pass.

One of the buildings contained suites of bedrooms. Bill took one after being certain the heavy steel doors that led outside the tunnel complex were shut and locked securely. He would sleep off the long flight, she knew, as she wished him a good night.

The cousins had other plans. Selecting one of the more sumptuously decorated chambers far enough from Bill that they wouldn't disturb his sleep, they locked themselves in. David secured the door while Michael led her to a plush couch in the outer room of the suite.

"Where are we?" Jaci looked around at the colorful fabrics and lush interior of the room.

"We saw this place when we did our run-through of the facility." Michael poured some water for her from the supplies they'd already stored in the room. "Dave thinks it was the base commander's suite and I tend to agree. It's the largest and nicest of the rooms we saw, but we can find out more tomorrow when we investigate further. Right now, we have other things to do that are much more important." His smile made promises that she longed for him to fulfill.

"Such as?"

"Well—" David tugged off his shirt, holding her gaze, "—we've never really made love to you, Jaci. Unless you have any objections, that's about to change."

Jaci stepped right up to him, boldly running her hands down his chest as she'd only been able to do in dreams. "No objections at all. Not a one."

"Good." Michael crowded in behind her, sandwiching her between two hot male bodies.

"Shards! This feels even better than the dream."

"Dreams are good," Michael said, kissing her shoulder as he undressed her from behind. "But reality is so much better. You taste even better than I remember, Jaci. We've waited so long to be with you."

She reached behind to cup his head, turning so she could kiss him with the yearning she felt. These men ignited her fires more quickly than anything or anyone ever had. In dreams, they were potent, but in the real world, they were...more. More vibrant, more alive, more cunning, more desirable. More everything. And she wanted them as she wanted no others.

The Hum increased as they touched, drowning her senses in that most beautiful, perfect tone. She knew the Hum was beyond human hearing and for a moment she wished they could hear the perfection of their union, but they could feel it. Every moment they touched, every second they loved, all three of them could feel the way they fit together flawlessly. The rightness of them—together.

David kissed her, helping Michael divest her of her clothing as she pushed and tugged at their clothes. They were much more efficient than she and before long, she stood between them, naked. Their chests were bare, at least, rubbing along her heated skin. The coarse fabric of their pants teased her lower body, but she wanted those pants gone. She wanted to feel their skin against hers, and their arousal.

"Take it off," she cried, struggling with the closure on David's blue jeans.

He laughed, moving back slightly to take over the job. "Your wish is my command, sweetheart."

Watching David, she reached behind to deliver the same message to Michael, but he was ahead of her. His fingers were already freeing his thick erection from the closure of his pants as they slid down his legs.

"I love the way your skin gets hot. You warm me, Jaci," Michael whispered in her ear as he moved in close behind her once more, the pants no longer a barrier. His cock settled in the crevice of her ass as if made to fit there, warm against her skin and pulsing with life. "You warm all the cold places in my soul."

David backed away to finish undressing, but he didn't return. When she reached out to him, he shook his head. "Mike gets you first this time, baby. He sacrificed a lot to let me join in the dreams. He deserves to go first this time."

"But I want you both. Together."

David's eyes flared at her bold statement, but he continued to shake his head. "This isn't a dream and you aren't ready for that kind of thing yet. We need to prepare you. And after all this time, I don't think either of us can give you the time you'd need to accommodate us comfortably. We'll save that for when we're in less of a hurry, okay?" He kissed her lips sweetly, coming close for just a moment to touch her face and offer reassurance.

She needed his touch. Craved it like a drug. She needed them both, and they appeared to share her desperate cravings, touching her, stroking her skin, fanning the flames of her desire.

Michael moved her into another room and David followed close behind. This was a bedroom, complete with a large, sumptuous bed, though it was decorated in utilitarian colors. Still, the rich, dark greens and blues pleased her senses and as David dimmed the lights, Michael lay her on the wide bed, coming down over her body.

"You know my dreams, Jaci, and the feel of you beneath me beats each and every one of them."

She ran her fingers through his short hair, loving the feel of his weight pressing her into the soft covers. "I agree. Oh, Michael! I've wanted this for so long."

He licked at her lips, settling his mouth over hers with intent before delving inside, tantalizing her with skilful sweeps of his tongue over hers.

Her temperature went higher still as his hands swept over

her body. She felt the bed dip and knew David was there, watching them, enjoying them.

Michael sat up, breaking the kiss. She watched him, noting the look that passed between the cousins. Undoubtedly they were speaking telepathically, hatching plots of some kind. In one way, she didn't like being left out of their thoughts, but in another, she enjoyed the tantalizing uncertainty of what they would do next.

This was far different from dreams. In dreams, they all shared their thoughts. But if she needed any further proof that this was no dream, the cousins' display of their human psychic powers brought it home like nothing else. This was real. They were here. With her. Finally!

David nodded at Michael—the men had apparently reached some kind of agreement—and then Michael turned his full attention back to her. He moved between her thighs, parting them with strong but gentle hands as he made room for himself. He sat back on his haunches, just looking at her, and his smile touched the deepest recesses of her heart.

"I haven't had a woman in a long time. And I've never been with one I loved more than life." His eyes met hers and held. She read deep emotion there, the kind that made her breath catch. "I can't wait any longer to be inside you, Jaci. I know it's too fast, but Dave will help us out. He'll help you enjoy it and if I totally mess up, he'll be there to make it up to you." Michael grinned at her, winking, then shared the grin with his cousin. "And if Dave messes up, I'll probably be ready by then to make it up to you."

"Speak for yourself, cuz." David moved closer on the bed, leaning up so that he was near her upper body while Michael ruled her lower half. "Are you ready for this, Jaci? Neither of us want to rush you, but you have to know, we're desperate men."

The twinkle in his eye belied his words and she felt a rush of affection for them both. She knew they'd had little relief for far too long and she couldn't deny them anything they wanted of her. She knew, deep in her heart, they loved her as much as she loved them—miracle that it was.

"I want what you want, David." She reached up to cup his cheek, coaxing him down for a quick kiss that turned to a gasp as Michael parted her folds and delved within, using his fingers to test her readiness.

David broke the kiss and looked down her body to his cousin. "Is she ready?"

"Oh, yeah." Michael moved closer, sliding his fingers through her wet folds. "I can't wait, Dave."

"Don't wait!" Jaci nearly screamed as David's hands moved to her breasts, followed quickly by his talented mouth. He sucked her while Michael replaced fingers with his thick cock. Her temperature spiked as he pushed inward.

"Damn, that's hot." Michael's breath came in harsh pants as he paused at her entrance. "I love the heat of your skin, Jaci. It's so different and sexy."

Different from a human woman, she knew. It was one of the things she'd worried about when she realized she'd be taking human lovers. Her body was different than a human woman's in subtle ways, but the most obvious difference was the way her temperature spiked when she came. She'd hoped they wouldn't notice, or if they did, that they'd be able to get past it. She never dreamed they'd actually like it, but that's exactly what Michael was saying. The thought gave her relief for a worry she hadn't actually realized she'd harbored.

"I love you, Michael," she whispered. "Please! Do it now!"

With a growl, Michael complied. He forged within her tight sheath with steady pressure, making way for his thick cock inside her wet channel. She thought she'd die from the pleasure and he hadn't even really started yet. This was way better than any dream.

"Jaci!" Michael stilled once he'd pushed all the way inside. She'd never been so filled. David backed off and Jaci opened her eyes, meeting Michael's hazy gaze. His eyes almost seemed to glow, so taken were they both by the moment. And then he began to move, breaking the spell.

His motions were jerky and rough and she loved every moment, every motion. David held her shoulders, anchoring her to the bed as Michael dominated her lower body. For her first true mating with the cousins, she wouldn't have changed a thing. Her temperature kept reaching new highs as her body flooded the path Michael forged inside her, changing her expectations of lovemaking for all time—most definitely for the better—and neither of them had climaxed yet. She didn't know if she would survive.

"Take him, Jaci. Make him yours. Make us yours. Forever." David bent near her ear, sucking the lobe into his mouth, whispering encouragement only she could hear.

Michael's movements grew shorter and more forceful and Jaci loved it. Guttural sounds were forced from her throat as she reached for the highest peak she'd ever seen, much less dreamed.

"Come for us now, love," David encouraged in a deep, urgent whisper. "He's about to lose it and he needs you with him. Go with him, Jaci. Go now!"

Pleasure exploded over her in waves that threatened to drown, but she was beyond caring. She felt Michael's seed warm her deep inside as he tensed and came inside her. She loved the feel of it, having never experienced unprotected male release within her. The thought occurred to her hazy mind that she could very well get pregnant from this kind of contact and the thought warmed her even more.

A baby. Their baby. She'd love it and nurture it as she'd love and nurture Michael and David for however many days she had left in this life.

She floated back to earth, luxuriating in the feel of Michael's heavy body blanketing hers. He kissed her and her eyes flickered open to meet his. The smile on his face was uncertain and she loved that he worried about her, even after his own momentous release.

"Are you okay?"

She smiled up at him. "Never better. *Never.* Oh, Michael!"

His grin widened. "That good, eh? Damn." He leaned down to kiss her sweetly, then backed off. "I'd lay here and bask with you for hours, but Dave has something he wants to give you."

"I don't think I can have another orgasm after that," she said honestly, making the cousins laugh as Michael moved to lie at her side.

"Oh, we'll get to that, Jaci," David promised as he leaned up on her other side to look at her. "But first, we wanted to give you this." Michael lifted her left hand and David slid a ring on the third finger. She'd seen some of the human prisoners with gold bands like this on the same finger and she thought she knew what it meant. "This is a wedding band, Jaci. It's the sign of our commitment. The sign of our love. Will you wear it and be our wife?"

Tears gathered behind her eyes as she sat up, flanked by the cousins. She fingered the delicate band of gold, gazing at the tangible symbol of their culture. That they would go to the trouble of procuring it for her touched her deeply.

"Ruth made the ring," Michael said. "She said if you didn't like it or it didn't fit, she could change it."

"Oh, no! It's perfect." Jaci felt the tears fall down her cheeks as she gazed at the ring that meant so much. Such a small thing to affect her so deeply, she thought. But it was the thought behind the golden band, and the love it represented, that brought on the tears.

David tipped up her chin with one gentle finger. "Will you wear our ring, Jaci?"

He looked so unsure, so strong yet loving. She flung her arms around him and kissed his cheek. "Yes! Oh, yes!" David drew back and she hugged Michael too, knowing the ring was from both of them, just as the love came from both. As she loved them.

"Now let's see about that orgasm I owe you," David said with a lusty grin as he lifted her with his hands around her waist. He positioned her on her hands and knees and went to his knees behind her.

She knew what came next from their shared dreams, but it had never felt this good, or this loving. She looked down at her hands, seeing the beautiful gold band glimmering there, reminding her of their love, of their care.

David pushed into her, his long cock sliding in deep and easy. She loved the feel of him and though she wouldn't have believed it a moment ago, she felt her temperature begin an upward climb. It was slow and steady this time, but no less powerful. It rose in response to David's steady thrusts and his hands on her ass. He stroked her inside and out, praising her responses and urging her on with lusty, low-pitched words.

Jaci squeaked when David reached around and pinched her nipples. The sound seemed to rouse Michael from his semi-stupor and he rose on one elbow to watch her. After a few moments, he moved on the bed, positioning his head under her swaying breasts as David's hands moved lower, to tease the place where they were joined together.

Michael took up where David left off, stroking her nipples with his fingers and tongue, following the sway of her heavy breasts as David pushed her back and forth with his thrusts.

The build-up was slow and steady, though she could feel the strain in David's tight muscles. He was holding back for her sake, but she didn't want that. She wanted him to enjoy this as much as she did.

"Faster, David!" she urged him in a choked voice. He complied and she tried her best to squeeze him on each inward thrust, drawing grunts from his throat that made her temperature spike. "Harder! Shards! David, please!"

The thrusts were fast, hard, and oh-so-pleasurable as he lost control. Michael held her by the shoulders, holding her up as he sucked her excited nipples deep into his mouth, one at a time. She needed him there, holding her up, or she would've been forced across the bed by the power of David's strokes.

And she loved every minute of it.

Michael moved away from her breasts to kiss her mouth. He moved back further, bracing her against David's almost-violent motions. "All right, Jaci?" he asked, worry in his expression.

She cried out, unable to answer in words as her passions rose higher. Her body was steaming now, hotter than before, more aroused than she would have credited given the amazing release she'd just had from Michael.

"I'm gonna blow," David warned. "Come now, Jaci. Now!" He swatted her ass just once, driving her into the most amazing orgasm she'd ever experienced. She screamed as she came, glad to hear the answering groan torn from David's throat.

She felt the warm torrent inside her as David's seed flooded her womb and again she thought of the children they could have. Incubated in her body. Such joy filled her that she felt tears wet her cheeks as her body jerked with waves of completion that were uncontrollable and incontrovertible.

Michael caught her as she collapsed, stunned by the response she'd given both him and his cousin. If he'd had any doubts whatsoever, they'd just been blown to smithereens. She was theirs, body and soul.

Dave left her, rolling over on the coverlet, totally drained. Mike knew how he felt. Jaci in dreams was fantastic. In real life, she blew his mind. If he had his way, they'd never be separated now. He'd give his last breath to see that they stayed together.

She was shaking as she came down from the climax. She was so beautiful, it almost hurt to look at her and Mike didn't know how he'd gotten so lucky to have a woman like this in his life. Sure, he had to share her, but it was a different world now and he had to live by new standards. Plus, if he had to share his woman with anyone, there was nobody he'd rather share her with than his cousin, Mike. They'd been friends all their lives—business partners, partners in running from the Alvians and they'd likely spend the rest of their lives working together and loving Jaci. It was as ideal a setup as they'd achieve in this brave new world.

Mike turned her in his arms, loving the solid feel of her after holding her only in dreams for so long. He tucked her into the big bed, realizing she probably would be more comfortable if he cleaned her up a bit before they all caught some sleep.

That thought in mind, he went to the attached bathroom. They'd checked the water system first thing, astounded to find it ready for use, though there'd probably be no hot water until they located and fired up the boiler. That would be the first order of business...tomorrow. For now, cold water would do.

The room was stocked with clean towels and for a moment Mike felt nostalgic for the old world. If he didn't think too hard, he could pretend he was staying at a hotel, stocked with familiar human items and creature comforts. But he wasn't. He and his cousin—Jaci too—had to come to terms with the new world. They could hide out here, sure, but eventually, they'd need to rejoin the real world.

But this is where they'd regroup. If and when the time came for them to contribute to the ongoing struggle, this place—the opportunity it presented for them to be together without any constraints—would give them strength.

Mike wet a washcloth and shook off his dreary thoughts, returning to the brightest part of his life to date—Jaci. He cleaned her gently, loving her, caring for her slightest comfort, knowing it was an honor and privilege to take care of her. It was something he enjoyed doing and would enjoy for the rest of his days.

Dave caught his gaze as he threw the now-dirty cloth toward the tile floor in the bathroom through the door he'd left partially open. One raised eyebrow spoke volumes.

"Give me a break, Dave. We have to take care of her." Mike used their shared telepathy so they wouldn't wake Jaci, now sound asleep.

"You like taking care of her," David accused.

"Can you blame me? Damn, Dave. I never expected to have a woman of my own. Not in this changed world. I'm going to enjoy spoiling her as much as I possibly can."

Dave chuckled quietly. *"I've never seen this mother hen side of you before, cuz."*

Mike got in bed beside Jaci, loving the feel of her warm body next to him. *"I never loved a woman before, Dave."*

Dave settled down on Jaci's other side. *"I never did either,*

Mike, but I never knew it until we met her."

Chapter Fourteen

When Mike woke the next morning, Jaci was still sound asleep and Dave was in the bathroom. Dave's movement must've woken him, Mike guessed as he sat up and swung his legs over the side of the bed, rubbing his face.

"Hey, Mike? You up, cuz?" Dave's silent call sounded through his mind.

"If I wasn't already, I am now." Mike scratched as the day's growth of beard stubble on his jaw.

"Come in here, you gotta see this."

"Dude, this better not be some juvenile prank."

"It's not. Mike, the water from the tap is hot. I mean, really hot."

That spurred Mike into action. He crept from the bed to the bathroom as quietly as possible. Dave had the presence of mind to shut the light before he opened the door for Mike to enter, in consideration of Jaci, who still slept soundly.

The water coming from the hot tap on the faucet was indeed hot, which brought forth a number of questions.

"You think Bill switched on the water heater?"

"It's a possibility, but I doubt human-built hot water heaters are much like Alvian systems. It's more likely that this system runs on some kind of energy that didn't need to be replenished

and was left on. Geothermal, perhaps? Though I'm no expert."

"This water does feel a little...sparkly for lack of a better word."

"Are you thinking what I'm thinking?"

The cousins looked at each other. *"Hot springs."* They said it at the same time, in both their minds.

"Damn, that would be awesome. No worry about power if it's coming directly from the earth. We gotta find the source. See if we're right," Mike said and Dave nodded in full agreement.

"All right. I've already had a shower. They left soap and shampoo stocked in the medicine cabinet. You grab one while I dress and we can start exploring."

David left the small room and Mike hit the shower, but they continued to plan telepathically.

"What about Jaci? She'll probably want to come with us and I think it's best we stick together until we've gone through this whole place. For all we know, we're not alone down here. Maybe there's somebody else who kept the hot water flowing."

"I think we would have noticed if anyone was in here by now, but you're right. For now we should stick together."

"What about Bill?" Mike asked.

"We definitely owe him for rescuing Jaci, but he strikes me as a lone wolf. We'll take him with us on the first run-through of the place, but after that, he's big enough to take care of himself."

"You trust him then?"

"As much as I can trust any Alvian, I guess, but it's in his best interests to keep this place secure. He saved Jaci once. He wouldn't mess that up now. I don't think he has any reason to betray us."

"Good point."

Mike shut off the taps, feeling refreshed after the hot

shower. He wrapped a towel around his waist and shut the light before heading out into the bedroom. Dave was dressed, sitting on the side of the bed, staring down at Jaci. The look on his face spoke volumes about the love he felt for this Alvian woman—their mate.

Mike cleared his throat and Dave sat back. "I guess it's time to wake her," he said aloud.

"I'm awake." Jaci stretched, her voice tempered with sleep as she moved under the covers.

David leaned forward and placed a smacking kiss on her lips. "Are you up for some exploring today?"

Her eyes opened fully and she rose up on her elbows. She looked around, as if needing a reminder about where she was. She was so adorable, Mike was hard pressed not to join her on that bed and show her just how much he loved her...again. Even though they'd spent half the night humping like bunnies in the greatest sexual marathon he'd ever experienced.

Down boy, he told his wayward dick as it tried to tent the towel.

"Much as I'd love to stay here all day and make love to you, Jaci..." Mike put one knee on the bed, bending forward to give her a good morning kiss, "...we really need to explore the rest of this facility today. For one thing, we need to find the source of the hot water."

"Hot water?" That seemed to spark her interest as she came slowly awake.

"Yeah, the taps are fully functional, which is something we didn't expect." Mike flung the covers off the bed, exposing her beautiful, bare body. "Go take a shower. We'll wait for you in the living room and then we'll pick up your friend Bill and go see where the hot water is coming from. What do you say?"

"Sounds like a good plan, though I also would have liked to

spend all day in bed. Still, I'm sore in places I have never been sore in before, so hot water and exercise is probably a good idea." Her blush stole his heart. How she could be even the tiniest bit shy after all they'd shared, he didn't know, but it was endearing.

He patted her shapely ass as she hopped out of bed and headed for the bathroom. "Hurry up. There's a lot of ground to cover today and the sooner we finish, the sooner we can come back here and make love."

She paused at the bathroom door to smile back at him over her shoulder. "I will hold you to that."

"Honey, you can *hold me* all night long."

A smile stretched his face as she disappeared into the bathroom and he turned to find Dave watching him with a grin on his face.

"What?" Mike groused.

"It's good to see you happy, Mike. That's all. It's been too long since we were both happy."

"Far too long."

They shared a moment of silent communication before Dave stirred. "I'll go roust Bill while you get dressed. I'll bring him to the living room, so come out when you're ready. We'll leave from here."

"Sounds like a plan, cuz."

Before they could leave the suite, a new but familiar voice sounded in the cousins' minds. Mick O'Hara sent them a mental "knock" before imparting his news and the cousins had to laugh at his tact. Mick knew damn well what they'd be up to after so many months away from their mate.

"Listen up, guys. I wish I had better news but Caleb sent a

warning through Harry last night and Justin went out into the woods at first light. Grady Prime is gone."

"Gone?" Dave felt a shiver go down his spine at the news. *"He's sure?"*

"He's sure. Grady had a ship stashed nearby. It was well hidden, but Justin found it. It's gone and all traces of Grady's camp sites have been erased."

"So he went back home to the city then?" Mike asked.

"Harry checked every which way he knew how to check, including hacking into Alvian military computers. Grady's still off the grid. Coupled with Caleb's visions of danger, I think you need to stay on your toes."

"Son of a bitch!" Dave was both pissed off and worried. Not a comfortable combination.

"Justin has no idea how Grady knew Jaci left or how he could have any idea where she went, but Grady's always been spooky. Justin wants you to be careful. Don't set foot outside the cave entrance until we know where Grady is."

"No shit," Mike grumbled. *"We've got a lot to explore in here. We won't go out, but we'll need to watch the entrance. We'll need to find out if there's more than one entrance."*

"There have got to be schematics of this place somewhere." Dave tried to stay calm but it was tempting to curse a blue streak at this upsetting news. *"We'll look for those first thing and secure the entrances as best we can from the inside."*

"Good idea. I'll be in touch as soon as we have any news for you. Stay sharp."

"Thanks for the warning, Mick. Your family has gone above and beyond for us in so many ways..." Dave couldn't finish the thought as emotion welled up.

"Don't mention it." Mick's tone held understanding and

compassion. *"We're all in this together, Dave. Humans have got to stick together and help each other when we can if we're going to survive."*

"Amen, brother." Mike's respectful words summed up Dave's feelings as well.

Bill was the one who actually found the schematics for the facility. The man was a cunning scout and even though he didn't know human tech as well as the cousins, he was a fast learner. Bill led them to what proved to be the nerve center for the entire facility. Inside were a series of manuals on every system in the place as well as the core of the giant computer that was in a low-power mode, maintaining bare minimums in the place in preparation for a new shift of inhabitants that hadn't shown up for decades.

With any luck, the computer would let them take up where the last residents of this place had left off, but Mike knew military computers could be fickle. Still, he decided to give this one a try. With a silent Hail Mary, he switched it on.

"Welcome." The somewhat androgynous voice sounded from small speakers built into the walls. Mike hadn't expected a voice interface, but then, this whole facility was unexpected.

"Thank you," Mike responded, unsure of what to say as he looked over at his cousin.

"You're late," the computer voice scolded, surprising him. "Last shift change was incomplete, so I scanned news databases and learned of the bombardment from space. I followed the news until it stopped being broadcast. Can you tell me what has happened since then?"

Mike sat back in his chair, astounded.

"Artificial intelligence?" Dave asked telepathically.

"A really advanced form, I'm guessing. We'll have to tread lightly here."

"You're the master where computers are concerned, Mike. Go for it."

"The bombardment from space was the precursor to an alien invasion. Most humans perished, but some of us lived on in the more desolate areas of the earth. The aliens built cities and engineering facilities. They took some humans captive, but a few of the aliens have begun to help us escape. My cousin and I are escapees from the nearest alien city. Our wife is an alien and she helped us, as did her friend here."

"I scanned your presence and noted the differences between your physiologies. They are not major, but enough so that I will be able to tell aliens from humans in the future." The computer continued to amaze. "Why did you come here and why did you reactivate me?"

"We intended to live here, if you permit it. This is one of the few places we can be free from detection by the aliens. To be honest, I thought I was turning on a regular computer. I didn't realize you were an AI."

"My name is BURTIN. Basic Underground Resident Type 1 Intelligence Net. I was designed to run this facility. Apocalyptic scenarios were programmed but I don't think anyone expected it to occur, or they would have been here when it happened."

"So you were alone during the bombardment?"

"Powered down, awaiting a new crew," the machine confirmed. "There were some budgetary changes."

Mike well remembered the way governments used to work and the bureaucracy involved. In many ways, they were better off without all that, but then, governments had brought order and accomplished great things when all their people worked together.

"Would you allow us to live here, BURTIN?" Mike asked outright. It paid to be clear with computers. Perhaps AI powered computer brains would be just as straightforward.

"Yes. One of my primary missions is the continuation and protection of the human race."

"What about our alien friends?" Dave asked, speaking for the first time.

The computer seemed to think before answering. "Your DNA has shared traits. I would like further analysis, but I think sheltering them would not be incompatible with my mission. They are very close to human."

That was news to the cousins, but it sounded promising.

"Our wife may be able to assist with your analysis. She was a genetic tech in the alien city before she escaped." Mike held out one hand for Jaci, noting her pale features.

"That would be agreeable," the computer responded.

"I'm Mike, this is my cousin, Dave, and this is our mate, Jaci and her friend, Bill. We're all pleased to make your acquaintance, BURTIN." It couldn't hurt to be polite, Mike reasoned.

"And to meet you, Mike, Dave, Jaci and Bill." Mike was right. The computer was very polite indeed.

"We may need your help, BURTIN." Dave stepped up, holding a large drawing of the facility in his hands as he scowled at it. "There are alien soldiers—one in particular—who may try to seek entrance to this facility in order to apprehend us. We'd like to secure the facility so that nobody can gain admittance without our knowledge and approval. Is that possible?"

"It is one of my primary functions," the computer replied. "I monitor the locks on all ingress and egress points. All are in good working order and secure at this time. I have a log of entries and exits that occurred while I was powered down that you can examine."

"That's great." Mike was impressed with the capacity of this amazing computer brain. "Can you give us active alerts if someone tries to enter?"

"Affirmative. Voice alerts are now active."

"This is going to be easier than I thought," Mike sent the words silently to his cousin.

"Let's not count our chickens before they're hatched." Dave, as usual, was the voice of caution.

Mike spent an hour or more talking to the computer before they realized the computer could "follow" them anywhere they went in the facility. There were speakers and pickups throughout the complex so the voice interface could be accessed from just about any location.

BURTIN led them to the hot springs that were the source of the facility's hot water. He also explained how the temperature was held steady by a geothermal heating system. Electricity was generated underground by a clever combination of hidden wind tunnels equipped with turbines that rotated when the wind whipped through the specially designed channels in the rocks near the top of the mountain. As power was generated, it was stored for future use in a series of batteries that were maintained by a fleet of specially designed robotic caretakers directed by one of BURTIN's many subsystems. It was ingenious. Renewable, clean, sustainable, and totally self-contained.

Air was purified through charcoal filtration units in the upper chambers and piped in through the tunnels, and there was a vast underground lake that supplied fresh, cold water for many different areas of the complex. The lake was one of the few places where BURTIN's speakers couldn't reach, so they explored it on their own, without their computer guide. They had flashlights from the facility's store room and a big hand-held spotlight that had been left in a water-tight locker near the edge of the lake. Dave shone the spotlight across the black surface of the lake, but they couldn't see the farthest edge. The cavern was enormous.

"The rock is different here," Bill noted, drawing their attention.

"Limestone," Dave said, taking a close look at the wet walls. "It's really porous. Rainwater must drip in here constantly, purified by its journey through the rock. Brilliant, really, to use this water for the place. It's pure and cold and as long as it rains up top, it'll never run out."

Bill took off his shirt and spread his wings. It was the first time the cousins had actually seen his wings and Mike marveled at both the wingspan and thickness of those feathery appendages. It was one of the strangest things he'd ever seen. It also reminded him eerily of descriptions of angels he'd heard in his youth.

"If that don't beat all." Dave's words came directly to Mike's mind. *"Any human sees him, they'll think we've got a divine messenger on our hands. Dude looks like an angel right out of the Bible."*

"I was just thinking the same thing."

"You remember what Caleb O'Hara wrote, don't you?"

"You mean the bit about the angel in disguise?"

"I believe his words were something like, 'a blond giant named for Hickok, who's an angel in disguise.' I think that fits our boy, don't you?"

"No shit. They call him Wild Bill. And he's supposed to lead the resistance?"

"Caleb called him the 'father of the revolution'."

"I wonder if he has any idea." Mike looked at the giant alien and his equally alien wings. *Wings*, for cripes sake!

"I don't think he has a clue. The man is still coming to terms with his past. He's got a boatload of guilt in him and still needs to integrate a lot of emotion. He's probably been in denial since the emotions started kicking in."

"Funny how he wound up here, with a mind healer ready and able to help him." Mike shot his cousin a knowing look.

"I've never believed in coincidences."

While the cousins conjectured silently, Bill took one of the high-powered flashlights and stepped to the water's edge. "I want to see how far across it is and how high this cavern goes."

"Be careful," Jaci warned him. "There may be obstacles in the darkness. Don't run into anything. And there could also be creatures in the water."

"Yeah," Dave agreed. "The Loch Ness Monster could be waiting below for a giant bird to fly across so he can eat you."

Mike laughed but the two Alvians had apparently never heard of Nessie. He'd have to enlighten them sometime, but Bill took to the air a second later and their attention was diverted by the amazing sight of a man with wings, flying across the mirror surface of a black lake.

They followed his progress with the spotlight, but soon all they could see was the pinpoint of Bill's flashlight in the distance. Jaci sidled over to Mike and took his hand, fearing for her friend. He tried to reassure her, bending to give her a kiss to take her mind off Bill's solo flight into the unknown.

Much to his surprise, the light level suddenly increased. Mike looked up to see flecks of crystal embedded in the walls, glowing as he kissed his resonance mate.

"Hot damn." Dave glanced around. "Kiss her again, Mike. I can just make out Bill in the distance. If we can get more light out of the crystals, we might be able to see the far walls of the cavern."

Mike didn't need any more encouragement. He pulled Jaci into his arms and laid one on her. The light level jumped again as he deepened the embrace.

"That's handy." Mike came up for air, looking around at the lit chamber. "We'll need to keep you around so we can see where we're going."

Jaci pushed at him, laughing. "It's the resonance." She glanced around in wonder. "The small remnants of crystal here respond to the resonance of our embrace. I've never seen the like before, except in news reports of Davin's interactions with his mate before the High Council."

"We've seen it first hand." Dave took her other hand. "Callie and her mates can light up a room with just a touch. As can we, apparently." Dave nodded to the glowing walls. "There's not a lot of crystal here. I bet if we find larger deposits, we'll be able to achieve daylight down here."

They put their theory to the test when they found a small crystal-studded hot spring cavern back near the main entrance to the complex, just outside the fortified doors. They'd debated before leaving the comparative safety of the blast doors that sealed the tunnel entrance to the complex, but the men wanted to explore the outside tunnels a little farther. As long as they didn't actually go outside the cave network, they reasoned, it should be reasonably safe with good ol' Burt on guard.

When BURTIN mentioned this spot, he'd assured them the spring that fed this small pool wasn't hooked into the water supply. He'd also said the former inhabitants of the facility used the small grotto for recreation—bathing and soaking in the revitalizing mineral water.

After a long day of exploring, that sounded like just the thing. Jaci, Mike and Dave left Bill behind on watch with the computer and took off for some splash therapy in the hot spring. They frolicked there for an hour before heading back into the safety of the blast doors, welcomed by BURTIN who was monitoring everything in the facility on a heightened basis.

The trio made love long into the night and rose the next day for another round of discovery in their new home. They couldn't perceive day or night while underground, of course, but BURTIN kept the clocks working and on the second day they discovered the true extent of BURTIN's very advanced and well-camouflaged security system. It came complete with cameras that kept track of what went on above ground. A monitoring station with multiple camera angles covered miles of territory all around the complex, though there were a few blind spots where cameras had malfunctioned over time.

"Why didn't we see the cameras?" Dave asked as they monitored the landscape above, marveling at the views.

"Most of the cameras were made to look like rocks," BURTIN answered in his androgynous voice. "A few have become irreparably damaged over the years. I have small robots I dispatch to perform routine maintenance on the systems and was programmed to run diagnostics once every year even while powered down. Some of the cameras look like tree limbs or sticks, but all are very small and well hidden so as to avoid detection."

"No kidding," Dave agreed with the machine as he leaned in to look at another row of monitors. "What's this?"

"Heat sensor," BURTIN replied. "There are also motion, radiation and infrared detectors."

"Amazing." Dave flicked a few switches, bringing up

different views. Mike had to bite back a laugh at his cousin's interest. In the old world, Dave had left all the tech stuff up to Mike. Now it seemed he couldn't get enough. How things had changed.

"What's this?" Jaci pointed to a monitor that showed a long, empty room with strange equipment inside. "This is an interior view, isn't it?"

"Yes," BURTIN agreed. "This is the hydroponics sector. There were plans to use the water from the cavern you saw yesterday to grow crops hydroponically. All the equipment is there and ready for use, but the last inhabitants never stocked any seeds. There were—"

"—budget cuts," Mike finished for the computer. "Right?"

"Yes, Mike," BURTIN replied. "But there are many ration packs here. Some of the stored food might still be fit for consumption."

"We brought supplies," Dave said. "And we may even be able to get seeds if that hydroponics setup is still viable."

"It is indeed viable," the computer replied.

"That could come in very handy," Dave said, looking to Mike for agreement. If their little community grew, it would indeed be useful to be able to grow some of their own food.

"Let's think about setting up a small test run for now," Mike said. "Maybe the O'Haras can give us some pointers and seeds to get started."

"Which reminds me," Dave turned back to the monitors, flicking through the channels until he found the view of the main entrance to the tunnels. "Burt, we are expecting a friend to join us here today or tomorrow. He's coming over land and will probably have a horse or mule. Maybe two. His name is Sam and he's human. Could you let us know if you spot anyone?"

"Yes, Dave. I will alert you to approach by any humanoids or machines within my active scanning area. That's what my former commanders elected. Will that suit you as well?"

"Definitely," Dave agreed with a huge smile. "It's a pleasure to work with you, Burt. Thanks."

"You're welcome, Dave."

Oh yes, their computer friend was very polite.

A few hours later, BURTIN alerted them to an approaching visitor. They all crowded around the monitors until they recognized Sam's stealthy approach.

"I'll go out and meet him," Bill volunteered.

Bill brought Sam and two pack mules through the main entrance a few minutes later. Sam seemed glad to see them all and wasn't very surprised to meet Dave and Mike. The O'Haras had warned him that their arrival was a possibility.

"Damned if I know what we're going to do with the mules," Dave mused as the cousins stood back and watched the reunion of Sam with his two friends.

"There are facilities for livestock on the fourth level," BURTIN chimed in, startling Sam until they explained about the intelligent computer.

They filled him in on their discoveries about the place as they took the animals down a series of wide, gently sloping tunnels that corkscrewed through the complex. They unpacked the animals, rubbed them down and left them with water and some of the grain Sam had brought with him. He explained that the mules were a loan and could be returned anytime or used for as long as they needed them. Justin O'Hara had thought some extra *horsepower* might come in handy depending on what they found inside the mine.

Sam had also packed some gifts from the O'Haras and he gave them out as he sorted through the packs. There were baked goods from Jane for them to share, other food items and perishable goods as well. Lengths of rope from Justin and medical supplies from Mick. All the things they might need for living on their own for a while. It was a treasure trove for them, considering everything in the complex was decades out of date. A few items could be salvaged, of course, and the physical plant seemed to be in good working order, but things like food and medicines were at a premium.

Sam handed one particular burlap sack to Bill, much to his surprise. "Caleb O'Hara sent very specific instructions to his brothers before I left. I was supposed to give this to you, Bill. Caleb says you need to nurture life, whatever that means."

Intrigued, they all watched Bill open the bag. It was full of seeds. Mike recognized corn, cucumber, melon and other kinds as well as smaller ones, packaged in paper with handwritten instructions on the side. Once again, the Oracle had foreseen their needs.

"What is this?" Bill asked, his expression nothing short of confused. Jaci was just as confused and it brought home how far the Alvians had gone from living off the land.

"Those are seeds, Bill," Mike said as gently as possible. "From those, food crops will grow. Caleb just sent us the beginnings of our little hydroponics experiment."

"But why did he send them to me?" Bill still looked confused. "I've never created life or nurtured it in any way. I have no idea how to make things grow."

"Maybe that's why," Dave said, understanding in his voice. Mike recognized that tone. This was Doctor Dave, counseling a patient who needed him. Mike stood back and let Dave work his magic. "A garden can be therapeutic. It can teach us things about ourselves and our world. I think it's important for you to take charge of the hydroponics experiment, Bill. Caleb O'Hara must have foreseen something that made him bother his brothers, Sam and us with this special request and that man hasn't been wrong yet. We've done well taking his advice and I think you would benefit from it too."

"If you're sure." Bill still looked uncertain.

"I'm sure," Dave's tone was reassuring. "Gardening is often a very solitary occupation. It allows time for the soul to commune with nature and is said to bring peace. I think you need that now, Bill. Even more, I think you'll enjoy it." Mike had noticed how quiet and introspective Bill was most of the time and he knew Dave had picked up on it too.

Bill held Dave's gaze for a long moment before stepping back into the shadows with a curt nod. He'd be their gardener for now, which was apparently what the Oracle wanted. Dave was right. They could do far worse than follow Caleb O'Hara's instructions.

They ate together that night, dining on the delicious food Jane O'Hara had sent along. It was a celebration of sorts, a time for the cousins to get to know the men who had rescued their mate. Dave found a bottle of whiskey in the commander's quarters that had only gotten better with age and shared it around. They only had a shot or two each—wanting to prolong the remnant of Earth's past glory—but it was enough to leave the cousins feeling pleasantly uninhibited and Jaci was downright naughty.

Alvians, it seemed, could not hold their liquor. She was fast asleep after only one round of loving, laid low by the combination of pleasure and very old Scotch whiskey.

Dave and Mike left her sleeping and did more exploring

around the huge facility, enjoying the quiet hours of the night. Bill was fast asleep, also done in by the Scotch, and Sam was tired from his trek, so it was just Mike, Dave and BURTIN. The complex was quiet, the lights lowered to nighttime levels to help the inhabitants keep track of what time it was in the world above.

Respecting the quiet, Dave and Mike spoke telepathically, used to keeping their innermost thoughts to themselves after years in captivity.

"Emotionally, Bill's a mess." Dave's words surprised Mike. He'd known the Alvian warrior was conflicted, but he'd never heard Dave assess someone so starkly. It had to be bad for Dave to lose his usual professional demeanor.

"In what way? Could he be a danger to Jaci?"

"I don't think so. The man is consumed by guilt and self-loathing, but he's got a core of steel, Mike. He's an honorable guy. If he weren't, he wouldn't have made it this far after they awakened his emotions."

Rick and Davin had told them a little about Bill's past on the flight up here. They'd been reluctant to speak of the man who'd been Sinclair Prime, but they'd decided—rightly so, Mike thought—that the cousins needed to know what they were walking into.

"Even knowing what he was, I feel kind of sorry for him, Dave. He didn't choose his life. He was bred to be a killer. Hell, they even gave him wings so he could drop in from above to silence his victims. What must they have gone through to give him wings? And what must he have gone through, hiding them all his life except when training with his keepers?"

"I think his instincts were always at war with his predetermined path. Anything with wings wants to fly free, but an assassin always has to keep to the shadows. It's a paradox

that must have created an internal, instinctual conflict in him even before they tinkered with his emotions."

"Poor guy."

"Yeah," Dave agreed.

"Do you think you can help him?"

"At this point, I don't think he'll let me close enough to even try. Maybe in time. I think Caleb's onto something giving him the role of head gardener. Bill needs to learn how to nurture. He's got the instincts or he wouldn't have been taking in strays like Sam and Jaci, or keeping watch over the O'Hara ranch. Give him a few hundred baby plants to develop those instincts more and maybe he'll start to heal on his own—at least enough to get him to the point where he'll accept my help."

"But do you really want to help him?" There was the big question. Bill was Alvian, after all. A soldier. A former Prime and master assassin. Did they really want to help him? Did he deserve it?

He'd saved Jaci's life and Sam's too. He'd pulled his shot at the last minute and missed Davin when he'd been sent out with orders to end the Chief Engineer's life. He'd changed from the ruthless Alvian assassin he'd once been. He had feelings now and nurturing instincts, though he didn't seem to recognize them at all.

Bill had a lot to learn.

But everyone deserved a second chance. Mike was a firm believer in that. As was Dave.

"I want to help him," Dave confirmed Mike's thoughts. *"Deep down, he's an honorable man. And on a practical note, with his skills, he could be a great asset to us and any other human refugees we might come across. And what Caleb O'Hara predicted keeps running through my mind. Bill could be the start of something...eventually. But for now, he could be a big help*

getting this place habitable."

"So you've given further thought to the idea of setting this complex up as a sort of sanctuary?"

"Yeah. Come on, Mike, you have to admit it's a perfect setup. We even have a smart computer that's kept the place functional all these years. It's like it was meant for us. I think, once we get used to the place and get it spiffed up a bit, we should seriously consider letting just a few select people know we're willing to take in those, like us, who are on the run and need a place to hide. It's what the O'Haras want and what Caleb expects, plus, it just feels right. You can't deny that."

Mike shook his head with a faint smile. *"No, I can't deny it, though I had no idea we'd start ourselves a half-way house for troubled fugitives, be they Alvian or human. The only things that worry me are Bill's wings. How are we going to deal with the predictable human reaction to seeing them? I mean, we can't ask him not to fly. After all the years he's had to hide his wings, he can at least fly around down here without fear of discovery. I wouldn't want to take that away from him."*

"You've always been a soft touch, Mike." Dave rolled his eyes at his cousin, but he was grinning. *"But I agree with you. The guy needs to fly. I guess we'll have to deal with our tenants' reactions—if and when we get any tenants—when we get to that point. It might even work in our favor. Angels are the good guys in most human belief systems."*

"They're also the harbingers of change and messengers of momentous events."

"I don't know how just yet, but we might work that to our advantage some day."

§

A few days later, Bill found Sam skipping stones at the edge of the vast underground lake. The lovers had been here earlier and the walls still glowed with echoes of their resonance. Bill had wanted to spend some time stretching his wings in the vast cavern above the lake, but Sam's mood spoke to him.

Bill was learning to read emotions better the longer he observed humans, and the more he became used to his own emotions. Each new revelation Bill achieved made him feel that much closer to sanity and reminded him of all he'd lost and all he'd gained. Each time he discovered some new way of reading people and recognizing that he had the same emotions in his own psyche, he knew every last trial was worth it. He wouldn't go back to the way he was—even if it could remove the pain.

For pain let him know he was alive. The pain of his past and the guilt that sometimes threatened to swamp him were reminders that he was still here, among the living, not the lifeless automaton he'd been before. He'd sooner die than go back to that featureless existence and he pitied any Alvian who had to exist in ignorance of the emotions the scientists had so cavalierly discarded for their entire race.

Bill cleared his throat to alert Sam to his presence, but Sam had already known Bill was near. Sam was almost as good as Bill was when it came to sensing others in his vicinity.

"What troubles you?" Bill hoped he'd struck the right tone with his query. He was still very new at talking about emotions and even newer at having human friends.

"Mike and Dave told me about my daughter. They've seen her. And Ruth." Sam pitched a stone across the surface of the water with expert skill, watching it skip seven times before it succumbed to the power of gravity and sank beneath the rippling surface.

"Is Ruth the woman in your journal?" The answer was suddenly vital to Bill. That woman's image had haunted him.

Sam nodded. "We were only together a few days, but I've never forgotten her. She's special. If I believed in your people's ways, I'd say she was my mate—I feel that strongly about her—but we're both human."

Bill wondered if true resonance mating could occur between humans and he suspected, given the evidence of the O'Haras, it could indeed. Though the idea that the woman whose image was etched in his mind was already mated, grated on Bill's new emotions. He didn't understand it at all, but then, there were lots of things he didn't understand about emotion. He'd spend his lifetime learning it all.

"I'm missing so much of my daughter's life." When Bill didn't comment, Sam continued speaking, skipping stones and studying the lake. "Hell, I didn't even know about her 'til I met Jaci. She told me that Ruth talked about me and she named the baby Samantha—for her daddy." Sam's voice broke and Bill thought the man might be near tears, but he wasn't sure. Sam cleared his throat and went on in a stronger voice. "I never thought I'd have a child of my own, much less a little girl. This world is so hard for humans, Bill, and it's really bad for females in particular. I don't want my baby girl in danger every waking minute, much less her mother. My only consolation is that they're with Davin. I know he'll do his best to keep them safe, though his position is as precarious in some ways as theirs. I wonder how long the Alvian High Council will let him get away with defying them?"

Bill knew the answer to that one. "As long as they need power, I would imagine. Chief Engineer Davin has something they desperately need. They won't dare to destabilize him. As a throwback, they think him too volatile. They'll humor him as long as he gives them what they want—energy."

"But then why did they send you to kill him?" Sam turned to gaze at him with accusing eyes. Bill sighed. He knew he had much to answer for. This was the least of his sins.

"It was a minority faction of the Council that has since been eradicated. Davin and Rick saw to that. The display they made before the Council and all those news feeds did the rest. Nobody will go after Davin again. He's far too powerful now."

Sam's eyes narrowed. "You're sure? You wouldn't just say that to make me feel better?"

Bill didn't understand the concept well, but he did see that Sam needed reassurance. "I'm positive. I would not lie to you, Sam."

Sam stood and clapped Bill on the shoulder. "I'm glad to hear it." He walked past him and made for the tunnels heading back toward the main complex. "Thanks, Bill. Enjoy your flight."

Bill nodded, surprised Sam realized why he'd come to the giant, high-ceilinged cavern. But Sam was very observant for a human. In fact, Sam was the closest thing Bill had to a friend among his new acquaintances. He genuinely liked the man and respected his abilities.

Bill had had friends before, among the men he'd commanded, but they were far away now, lost in another life. And Bill couldn't be sure the camaraderie they'd shared had ever been true friendship—not the way he now understood the concept. They'd shared experiences and training, but they had never shared emotions of any sort. The emotional connection is what made friendship feel good, Bill realized as he took to the air with one powerful thrust of his wings.

His former comrades may have shared his physical attributes and abilities, but they'd never shared his feelings.

Chapter Fifteen

The four of them settled into a routine of sorts. Each day they checked the perimeter they'd set up within the tunnels and worked on restoring the facility. The mules came in handy for some of the heavy lifting that needed to be done, since they didn't want to dip into the gasoline stores to run trucks and other vehicles that had been left behind, if it could be helped. Plus, most of the vehicles would need major mechanical work to function properly after sitting dormant for decades.

BURTIN was a wealth of information, giving Bill step-by-step instructions for setting up a small corner of the hydroponics area. The others helped him move the bigger pieces of equipment into place and saw him through the first planting stages, but left him to the task when it seemed he had it well in hand.

Jaci had become something of a scavenger, locating odd bits and pieces from the various bedrooms that had once been inhabited by a large number of men and women. She took it upon herself to freshen and clean each of the chambers, though there really was no need. Dave thought it was because the tasks were familiar to her, and therefore comforting. She'd done much the same in her work performing upkeep of the cells below the Alvian city.

Each night, they'd adjourn to their chamber and make love

long into the night. Sometimes they'd venture outside the complex, just to the hot spring and make love under the waterfall that brought cold water from above to the hot below and made the pool the perfect temperature for bathing...and other things.

On this particular night, the cousins left Sam and Bill far behind in the main complex, taking their time bathing in the hot spring and making love to their woman. Jaci loved the place, as did her men. They'd spent hours here, showing her just how much they loved her and making the small crystals embedded in the walls glow like little stars from their passion.

§

Grady Prime was on a mission. Perhaps it would prove to be his last mission, but he welcomed the unknown future if it meant a change from the endless monotony of his existence. Still, this mission had delayed the experiment for him. He needed to be off-duty in order to administer the experimental treatment, and he was most definitely on duty until Jaci 192 had been apprehended and returned to the city for questioning.

He'd known there was something different about her, but he hadn't been able to put his finger on exactly what it was. Now that he knew she'd already taken the treatment, albeit accidentally, he wanted to talk to her about the changes she'd undergone as the agent reshaped her DNA on a molecular level. Maybe she'd speak with him on the shuttle trip home, though he knew she'd have little incentive to want to speak to him after he captured her. Especially since he'd be delivering her into a prison cell at the end of that journey. Still, he liked the woman and hoped she would speak with him. She'd already been through the journey he would be undertaking as soon as he got back to base.

Of course, he had to find her first. She'd led him a merry chase, but he thought he had her now. She had to have help, and following the human male had led Grady Prime to a place he never would have expected. It was an unknown human base of some kind that had weathered the apocalypse in surprisingly good shape.

He and his men had found other places like this from time to time, but he'd never suspected there would be one here in the middle of the mountains they'd already searched in every way possible—with every instrument they had.

But Grady Prime had always had an instinct for the hunt. He could feel when he was being observed and he could sense prey long before they showed up on sensors or were picked up by other hunters. He felt eyes in the woods now and picked his path carefully. He also sensed his target nearby. How he knew these things, he'd never bothered to ask. He just took it as the natural ability it was and used it to his best advantage. It was part of what had helped him become Prime at so young an age.

Grady Prime observed the human male entering a small, unremarkable cave and staked out the area. There were undoubtedly sensors in the area. They'd found such at all the previous installations they'd reconnoitered. The secret here would be to lay low and wait until they were lulled into a sense of security. Grady Prime would bide his time under cover of the woods, watching and waiting for his opportunity.

He waited for deepest night to make his move. He followed where the male had gone, examining the ground carefully, but moving as quickly as possible. If any of the hardware in the facility were still working, they could have been alerted to his presence already. He was counting on the lateness of the hour, and the fact that there couldn't be that many of them, to aid him in his mission. He would find them now, but the tracks would tell their own story, letting him know what he was up against.

Sure, he could call for backup, but this was one small woman whom he had once considered a friend and one, perhaps two, humans. He knew he could handle this situation alone and truth be told, he wanted to give Jaci 192 a chance to speak to him away from the rest of his men. He wanted a moment to talk with her and see for himself the changes that had come over her. He had to know if she was irrational or insane. He had to see his possible future for himself.

What he found was not what he had expected. Instead of a madwoman on the run, he found her frolicking in a steamy, mossy cave that had water running swiftly through it from a waterfall above that dropped away into a shallow, bubbling pool below. It was a hot spring of some kind, lit with crystals embedded in the very walls, glowing brighter each time she touched one of the two men who flanked her. Grady Prime crept inside, disabling the small proximity alarm which had also been taken, or perhaps supplied, by her unknown allies, and two other backup sensors that they had put near the entrance to warn them of anyone approaching.

He recognized the two males with Jaci 192. He had pitted his skills against this pair before. They had led him in circles, but his tracking skills had prevailed. He had almost hated to see them captured, but he was only doing his job. He respected the men, though they never knew it. They had challenged him and stumped him a few times, but in the end, he won as usual, and they had lost their freedom.

Grady Prime crept slowly into the cave, rounding a corner that arched sharply away from the nearly hidden entrance to a main tunnel. It was well lit and all but unseen from the outside. He watched from the shadows, knowing his quarry was trapped. He would take a moment to observe them, to see how Jaci 192 interacted with the Breeds now that he knew she had taken the experimental agent. This was purely for his own edification and he would never admit to delaying the performance of his duty to his superiors, but he had to know. It was his life on the line, his future. He had to know if the agent made her unstable or insane, or if it even worked at all. So he ducked silently behind a rock formation to observe.

The males stood at the edge of the pool and Jaci 192 was already in the water. The men joined her with sighs of pleasure as the warm water lapped at their muscles. Immediately, one of the males took her naked form in his arms and kissed her soundly.

Grady heard the Hum first, then saw the flicker of orange light in the tiny crystals that lived in the walls of this cave. They glowed for Jaci and the Breed, stealing Grady's breath as their kiss deepened and they truly Embraced. The crystals glowed with bright yellow sunlight. They were indeed, resonance mates.

Grady would not have believed it had he not seen it with his own eyes. But even as he thought this, the first male let her go and the other male took her in his arms, repeating the Kiss and Embrace. The Hum intensified again and the raw crystal in the walls of the cave shone brightly for them. Both of these men resonated with Jaci 192 and were her true mates.

By rights of ancient Alvian law, these three could not be separated, even by ruling of the High Council. Grady knew what his orders were, but he also knew what was right. Decision made, he stepped out from behind the rock formation.

"Holy shit!" Dave's tone had Mike lifting Jaci and putting

her behind them. Something was very wrong. "Where did he come from?"

Jaci pushed her way out from behind her men.

"Grady Prime?" Dismay filled her tone.

"Yes, Jaci 192. I've been sent to take you back."

His voice was like winter, cold and unfeeling. It didn't give them much hope.

Jaci surprised them all by stepping from the pool and calmly wrapping her towel around herself. She faced Grady with anger in her eyes.

"You'll just have to kill me now, Grady Prime. I will not go with you any other way. I would rather die."

Grady lifted the large weapon strapped around his shoulders and the two men started forward, but he only lifted the gun clear and tossed it back toward the tunnel entrance. Three pairs of confused eyes regarded him.

"I didn't come here to kill anyone."

"Then why did you come?" Dave had a towel around his waist as he faced the alien warrior, but Grady had eyes only for their woman.

"I came for answers," the warrior said softly, just an echo of humanity in his deep, melodic, alien voice, "and I've found only more questions."

Jaci breathed what sounded like a sigh of relief but the cousins weren't letting their guard down just yet. They had a history with this soldier and they didn't trust him.

"I tried to tell you what I could when I gave you the skinpatch. Grady Prime, I consider you a friend and if what I believe about your character is true, then you should, by all means, go forward with the treatment. It will change your life forever."

"As it has yours? I saw the crystals glow. You have found not one, but two resonance mates. How is this possible?"

Jaci shook her head. "Davin has theories. You should find time to speak with him privately if you seek that answer. I only know that these men are my true mates and I will not part with them for any reason ever again. I love them."

"You can feel? You feel love?" Grady asked his gaze intent.

Jaci nodded, a smile curving her lips. "Love, anger, pity, sorrow, hope, excitement, joy and so much more. Grady Prime, our people don't know what they're missing!"

"Perhaps you could show them. If you come back to the city and tell them what's happened...show them the proof of your mating with these men. They might listen."

But Jaci shook her head. "That's not my place, Grady Prime. Not yet. Perhaps not ever. I would not have been chosen to participate in the experiment. I don't hold high enough rank. But you might have that chance. You're among the best of the best, and they'll listen to you. They won't want to lose your skills and they'll listen and hear what you have to say."

Grady stepped right up to her and placed one large, calloused palm on her cheek. The cousins flanked her, letting him know that he was getting too close to their woman, but he would not be cowed.

"You are much more than you think, Jaci 192. As a soldier, I've come to believe in fate. I think it was fate that stuck that skinpatch on your arm and fate that brought you to your true mates. I don't think fate is done with you yet, either, but I'll respect your wishes for now. According to the ancient laws, you would have one month of freedom to be with your true mate after Joining before having to resume your duties and no one—not even the High Council—has authority to separate true resonance mates." He stepped back from her, smiling faintly. "As a warrior, I can do no other than obey the law."

"But what about your orders? Didn't they send you to take us back?" Mike asked with a hint of challenge.

Grady turned laser-like blue eyes on him. "The ancient law supersedes orders given by a mere scientist. True mates may not be separated for any reason. Only my direct chain of command can issue capture orders in conflict with other laws and even then, they could be appealed to the High Council on grounds that they are superseded by superior law. Since I'm Prime, I am the highest authority before the High Council. I've decided that Mara 12's orders are illegal now that I've seen the proof of resonance. I can leave you here with no harm to my honor."

"Very tidy," Dave commented from the side.

Grady bared his teeth in what passed for a smile. "Yes, indeed." For a short moment the three men shared a bit of camaraderie, but it didn't last.

"Will you tell them?" Jaci's voice bit through the quiet. She was clearly worried.

Grady shook his head. "Your trail is nearly invisible. I tracked you alone. No one knows I found you and they don't need to know as far as I'm concerned. Jaci 192," his voice dropped, "you've found what many of us seek. You've found your true mates and you have my congratulations and envy."

"I thought your kind couldn't feel such things?" Dave's voice challenged him, but Grady didn't appear to take offense.

"Because I'm a soldier, I feel more than most. I feel...echoes. And I want to feel more. It's always just beyond my reach and it has taunted me most of my life. That's why I volunteered for the experiment."

Jaci lowered her eyes, sighing heavily. "You won't regret it,

Grady Prime. But it's overwhelming at first. Do not despair. Seek help from those with emotions who can understand what you're going through. My friends among the humans and my mates helped me through the initial disorientation. You'll need someone to help you too."

"But I'll be watched closely as part of the experiment."

"But you are also Prime. Very few of the Maras will argue with you should you want to talk to someone other than one of them."

Mike touched her arm and the Hum sounded to both pairs of Alvian ears. Grady's eyes shot to hers as she smiled.

"Maybe he could talk to Harry," Mike suggested.

"And Caleb," Dave added from her other side.

"The Haras?" Grady nodded, thinking. "I have known them for many years. It would not seem too odd if I were to seek them out."

Jaci touched his arm. "Then do it. You could have a worse reaction than I did because of your warrior DNA. For me, the emotions started to intensify on the second day, then became progressively worse for the next few days. I was feeling overwhelmed and didn't know where to turn, but David and Michael helped me. Perhaps Hara and Caleb can do something similar for you."

Grady saw the wisdom in that, already thinking and strategizing ahead. "What you suggest has merit. I will consider it closely and thank you for your candor."

"So that's it? You're letting us go?" Mike asked, just to be sure.

"That's it, as you say. I stayed on in the woods alone after I sent all my troops back to the city. I wanted to find Jaci 192 for my own reasons. I wanted to see what the skinpatch had done to her before I embark on the journey myself. I've satisfied my curiosity now. She is neither insane nor unstable that I can see. It gives me...hope...if that's the right word for the echo of feeling."

"You'll find out soon enough," Dave said. "And just so you can be certain, Jaci is becoming better adjusted to her emotions every day. In the old world, I counseled those with mental and emotional problems. What we called psychiatry was my field of expertise." Mike knew from his cousin's tone that the doctor was definitely *in*. For whatever reason, Dave had decided to help the man who'd once captured and imprisoned them, and who'd had sex with their mate. Remembering that didn't sit to well with Mike, but he didn't say anything. He just stood back and watched. If Grady made the slightest move, Mike would give him something to think about.

"I can assure you..." Dave put one arm around Jaci's shoulders, "...she's as well grounded as anyone in her position could possibly be and she integrates more of the emotion with each passing day. I like to think that Mike and I have some influence on her progress." Dave gestured toward his cousin. "But I also believe a balance can be reached—given time—on one's own. Talking to the O'Haras would be beneficial to you, but try to keep your spirits up and don't despair when the emotions start to feel overwhelming. There is hope for you. And hope for you, Grady Prime, means hope for your entire race. Keep that in mind."

"You seem to have given this some thought," Grady said, watching Dave with measuring eyes.

"It's been on my mind since I found out about the experiment. I think overall, it's a positive step forward for both our races." Dave smiled at the warrior, but Mike wasn't so forgiving.

"Now that you know where we are, we'll be taking greater precautions," Mike stepped forward to face the soldier. "You won't catch us by surprise again."

There seemed to be a trace of respect in Grady's eyes as he returned Mike's gaze. "If it's any consolation, you two were a great challenge to me. I almost regretted taking you in, but it was my duty. I know you'll be more vigilant with your mate from now on. But rest assured, you have my word as Prime that this location will never be divulged by me to any Alvian." Grady put his hand over his heart and bowed slightly. Jaci put one hand on Mike's forearm, squeezing lightly and he took that to mean that Grady's actions had some significance to her.

He hoped Grady could be trusted, but he didn't see they had much choice. If he disappeared, the entire Alvian army would be out searching for him.

"Thank you, Grady Prime." It was Jaci who acknowledged the warrior's words with a slight bow of her head. "I and my mates thank you for your discretion and we wish you well."

"As I do you, Jaci 192." Grady looked at all three of them for a final moment before turning on his heel and leaving the chamber.

Long minutes later, after the trio had cleaned up and dressed, Sam signaled them from the cave opening.

"He's gone. Bill and I followed him all the way out to be certain, then Bill went after him and sent me back here to let you know what was going on. BURTIN alerted us when he got in but we were too far away to warn you in time. Then, when we got here and saw him throw down his weapon, Bill held us back, out of sight."

"Good move," Mike agreed. "Better that Grady Prime thinks it's just us down here. He doesn't need to know about you and

Bill."

Bill moved into their line of sight from the outer tunnel. "Thank you for that." He nodded at Mike in acknowledgment. "I followed him to his ship. He stowed his gear and took off toward the city. He did not see me."

"I'm glad," Jaci said, stepping between the cousins. "I think he will keep his word. He won't tell anyone about this place. He swore it."

"I saw that, "Bill agreed. "You must have made quite an impression on him, Jaci. Grady Prime does not give his word lightly."

David growled and Mike held back, just barely. "We have interacted several times. I know he had a sort of...fondness for me."

"It's more than that, Jaci," Bill said. "He respects you. That is rare between a soldier and a science sector tech."

"Then that gesture he made...?" Mike asked the leading question.

Bill turned his focus to the cousins. "That gesture is a symbolic promise among soldiers. It is not lightly given. Grady Prime will not divulge the location of this complex to any Alvian. He will take the secret of it to his grave, if necessary."

Mike whistled between his teeth. Dave just looked grim. Jaci took them both by the hand and led the way inside, leaving Bill and Sam to secure the blast doors behind them.

"I know we owe him for not even trying to capture us this time, but I'm jealous as hell that Grady Prime has a soft spot for my girl," Michael admitted as he cuddled her in his arms on the soft bed in their quarters.

"Don't be jealous, Michael." Jaci smoothed the hair back

from his brow as she looked up at him. "He may have wanted me, but I never wanted him. I've only ever wanted two men in my whole life and they are both with me now."

She reached out with her other hand to touch David, reveling in the instant Hum the blessed resonance created. They couldn't hear its perfection, but it was enough that she could. The Hum was the very real evidence of their compatibility…it was evidence of their love.

Epilogue

He'd seen them together and both heard and seen the evidence of resonance for himself. Grady Prime knew theirs was a union of true mates that would last for all time. He wanted that—or at least the chance of finding that—for himself. It might not happen. He might go mad from the emotion, but it was a chance he had to take.

Somewhere out there, there might just be a woman meant for him. A woman he could resonate with and pledge his heart and life to. A woman who would temper his aggression with her love.

With that oddly comforting thought in mind, Grady Prime placed the skinpatch on his thigh.

About the Author

To learn more about Bianca D'Arc, please visit www.biancadarc.com. Send an email to Bianca at Bianca@BiancaDarc.com or join her Yahoo! group to join in the fun with other readers as well as Bianca! http://groups.yahoo.com/group/BiancaDArc

He's waited centuries for her rebirth.
Can he persuade her to love again?

Night Rhythm

© 2008 Charlene Teglia

A Sirens story.

Once, Valentine had everything: Position, wealth, love and happiness. Then tragedy struck. Over the centuries, he has clung to the prophecy that his love will be reborn, but when he meets Lisette, she's no longer his wife, no longer his love. She no longer remembers their life together.

After a chance meeting with Valentine, Lisa can't shake the lingering impression he leaves behind—or the odd feelings he stirs. He gives her two gifts: A necklace, and a dream of passion that awakes her memory. But are these memories she can trust?

After all, Lisa isn't the woman she once was. And Valentine is no longer human.

Available now in ebook from Samhain Publishing.

Enjoy the following excerpt from Night Rhythm...

A restless movement in the bed woke him. A wayward elbow nudged his ribs and the fringed end of a thick braid tickled his nose. Valentine smiled at the disturbance, now fully awake although his eyes remained closed. He had no need to open them to know what he would see. His arm tightened around the slight form bumping into his side, drawing her closer. "Having trouble sleeping? I have the cure for that malady."

The cure he spoke of rose thick and full from his groin, drawing his sac tight. That part of him had woken first in response to her nocturnal stirrings. It jutted forward when her bare thigh brushed against it, as if eager to volunteer its services.

A musical giggle answered him. "I wonder which of us has a malady. You seem to suffer from a great swelling this night."

One small hand splayed against his chest while another closed around his cock in a bold grip. Valentine felt himself growing even thicker in her hand, swelling with lust and need that never fully slept and woke easily to her lightest touch. If he was honest, it took far less than her touch to rouse the slumbering beast inside him. The scent of her perfume, the sound of her skirts rustling when she moved, the sight of her. Any of these things would suffice to incite him. All of them together could madden him.

The most innocent gesture she made aroused him, and when she deliberately inflamed him, running her tongue along her lower lip when she knew he was watching her, or stretching to display herself for him with her eyes full of mischief and daring, she was likely to find herself with her skirts tossed up and her legs spread at any hour of the day and in any opportune place.

"A great malady," Valentine agreed in a solemn voice. "You torment me all day and then all night, waking me from a sound sleep because you must have more of me. I am never safe from your demands."

She let out a soft snort. "You were the one lunging about in this bed like a rutting beast. I was having the most wonderful dream." Her hand stroked up and down the length of his engorged shaft in a slow caress as she spoke.

"A better dream than this?" Valentine asked.

"Nothing is better than this."

She slid onto him, all satin skin and heat, thighs parting for him, lips reaching for his kiss. Hunger leapt up like a flame given air and roared through him. The scent of her desire told him she was flushed and eager, her heartbeat increased, rich blood pulsing through her veins just beneath the surface of that delicate skin. His fangs lengthened as his cock throbbed, all of him ready to take all of her...

The doorbell rang again. More insistently this time.

He wanted to roar with rage as the phantom memory that was all he had of her now slipped away, the past shattered by the intrusion of the present.

CPSIA information can be obtained at www.ICGtesting.com
Printed in the USA
LVOW101756031012

301360LV00003B/55/P